HIDDEN

THE SWAMP

REBECCA ROYCE

Hidden (The Swamp #1)

Copyright @ 2019 by Rebecca Royce

Ebook ISBN: 978-1-947672-91-8

Print ISBN: 978-1-947672-96-3

Cover art by Syneca Featherstone at Original Syn Designs

Content Editing: Heather Long

Copy/Proof Editing: Jennifer Jones of Bookends Editing

Final Proof: Meghan Daigle

Formatting: Ripley Proserpina

Published by Rebecca Royce

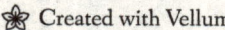 Created with Vellum

ACKNOWLEDGMENTS

As nothing gets written in a vacuum, I am very happy to acknowledge that this book couldn't have been written without the help of some very talented people who take the time to help me with my books. Ripley Proserpina, Rachel Feuerstein, Sara Vermillion, Autumn Reed, Chandra Ryan, Tate James, Heather Long, Jennifer Jones, Meghan Daigle, Syneca Featherstone, and Michelle Duke. Thank you so much. I couldn't have done this without you.

This one I am dedicating to my ARC team. Thank you for all that you do for me. I truly appreciate it.

FOREWORD

Dearest Reader,

Thank you so much for picking up Hidden (The Swamp #1). This is the first book in a paranormal, shifter trilogy. It's hard to get readers to check out a new series, so I'm grateful to you for taking a chance on this one. For information about the next book or any of my books, please check out my note at the end. You know I always get to a happy ever after, or if you haven't read me before... I promise I do. But we have three books to get there....

I hope you like MacKenzie and the Lejeune brothers as much as I do!!

Hugs,
RR

CHAPTER 1

EVERYTHING SMELLED... wrong.

I didn't know how I knew that, but I did. I rushed forward, growling at the man in front of me. I would tear him apart, destroy him if he got in my way. I would... I would...

I jolted awake, my heart in my throat. Sweat drenched my body, dripping down my neck onto my back. I looked left and right, trying to get my bearings. Where the fuck was I? What was happening? Panic warred with the fatigue threatening to take me back under as I forced myself awake. I couldn't sleep. Not until I knew where I was, what was happening, or even who I was.

I caught my breath. Who was I? I... I...

"Easy, girl." A voice from the front seat of the truck I was in caught my attention. I caught his eye in the rear view mirror before I immediately dropped my gaze. I didn't want to look at him. It seemed integral that I didn't. Not until I understood... what?

"I..." I tried to speak and stopped. Shame rode through me at my confusion. This was my weakness, my lack of... something.

The man driving was old, his hair gray both on top and in his beard. He tilted his head to the side and continued to stare at me instead of the road. I had to watch this from under the tops of my eyelids since I refused to look up and stare at him straight on. I wanted to. I just couldn't. Something was wrong with me.

"What you're feeling, girl, it's normal. I can smell your distress in the same way you can scent that I have no ill intent. You can, can't you? Take a deep breath and see what your big brain tells you."

I did as he said. I wouldn't have been able to resist doing it if I had wanted to. It would probably have been hard to tell this man no to anything, and that in it of itself made my already buzzing anxiety worse. Still, a deep breath did release some of my tension. He didn't want to hurt me; he was worried about me, concerned. And on my side. He was a friend. No, more than that. He was in charge.

That was all very helpful, except that I didn't have the slightest idea why I knew any of that from just breathing. I might have lost my mind—literally—but I was still in possession of some faction of my good sense. People didn't get that load of information simply from taking a deep breath.

"Mister, I—"

He shook his head. "My name is August Lejeune. You can call me Gus. Almost everyone does."

"Okay. Gus. I don't know my name and that is a problem, but only one of the bigger ones I have going on. Something is wrong with my brain. I can't think. Everything is..."

He interrupted me. "Too much."

I nodded. That was entirely it. Everything was too much, and I couldn't make sense of any of it. "Your name is MacKenzie Harper. You're twenty-two years old." He pulled over to the side of the road. The pickup truck groaned to a stop, shaking as it did. "You're from Colorado. Way high in the Rockies. Much higher than I like. That kind of elevation makes me dizzy. Anything over 8000... never mind. That's not important right now. You've been missing, and I found you. On behalf of your family... in the Outer Banks of North Carolina. The Albemarle Peninsula. You've been through an ordeal. Your memory will come shortly. Tonight, tomorrow at the latest, and until I figure out exactly what is going on, I will see to it that you are safe. I have to find the others that have gone missing."

I appreciated the information. Yes, the name tasted right in my mind. That was my name. MacKenzie. No one called me that but there it was. My mother put the name on my birth certificate, so it was mine. I rubbed my eyes. Tiredness pushed through my adrenaline.

"Where am I? Who are you, Gus?"

He smirked. "When you can look me in the eye, and I imagine that will happen sooner than later if you are what—who—I think you are, then I will tell you all about me. Until then, what you need to do, MacKenzie, is get some sleep. We're on our way to my home. In the Bayou. You'll be safe there. Take a deep breath. Am I lying?"

I did just what he said even though it made so little sense. Following orders was about all I could handle right then. I breathed in slowly, exhaling the same way. He really only wanted the best for me. I was sure of it. "No. You're not lying."

"That's good. Put your head down. Get some sleep. You're safe. That's all that matters until more of it makes sense."

I had to do what he said both because he'd ordered it, and also because I couldn't keep my eyes open. Everything was just... too much.

He started the pickup truck back up again, and although it shook like we were in a popcorn machine, he pulled us back onto the two-lane highway.

"You're not sleeping. I can scent it." He had a laugh in his voice. "I guess I told you to put your head down, and you did that, but ordering you to sleep... well that would be above my pay grade, so to speak. Someone else, yes, but who that might be is beyond me. Everyone is going to want you."

I didn't like that. I lifted my head, and he tsked. "Head back down. You need to rest if you're not going to sleep. Don't worry about what I just said. No one will likely be ordering you to sleep. Not unless you want them to." He sighed. Gus was tired. I could smell it. But underneath the exhaustion lay strength and determination. He would get us wherever we were going.

"I've got to use this cell phone to call ahead. I hate this thing. Feels like a leash. But... fine. Right now, I need it."

I smiled. He wasn't really talking to me as much as he mumbled, and that seemed familiar as though I knew someone like that, too. A person who chatted to himself. It was comforting in the same way that hot soup or coffee might be.

After a second, he spoke again. "Yeah, boy. It's me." He paused. "No, I'm fine. Stop speaking. I'm bringing you someone. You're going to watch her for me. Be at the house in an hour. Make it work."

Darkness sucked me under.

"There's a female in there?" Someone shouted. Not a voice I recognized. My head was foggy as though I needed to emerge from under water.

"Stop shouting." Gus shut the front door behind him, muffling some of the sounds outside. I moaned. My whole body hurt. Gus swung open the backdoor, and for a second, the door itself was balanced in his hand, clearly having detached from the vehicle. That didn't speak well for the safety of this car. It was also bizarre that he held the door like it weighed nothing at all. "... ordeal." I'd missed something he'd said. "And you're going to watch her for me because I'm telling you to. Did I expect to find all four of you here? Absolutely not, but I'm glad for it. That's four times the protection. I saw things I couldn't imagine. I'm going back to get the others who have to be held there. You'll keep her here until I get back."

Gus picked me up. "You're going to be okay, MacKenzie, and when this is over, if you want to call me Parrain like the other kids who grew up around here other than my sons, you can."

"Sir," another new voice spoke. "This is not what we're supposed to be doing. If you would just go home and see our mother, settle in, you'd see that they're right. There is a better way to live."

"Your mother knows where to find me, boy, if she or any of the others need me. Don't worry, MacKenzie, you're safe with these fools. They are, after all, my sons." He walked toward the house, and I only got the slightest look at the four—I thought it was that many—men behind him. "Or at least they used to be. I don't know what they are now. Or who they belong to. But they will keep you safe. They still have that much honor. I can smell it."

I was getting a little tired of all the smell talk. Gus sniffed the air. "That's good. You should have a temper. This whole thing sucks. And if it didn't make you mad, it would make you scared. None of us need anything to do with any more terror. We've all had enough."

"Sir," a third voice boomed. It was the most demanding of the ones I'd heard so far. "What happened to her?"

Gus shook his head. "You might be what saves them, or you might be what finally makes them disappear from themselves altogether. I don't know which yet."

"Well none of this makes any sense to me. If you were hired by my parents, shouldn't you give me back to them?"

He shook his head. "They lost you, and right now we don't know how that happened. Before we put you back in that den of potential pain, we will make sure you are safe. There aren't enough of you left to be losing you at this point. Don't try to make sense yet. It will be clear enough in the morning."

The house he brought me into had seen better days. It was huge, and as he tore up the stairs, I only got the quickest look at it. It was white, with peeling paint and creaking stairs. The door itself was red. I stored that information away as interesting. Red was often a sign of welcome in certain cultures. I blinked. Well, that was interesting information to know. The color made sense in that regard; it was why people used it in their kitchens on the walls to stimulate hunger, to make people want to eat the food. Again, that was interesting.

"I could probably walk." Discomfort at being carried around like some kind of wilting flower filled me until desperation to actually use my feet made me squirm. Gus tilted his head like he'd done in the car before he set me down. He didn't move his arm for a second. "You're strong. That's good. This one right behind me fell on his face so many times the next day after this happened to him that I wasn't sure he'd ever walk again."

Gus set me down. My legs wobbled for a second before I righted myself.

I looked where he indicated. One of the men from outside stood there. He was taller than Gus and incredibly angry. I shuddered, the heat of that feeling almost bringing me to my knees.

"Good," Gus nodded at me. "Keep using that nose. His anger isn't directed at you. Or it better not be." The older man lifted his eyebrows.

The man whose anger was in question crossed his arms over his chest. "I've got nothing against this fem— girl."

"Now, now, brother." A man almost as tall as the one in question sauntered into the room. The gold tips of his hair immediately captivated me. Did he do that to himself? "You know as well as anyone that she is old enough to be called a woman. Not a girl. Or has Mother not managed to civilize you yet? You are always welcome to stay here with me in the swamp."

The swamp? "We're in a swamp?"

I hadn't noticed on the way in because I'd been asleep.

"Come on." The blond tipped man walked toward me. "I'll take you to where you're going to be staying. What's your name? My father didn't introduce us. He used your name but," blond guy took my hand in his as he continued, "it's always polite to be officially introduced."

I groaned. He smelled really good, but I was unimpressed. None of this was sincere, so the sweetness of what he said just made me want to roll my eyes. "I'm MacKenzie Harper. I know that because he told me." I nodded toward Gus. "So I guess that might be a lie, but it doesn't seem that way. It feels right. What's your name?"

He touched his nose. "You know that it's your name because it smells right."

"Preston," the angry man spoke without looking at the blond one. "Knock it off. She needs not to do this. Whatever has happened, I can guarantee this isn't right. Don't encourage the nose."

The one in front of me shook his head. "Ever the stick in the mud, Rainer. Ignore him. He'd have you lose all of your fun abilities. I'm Preston, as he told you. Preston Lejeune. That's my brother Rainer staring down our father like it's his job—because maybe it is—and those two hanging by the doorway like they've never seen a woman before are Jarret and Anton."

I glanced to where he indicated and sure enough the last two men watched, practically in the shadows from the door. Suddenly, self-consciousness burst its way into my head. Everyone except Gus stared at me.

What was I even doing here? "I'm not sure what's going on or why I'm here. I certainly don't want to put anyone out. If you want to point me to where I can pick up a bus I can..." I didn't finish that sentence because I wasn't sure what I could do. I had no money, and I didn't even know what destination to pick. I couldn't exactly say take me to Colorado, somewhere above 8000 elevation. I was stuck here until my mind cleared up.

And for whatever reason, every dominant scent in the room told me that here was not some place I was particularly welcome.

"You're fine." One of the guys—Jarret—strode toward me. "You're more than welcome to stay here. You'll be our guest until this is all worked out. Come on. You're exhausted. I've never been through it, but I can imagine, sort of. Are you hungry?"

I touched my stomach. The idea of food was actually repulsive. "No."

"Probably not till tomorrow." Rainer sighed and stepped away from his father. "Then she'll be starving. I'll go to the store. I can't believe you did this, sir."

"You'd have done the same."

That was the last thing I heard before Jarret, who was handsome in a severe way because his eyes were so angry, led me up a staircase. It groaned under our weight, and I stopped walking. "Is it okay to walk on this?"

"Okay enough." He shrugged. "This is our ancestral home. It's been in the family a long time. We come from the swamp, the Lejeunes. I don't know if an architect or an engineer would call this place sound, but you'll be fine."

He didn't fill me with a great deal of assurance. Still, with no other choice, I continued to follow him up the stairs. I was tired even after my nap in the back of Gus's pickup. So much so that I might very well fall over. I should probably have let Gus carry me. I grabbed my head. It ached. And everything was just...

Jarret's hand shot out, touching me, bringing me back from the brink of whatever that was. "You okay, MacKenzie?"

I liked how he said my name but there was something about it that screamed wrong in my mind. "My friends call me Kenzie."

"Kenzie. Okay. Same question. You all right?"

I shook my head. "No."

He didn't pick me up like his father had done, although I was sure he could have. He was significantly taller than me with visibly strong muscles stretching his black t-shirt. Jarret had strong leg muscles too, on display with his black shorts. I lifted my head. I was in no condition to be looking at him like that.

Jarret tugged me against his side, his arm coming around

my shoulder. "We'll go slower. I won't let you fall. I promise."

I believed him, and we walked together silently up the long, nearly destroyed staircase until we reached the top and turned left. Jarret finally spoke again. "I'm going to put you at the end of the hall. It's the quietest. This house is noisy. I find it hard to sleep here. I jump at every sound. But it's quieter on this side, and I imagine with the way you are feeling, less will be more."

I wasn't sure I followed everything he'd said to me. But he was being considerate, and since we'd gotten up the stairs, I wasn't getting as much hostility from him in his scent. It was like he cooled but not in a hostile way, just the opposite. His blood pressure had lowered. How did I know that?

"There's something wrong with me."

We reached the room where he obviously intended to leave me. Jarret tilted his head to the side, regarding me the way Gus had. They didn't look alike or even particularly smell alike. Gus was like the wind, and Jarret was more like cloves. I shook my head. What was the matter with me?

He visibly swallowed. "There's nothing wrong with you that some rest and time won't heal. What happened to you, it doesn't ever have to happen again. I've never been through it. It's a choice. And with some instruction, you can make sure you never feel like this again. Everything will fade."

"Don't tell her that." Preston strode toward us. "My younger brothers don't know of what they speak. They've never felt like you do now, and they never will if they don't get their heads out of their asses."

Jarret shot Preston a look that could only be called

hateful and stepped back from the door. He nodded toward me. "Let me know if you need anything."

These men all had southern accents so far. So had Gus, but he sounded more like Preston, whereas Rainer and Jarret were more genteel. I still hadn't heard Anton speak at all. All in all, it was a little bit like being in a movie. I didn't know if I'd ever been around people with accents as thick as this before.

"This is my house." Preston took another step toward me. "If you need anything, you let me know. I have some business to do, but I'll be around."

Jarret shook his head. "It's all our home."

"Really? Because before today I can't remember you being here for years. If you hadn't made a trek out here today to insert yourselves into my business, you'd have never been here with Mac to begin with. So I'm going to say that since you will likely be gone first thing in the morning, leaving me once again in your taillights, little brother, that she should probably look for me since you'll already have forgotten her."

Jarret's eyes seemed to flare, and the heat of the anger that had been downstairs wafted toward me again. I took a step back. "Don't talk to me like that." He pointed at Preston. "You *never* listen."

Preston ignored him, his attention turning toward me again. "Don't be afraid. I'm sorry you've arrived in the middle of our family hate fest. It'll be much more pleasant tomorrow when my big brother takes the two littles with him and disappears back into New Orleans for the next however long. You and me? We'll get along great. How you're feeling now? That will happen to you for the next ten to twelve shifts. Less and less with each one until it won't happen at all. Jarret can't tell you about it. He's too much of a coward to try it. The bathroom in this room works just fine. The water runs, and it heats up. The bedding is clean. You should be fine. If you see any ghosts, ignore them." He winked at me.

I swallowed. "Ghosts."

"Oh sure. These old places in the swamp are always loaded with ghosts. Vampires. Swamp monsters. Werewolves."

I shook my head. "I don't know what I do when I'm not confused and in the house of strangers, but I don't think I was born yesterday. There are no such thing as monsters."

Jarret took two steps back before he turned and headed straight for the stairs, as though he couldn't move away fast enough.

Preston's smile was harsh. "Oh, make no mistake, Mac. There are monsters in the swamp. If you only believe in what you can see, hear, and... smell, then fine. Watch out for the gators. They'll eat you and we'll never find your body. Not even pieces of it. But there are other things too, and the Loup-Garou, he'll eat you up until they never find your body either. Best to stay inside. Unless you're feeling like you want to run with the wild things."

I rolled my eyes. "You're a very strange person. Thank you for your hospitality, but I can't figure out what to make of you. You smell like... lemons. It's a clean, fresh scent, which goes in direct contrast to the things you say and how you're behaving."

He leaned against the wall. "You smell like honey. But I don't make the mistake of thinking that means that you're sweet. Go on inside. I'm going to watch you close this door."

I didn't have to listen to him. It wasn't the same compulsion I'd had with Gus. No, with Preston it was as though I could tell he was strong, and I could drop my eyes and do as he said but there was also a part of me that didn't want to, that wanted to challenge him by standing right where I was and not moving.

But tiredness won that strange argument, and in the end, I did drop my eyes and head into the bedroom. I needed to sleep. Then maybe this strange smelling-everything compulsion would stop, then maybe I could remember where I came from. I turned toward Preston before I shut the door. "No one calls me Mac. My friends call me Kenzie."

"I call you Mac." He grinned, and I got my first taste of laughter on my senses even though he didn't do that, at least not on the outside. Preston had teased me.

I shrugged. "Suit yourself. Thank you for your hospitality."

His mood abruptly shifted. Maybe that had been the right thing to say because there was something in his scent that was hard to identify. It was longing... sadness... I couldn't quite grab onto the word. "You're welcome. You're safe here. We'll keep you hidden until it all gets worked out. I promise you that."

I believed him. "I don't know what has happened, and I should be more afraid that I don't."

"No, you are feeling just as you should be. Somewhere deep inside of you, that part that always knew this was coming, that needed this, craved it, that part knows you were supposed to go through this time. It won't let you panic. It won't let you lose your mind. It'll just make you calm, force you to lean into this, until the clarity comes back. Get some rest. You're not crazy. Well, maybe you are. How would I know? All I know is that when it comes to shifting, you're totally boring and normal in your response."

I scrunched up my face. "I can't decide what to make of you."

Preston threw back his head and laughed. "Smart. Don't trust anyone. We're a hateful, difficult, selfish bunch who should probably all be taken out in our sleep. I'm the worst. That being said, you've never been safer in your life. Night, Mac."

I didn't really understand what was happening, but I could sincerely say this had to rank among the strangest days of my life. I could be sure of that, even without knowing who the hell I was.

Fuck. I closed the door.

CHAPTER 2

I RAN, snarling forward, my fangs ~~tearing~~ into the neck of the man who had been trying to hurt me. I wouldn't let anyone put their hands on me again. Not like that. He fell to the ground, my tongue coming out to lick his blood. I hated the taste, but not because I didn't enjoy the sensation, rather because I hated who it belonged to. I raised my eyes and saw him.

Family.

That thought struck me. I wasn't related to this man. But he was family. He was... pack.

I jumped to my feet. I had to get away. The wolves were coming, and my family had been clear... I was never to shift into a werewolf. We had to let our wolf side die, that was the only way we'd survive. The men with needles were going to hurt me again. I had to get away. I had to get home and tell my parents what happened. They'd know what to do, how to handle this. Surely there had to be a way to put the wolf back in the bag, as it were.

I ran forward, not even knowing where I was going until I collided with a hard body in the dark. I made an oomph, and strong hands kept me from falling straight down on my face. The moon lit up the room around us, showing me the huge brown eyes belonging to Anton Lejeune staring back at me.

His gaze was kind, and he didn't say a word to me, just standing there in the darkness as my heart wouldn't stop racing.

I swallowed. "Sorry. I have to go. I have to get out of here."

He shook his head. Once then twice. Still, he didn't speak. The truth dawned on me. There were things I knew about the Lejeunes. They were a famous werewolf family, one of the last to agree to the Accords, to agree to put their wolves away, to stop being werewolves. What had happened to them had been so awful that it had only made my parents surer about their decision to step away, to struggle through the 'unbecoming' that they went through on a daily basis.

Or so I'd been told. I'd been a baby at the time when Anton Lejeune had been stolen from his crib on his first birthday and tortured by the werewolf Hunters who were after their family. Those Hunters no longer breathed air. They'd been killed, brutally, by the Lejeunes, who had ended up losing one of their adult males in the battle. Like all werewolf families, the female had more than one husband.

The truth dawned on me hard. I was in the house with the Lejeunes.

I had to hide my truth from the humans around—calling several of my fathers 'uncle' in public just to keep anyone from knowing.

And now here he was... the famous Anton Lejeune with his huge brown eyes, long face, and utter silence. The rumors were true, even though the Lejeunes had hidden him away from scrutiny, he didn't talk.

I dropped my eyes from his. I couldn't look at him. With my mind back and not foggy, I could identify this for what it was. He was dominant to me in pack order, if he'd actually allowed himself to be a wolf, as I'd somehow managed to do.

"I'm a werewolf. I tried not to be. But... they made me. I shifted because they were going to kill me. I was terrified. I couldn't help it."

He nodded before he drew me closer to him. I stared at him from under my lids. What did he want from me? A second later he hugged me tightly, placing his head down on my shoulder. It should have been a weird thing. People, not even werewolves pretending to be humans, didn't go around hugging each other like this.

And yet... I loved it. It wasn't just that he hugged me; he clung to me like he needed me more than he did anything else in the universe. Before I could overthink it, I hugged him back just the same way.

He smelled like pinecones and smoke. The woods. Clearly my brain had been storing information about scents, even in the years I'd resisted the wolf, and seemed fine presenting it to me now. Having just shifted, everything was very potent.

As far as I was concerned, I never had to move.

Dizziness wafted through me, and my stomach rumbled. He lifted his head and caressed his thumb down my cheek. It was a gesture made for someone you knew, someone you were intimately familiar with. The way he hugged me had been the same way, too. All of it should have made me tell him to go to hell. I'd certainly told others to fuck off. But standing there in the hall of the falling-down-at-the-seams home in the swamp, the only thing I wanted was to let this man hug and caress me like we were deeply connected.

He strung his hand into my own, linking our fingers. With a gentle tug, he brought me downstairs. It was easier to descend the stairs than it had been going up. My legs had decided to work.

Anton switched on the light in the kitchen. It flashed a few times before it came on. He looked up at it with a scowl and then shook his head. He pointed to the counter.

"You want me to sit on the stool?"

He nodded and picked up the tablet. With swift movements he typed, and a word came out of it. "Bacon?"

I smiled. That must be how he communicated. "Bacon sounds like heaven."

He walked away from the tablet and toward the stove. "I can sign. ASL. If you want to talk like that." My best friend growing up had a deaf mother. I'd learned how from an early age. Not that I'd had anyone to practice on since they'd moved away. My parents hadn't loved the friendship to begin with.

Anton looked over his shoulder but just shook his head. No, he didn't want to sign or no he didn't sign? I'd have to ask him when his hands weren't busy cooking me breakfast in the middle of the night.

"Thank you for this." I wasn't sure I could stand at the stove without dizziness or I'd have attempted to make the food myself. For years, while my family worked, I'd taken care of myself and everyone else when needed, even if I'd done a disastrous job. Being catered to wasn't exactly my way.

He nodded; I could tell by the jerking of his head. It was hard to take my eyes off the strong steel of his back. Anton Lejeune. Where had he been this whole time? New

Orleans with the rest of his family? My mother would have had a field day standing in this kitchen. At some point, generations earlier, my family had left Louisiana for cooler, more mountainous lives, but they were still absolutely obsessed with the goings on here.

Anton looked over his shoulder and winked at me. Mind reading wasn't a power for werewolves as far as I knew. Otherwise, I might have been worried that he could actually read my mind and know that I was checking out his backside.

This was very unusual for me and had to be another reaction to the shifting. I rubbed the back of my neck. It would ease. I'd get the wolf issues back under control, never shift again, and that would be that.

I could return to my normal life where smells were just smells, and I wasn't checking out near strangers for their potential sexiness.

Finished with the bacon, he set it on a plate and brought it down to me. It was crisp, just liked I liked it. Clearly, I wasn't craving it raw and there was something relieving about that. I didn't want to be craving bloody things all the time. Not like...

My dream rushed back at me. I had lapped up blood. My stomach turned. Wearing four feet, I hadn't cared about how gross that was but now...

Anton nudged me, catching my gaze once again. He held up a strip of the bacon, bringing it to my mouth. I wasn't sure I could eat at all, not with the blood memory, but the closer it got to my lips, the less I cared about what I'd done and the more I wanted that pork in my mouth.

I chewed, closing my eyes. Yes, that was the greatest taste in the world. I opened my eyes in time to see Anton smiling at me. He held up another piece.

"You don't have to feed it to me. I can hold it myself."

He nodded his head but didn't set down the bacon. Instead, he brought it close to my mouth again. I smiled. "You're dangerous aren't you, Anton? Flirtatious."

This time he shook his head, and I laughed, the feeling bubbling up inside of me. "Oh sure. You're denying it."

"Is something burning?" Jarret rushed into the room. He skidded to a stop. "Fuck. Sorry. Okay. It's bacon. Of course it is. Because who wouldn't be cooking bacon at three in the morning."

I turned in my chair. Jarret was shirtless, which made me fully aware that Anton was, in fact, still dressed as he'd been all day. What had he been doing in the hallway? Jarret was built like he'd been carved out of stone. I wouldn't have guessed that when he was dressed, he'd looked slender, which was only because his muscles were lean. My mouth watered. Okay, yes. Totally a result of the shifting.

Jarret stepped toward us, nudging his brother with his shoulder. "You're cooking in the middle of the night?"

"He's helping me out. I got up, and I was a little out of my mind and starved." That sort of made the whole thing concise. Maybe.

Jarret walked to the fridge. It squeaked and groaned when he opened it. Everything in this house was falling apart. I'd hardly paid attention earlier, but my room was clean, yet still a disaster. The walls were peeling, and I suspected the paint was lead. In my current state, it made my nose burn.

I sniffed and went back to ignoring it.

"He doesn't talk. It's not an affectation. He can't." Jarret supplied without turning around.

"I gathered that," I answered him, raising my eyebrows as Anton slipped another piece of bacon into my mouth.

Jarret pulled orange juice out of the fridge and walked over to us. If he'd seen the bacon exchange, he didn't indicate it. I sniffed the air. I could only smell the bacon. And with Anton so close now, his natural, woodsy scent almost overwhelmed the food. Jarret's cloves smell wafted over to me as well. I still wasn't getting any idea of how they were feeling.

They were both staring at me, and once again, my dominance issue hit me hard. I looked down. Next to me Anton made a disgruntled sound. He tapped my cheek until I raised my gaze to meet his. His smile was slow and moved through me like a gust of warm air. "You want me to look you in the eyes."

"He could talk, or communicate," Jarret held up the tablet. "If he wanted to. I bought him this, but he's never used it."

I lifted my lids. "Never, huh?" He'd just used it for me.

"Nope." He smiled at us. "How are you feeling?"

"Well, I gave into my werewolf and shifted so now I guess I get to live with the discomfort of the wolf wanting to come out and play until it goes away again. However long that takes."

Jarret nodded. "I wondered if you knew or if you were one of those humans who didn't know you were a werewolf. Much easier that you know. You're not going to have a nervous breakdown."

"Well, not tonight." I laughed at my own joke and then stopped. No one could do cheesy as well as I could.

Jarret met my gaze, and I dropped my own. This was going to get harder and harder. At home, I'd sometimes had this happen but rarely. Without the shift, I'd pretty much felt like a regular human most of the time. I must have been really far down on the food chain to be unable to really look at anyone.

"Kenzie," he said my name, and I forced my eyes up in time to see Anton smack his arm. "What?" Jarret asked his brother. "She told me that is what most people call her. It's fine. Right, Kenzie?"

I nodded. "More than fine. I'm comfortable with it."

Anton's shoulders sagged. What was wrong? I turned to him. "You okay?"

He nodded, a smile coming back to his expression. He held up the bacon, sticking it back in my mouth. I chewed and swallowed. I liked bacon, but I don't know that I'd ever liked it this much. Had anything ever tasted this good?

"I've never shifted." Jarret passed a glass of orange juice to me. "What was it like? Anton and I weren't old enough to have had the shift when the Accords were signed. We never got the chance."

"I was also too young. But then those people kidnapped me and hurt me. It just happened."

Jarret sighed. "That's always the risk. That's why we have to be careful with ourselves. Not get ourselves into situations that present that." He held up his hand. "This wasn't your fault. It's good you shifted. I bet you protected yourself."

"It was more like I stumbled around. Drank some blood and stumbled into Gus who saved me. If he hadn't gotten there, I might have found myself shot in the head."

Jarret lifted his OJ. "Well, then here's to Gus."

I smiled. "Here's to Gus. Where did he go?"

"He left." Jarret set down his glass. "Lately, that's what he does. There was a time we were all very close, but the last two decades, for at least as long as I can remember, Gus doesn't stick around long. He can't take the Accords. He runs and runs."

Anton pushed back from the table. Jarret stared at him and something unsaid seemed to pass between the two of them. Preston had called this place a hatefest and my nose could finally pick up the low taste of anger clinging on them. They'd been pleasant, but that low frequency could quickly pick up into another explosion. There wasn't enough bacon in the world to get me through that at the moment.

"You guys don't see each other much, right? Preston said something like that. You're regularly in New Orleans?"

Jarret nodded. "We were all born here but the last... eight years or so... Preston has mostly been here. We're only here now because every so often someone," he said, nodding toward Anton, "gets a bug up his ass to come try to convince Pres to come home. We all turn around and do that because none of us can ever say no to Anton."

The aforementioned brother grinned. He linked our fingers again. This time Jarret noticed. He stared down at our linked hands and then back at me. Once again, I lost my ability to look him in the eye.

"You're very pretty," Jarret walked toward us, until he stood on my other side. "Your brown hair has all kinds of colors in it, and those blue eyes."

I wasn't vain, but I'd heard this before. I knew I was pretty enough to gather male attention whether I wanted it or not. But hearing Jarret say it or noticing the way Anton looked at me made me warm inside. Still, there was nothing to be done about any of this. We were all werewolves, and if the Accords were to work, we all had to figure out how to be in relationships with regular humans as we tried to breed the wolf out of our bloodlines genetically. Those were the rules.

Even if our parents hadn't managed to follow them. The Lejeunes, if I knew enough about them, had been a family of one woman and six men before they lost one male. That didn't count their four sons. I had five fathers, one mother, and three older brothers. We did tend to make more boy werewolves than female, but given that our wolves didn't mind sharing mates, it had all worked out mostly well.

But we were going to be asked to mate with a human, one-to-one and pretend that all was well. Fake it our whole lives. This was why I didn't date.

"My wolf nature, it's very high right now. I'm feeling off."

Jarret touched his nose. "I'm not able to scent anything that a human can't."

Anton nodded.

That made sense. That had been me up until recently, and hopefully, if I could pull this off, I'd be like that again. How else was I going to survive?

Jarret rubbed my arm. "It's very, very late. I don't know anything about shifting, but you've eaten. Maybe you should go back to sleep."

Anton stepped away. He crooked his finger as though we should follow him, and without another thought, I did just that. We walked together into a room I hadn't been in yet. I would have called it the Great Room back home, but I didn't know what it would have been referred to as in a house like this.

A fireplace was on one side of the room with a couch facing it. Other than that, there was a red rug in the center and no other decorations or furniture at all. I smiled. No one had taken any time to decorate this place. Maybe

Preston, who was usually here alone, just didn't have the time or money to do it. Or maybe he was just trying to fix up the house itself before he furnished it.

Anton took the pillows from the couch and threw them down on the ground. He walked past us out of the room and came back with a blanket. I didn't know where he'd grabbed it, and I wasn't sure I wanted a blanket anyway. It was hot outside and humid in here.

Anton held out his hand, and I walked toward him not even sure yet what he was proposing. Did he want me to sleep downstairs on the rug? He lay down on the rug and tapped the floor next to him.

Jarret grinned. "I think we're all camping out down here tonight."

How was that going to work? "Where should we all lie?"

I actually liked the idea of being here with them. It was a wolf thing, like everything else that was weird about me at that moment. Wolves liked company. They didn't want to sleep alone. I'd seen it with my parents. We'd tried to climb into bed with them every night until they ousted us when we were each about eight. Still, we never did lose the instinct to want to sleep like a pile of puppies.

Anton patted the floor next to him, and I lay down where he'd indicated. Jarret came down on the other side. Anton had really set this up perfectly. Three pillows and a big blanket, but I didn't want the blanket.

"I'm hot." I sort of blurted that right out.

Jarret laughed. "You are."

I snickered. "That's not what I meant, although, thanks." I rolled my eyes, but my cheeks heated up. "Would it be okay if we didn't use the blanket? Or you know what? I can go upstairs if you want the blanket.

Anton picked up the blanket and threw it across the room.

I grinned. "Or you could handle it like that."

Jarret laughed, and Anton made a noise that had to be called a snicker. It was the first noise I'd heard him make. I hardly knew these guys, but I was going to spend the night on the ground with the two of them, in between them as though we were old friends. It must be a male werewolf thing. Of course, I'd never had any of this comfort around the ones I knew back home. But then there was the whole shifting thing...

Jarret touched the side of my face. "You're thinking really hard. I know it because I do it myself."

"You smell like cloves." I looked over at Anton. "And you smell like the woods. I know I shouldn't really be able to know these things unless I pressed my nose to your clothes or something. The way humans do. But now that I have it?" I stared up at the dark ceiling. "How do I give it up?"

Anton scooted over and rolled over until he had his head on my shoulder the way he had in the hall. He sat up suddenly and the movement was so jarring I actually sucked in my breath. What was he doing? He quickly took his shirt off, throwing it aside the way he had with the blanket before coming back down to put his forehead on my shoulder again.

He scooted closer so that his body was as close to mine as it could be. Jarret met my gaze in the dark. "Rainer and Preston both gave up their wolves. Maybe they could help."

"My parents did, too. And there is the odd thing about this whole thing. I was kidnapped from my job. I..." Those memories made me dizzy. "I should be really upset; I mean really upset. I should be crying and trying to deal with that time. But I can hardly think about it, like the whole thing was a fog. What is the matter with me? And I need to call my parents. Why haven't I done that?"

Jarret linked our fingers together. "Hate to point out the obvious, but it's three forty-five in the morning. That is probably why you haven't called them, and you've been out of the shift fog for like an hour. It'll all come back, most likely. And you'll deal when you deal. Or..."

His voice drifted off. "Or?"

"Or maybe you are dealing. You're lying here with us. Company is sometimes how we cope."

I knew something right then. It must have been the way he used the word cope. The way his voice dropped when he said it. Anton clearly had things he had to deal with, having no voice. But Jarret had his own demons. He was a guy who maybe knew how to cope. Maybe tonight we were both dealing, and Anton had brought us both into this dark place with him so that all three of us could lie here together.

Fuck. Maybe I was overthinking it.

Next to me, Anton's breathing deepened. I couldn't see him because of how his head was positioned on my shoulder. He moved slightly, his hand coming onto my side where he splayed out his fingers.

"He never sleeps," Jarret whispered. "Maybe a couple of hours every four days. He just keeps himself constantly busy. He's actually asleep."

Well, I didn't think Anton was faking it. I looked over at Jarret. "What do you do when you're not having to hide me in the swamp? And for that matter how can you possibly hide me in this place? I'm sure you have a life you have to get back to."

"I'm supposed to start law school in the fall. I went to college and then spent the last two years running one of my father's clubs in the Quarter. But I applied and got into law school. So in a few months that'll start. I'm sort of at odds right now. Guess it's the perfect time for me to hide you."

So he did have a plan. That was nice. I'd had one too that I was pretty sure I was going to have to let go of, considering the kidnapping and now the fact that I was going to have to figure out how not to be a werewolf after being one.

"I'm a stranger to you. You don't have to spend your free months before grad school babysitting me. Gus was sweet to ask you guys to help me but... I can't ask it. I'll have to figure things out."

He scooted closer. "Close your eyes, Kenzie. Everything will be okay. We may never get to be all that we could have been since there aren't any Omegas to keep the pack healthy, but werewolves, whether they shift or not, take care of each other. I want to be here with you until this gets sorted. I want to be your friend. And obviously, Anton does, too. Let's try to sleep."

That seemed like great advice, just close my eyes. I tried to do that. And not for the first time in my twenty-two years I wondered why there weren't any Omegas left and how in the hell all of us were supposed to live a half-life.

CHAPTER 3

I RAN THROUGH THE SWAMP, my nose down on the ground as I breathed in home for the first time. This was what I'd waited for. My paws ached. I had been gone too long, and I wasn't used to this. Still, I knew he would find me. Alpha always found me. They would all come. My years of being lost were over. I followed the scent that had caught my attention. It might have been a rabbit. My mouth watered. I loved them.

Abruptly, I came up short, it was hard for me to look up. There was someone powerful here, someone who waited for me.

I hadn't seen her before, and somehow, I managed to lift my head to look.

"MacKenzie, where have you been?" The old woman asked me. She knelt on shaking legs. "Where have all of you been?"

I came awake slowly, the dream floating away. That had been weird. The smallest swathe of sunlight trailed into the room, and I was warm, pressed between two very hard werewolf bodies. That should have been weird too, only it wasn't and maybe that was because I was still riding the werewolf high from having shifted.

"If you spent any time around us you would know how significant this is. I'm not sure either of them has slept... not really... in a year."

Rainer's voice reached my ears even though I was pretty sure he was trying to be quiet in the hall. He spoke in a hushed whisper. If I hadn't woken up, I wouldn't have heard it. As it was, neither of my werewolf companions budged at all. Anton breathed deeply; his hand had moved from my side to my stomach, but his forehead remained on my shoulder. This seemed to be his thing. For all I knew, he did it to every female werewolf he encountered—or maybe every female period.

Although my ego kind of hoped it was just me.

Jarret breathed quietly. Neither one of them snored, which was incredibly nice, considering I'd always had a terrible time sleeping through noise. Jarret lay on his back, his head turned toward me. His foot twisted against mine. They were both shirtless, and now that we had light in the room, I could see that Anton was tattooed right above his hip, twisting onto his abs. It was a moon obscured by the clouds. I had the strongest desire to reach out and touch it. I didn't, but a quote from George Carlin, the comedian one of my fathers had loved, struck my mind: "There are nights when the wolves are silent and only the moon howls."

The older brothers' conversation drifted in again. Rainer whisper-talked again. "So sad, lately Mom has been thinking about sending him to a psychiatrist."

"What is Jarret going to tell the psychiatrist? I am always going to feel like half the person I should be? There is literally nothing I can do." Preston sounded unimpressed. Footsteps passed by. "I'm very glad they're all sleeping so soundly. Frankly, if I didn't have to work, I'd crawl in there with them. I'd even drag a mattress in to get everyone off the floor."

Rainer was visible for a second in the doorway. "You're missing the point."

"I'm not missing it. I know you want me to care about this, and there is nothing I wouldn't do for the three of you even if you all hate me."

"Hate you?"

The rest of what would have been said was obscured from my hearing. In the meantime, Jarret rolled over as he threw an arm around my shoulders. He muttered something unintelligible. His family was worried about his happiness, and Anton almost never slept.

I guessed I wasn't the only one with lots of issues to fill my days.

"What time will you be leaving?" Preston was within earshot again.

"Why would I be leaving?" Rainer sounded confused. I didn't know him well enough to know if that was real or put on. My nose was telling me nothing from this distance away, considering I was wrapped up in his brothers and their over-whelming and very appealing mixture of scents. Oh, and Jarret was totally hard. I tried not to notice. Most men got hard in the morning. I was pretty sure that was true of were-wolves, too.

"Because you always leave. I have to go set up four boats today, and I'm expecting four or more drop-ins. I won't leave her here alone, so I need to know what time you're leaving so I can be back."

Something fell in the hallway. "Gus asked me to help watch her and keep her hidden. That's what I'm going to do."

"Oh, because you're always so concerned with what Gus wants. That is your utmost concern."

I expected more yelling, but this time when Rainer spoke, he just sounded tired. "I'm so sick of having this argument with you. I want my brother back. I miss you."

Anton shifted slightly, his hand coming into my hair. His eyes were open, slits really, but he smiled at me so sweetly my heart clenched. I didn't know what time it was, but I knew it had been more than just a few hours of sleep, which meant that was quite a lot for Anton. He looked over his shoulder toward the door and then shook his head. He curled back down, his forehead on me again. I smiled. I might have brought it up if I wasn't afraid he'd stop doing it, and I liked how that felt.

"Good morning," I whispered.

He nodded, and his hand in my hair brushed my scalp gently. He opened his eyes wider and moved his head so we could look at each other again.

"I meant what I said last night. You're a flirt, aren't you?"

He shook his head, and I rolled my eyes at him. "Deny it all you want."

Anton took my hand and placed it over his heart. For just a moment, we lay there like that, his meaning very clear to me, which meant that he was either the most romantic person I'd ever met, or he was completely full of shit and the biggest player—voice or no voice—I'd ever encountered. And his brown eyes were so filled with... I wasn't even sure what. His scent changed, deepening, calling to me. It would be so easy to give in to this. To press my mouth to his and go with whatever was calling to both of us. But I'd already broken a rule by shifting, even if I was pretty sure I'd had no choice.

I wasn't supposed to mate—in any form of that word—with werewolves. It was too risky we'd form a real bond, call to our wolves, and then eventually make more werewolf babies. With the Omegas gone, that couldn't happen. We were all one mistake from madness and discovery. We'd given this up for our own protection and to save humanity from us since we couldn't control ourselves anymore.

He didn't push, didn't join our lips, or make any moves to show he would. We just lay there together, my hand on his heart as the minutes passed.

Jarret tightened his hold on me, and I turned my head to regard him. His face wasn't passive anymore. Instead, he looked almost pained. He made a sound in the back of his throat that might have been a growl before his head went back and forth. Anton lifted his head, furrowing his brow at the same time. He didn't like this any more than I did.

I let go of Anton and rolled toward Jarret. My hand seemed to burn. I didn't even give it any thought. Instead, I just had to hold Jarret for a second.

"Sshh," I whispered in his ear while I stroked his back. "You're okay."

He settled and didn't wake. The burning sensation in my hands lessened, and I let out a breath. That was weird and concerning. I didn't know what was happening but...

Anton scooted closer to me, pressing into me from behind like he was the outside spoon.

"That... I'm not sure what just happened," I spoke low to Anton.

He rubbed his nose against the back of my hair. It was comforting. I might have been reading this wrong, but it was like he didn't want me to worry about it.

Footsteps entered the room and soon a pair of legs came into my view. I lifted my head to look up at Preston. He smiled down at me and crooked his finger at me. "Anton, let go of the beautiful brunette so I can speak to her for a minute."

He rubbed his nose against me again but let go. Anton stumbled to his feet, stretching his arms over his head. Preston shot him a look for a second before looking back at me. He squatted down. "He's really out of it. Is he okay?"

I let go of Jarret. "I think so. Something weird just happened."

"Weird?"

Anton shook his head several times, and Preston looked between us. "He clearly doesn't want you to tell me."

That much I'd garnered. The question was why. I got to my feet, slowly. Jarret sighed, and his eyes opened. He sat up, his eyes still not clear, but he smiled at me like I was the best thing he'd ever seen. "Hey, Kenzie."

"Hey, Jarret." I smiled back at him. "Um, Preston. Did you need something? Or want something? Or... how can I help?" The last one was the one I wanted. It was like I couldn't make my mouth work.

He put his arm around me. "Well, I'm going to get you some coffee. And then you and I are going to figure some things out. You don't have a phone so I'm going to leave you mine. You need clothes. You can't keep staying in those that Gus found so you should go into my room, it's the one with the balcony, and take whatever you want out of my closet. You're tall but thin so it'll be huge on you. Still, it'll do for now."

He handed me his cell phone. I tried to keep up. Yes, coffee sounded wonderful.

Preston kept talking. "I have a work cell phone that you can reach me on. When Rainer and the boys leave..."

"I'm not leaving." Rainer entered the room. "But please

go on giving instructions to the poor girl who shifted yesterday and hasn't had any food since whatever time someone fed her bacon."

We hadn't cleaned up after ourselves, and the pan Anton had used was in the sink. I scurried over to it. "Sorry, wasn't thinking about cleaning up last night."

Anton beat me to the sink, coming from behind me to get to the dishes.

I nudged him. "You cooked. I'll clean."

"He cooked?" Rainer and Preston asked at the same time.

I looked between them. "Is that weird?"

"Yes," they answered together with Preston adding, "unless something has changed."

Rainer shook his head. "I've never seen him cook anything."

"Well, maybe he just knew I was really, really starved." I nudged Anton away. "Let me do that, please."

He shook his head and didn't budge. I growled at him, but I wasn't angry, more like I wanted to play with him. Every eye in the room turned to gaze at me. My cheeks heated up. Yep, I'd just growled.

"Sorry." I looked down. All of the gains I'd made fled. I didn't want to make eye contact with any of them. "I was being hurt. It's hard for me to remember; it's more like impressions. Someone took me and they hurt me. I can remember being a wolf, drinking blood, tearing skin. And Gus arriving. But other than that I can't really seem to focus on what happened."

Preston rubbed my back, a long stroke down my spine with the tips of his fingertips. I shivered. He spoke in a low soothing voice, his ordering tone from moments earlier now gone. "You are just over twenty-four hours from the shift. I barely functioned for days. Sure, your memory is coming back, but what happened to you wherever Gus found you will come back differently. The wolf plays with memory. It changes everything. Makes you growl if you're not careful, even playfully, which is all that growl was, boys." He eyed his two younger brothers. "In case you can't hear the difference in the tone. That's why when we go through the shifts—usually sometime between fifteen and twenty-five—we have to hide away a bit. Because sometimes we growl."

Rainer nodded. "You won't shift again, and it'll fade fast. One turn? It shouldn't mean you have to hold back for too long. This time next week? You'll feel back to normal."

Speaking of that. I had no idea if Gus had called my parents or not. "Can I please use your phone to call my parents? When I get back to work, I can pay you back for the cellular data or..."

Preston waved his hand. "I have unlimited calling. This isn't the boonies."

Jarret snorted before he handed me a cup of coffee. I hadn't realized he was making it. So far, I'd seen this happen twice. Preston would start an idea, and Jarret would finish it. "Thanks."

Anton turned off the sink water and relaxed against the counter, seeming to watch us all. Jarret touched my shoulder. "You're welcome."

The scent of anger from the night before was nowhere to be found. They all seemed to be in better moods. I took a sip of the coffee. It was a little sweeter than I liked it, but I was grateful to have it.

Preston stopped rubbing my back, and I immediately missed the sensation. Yep, I was needy. That was for sure.

"Call your parents. I might not tell them where you are.

That's up to you. Gus said to keep you hidden and since you got taken at home..."

I nodded. "Right. That makes sense. I won't tell them where I am or who I'm with. Just that I'm safe." And that I missed them, and the sound the wind made this time of year passing by my window of my bedroom. I'd thought about moving out, but standing here now, thinking about that wind, I wanted to hear it one more time before I did.

"Come outside when you're done." Rainer smiled at me. "I'm going to sit on the dock. Sunshine helps a lot of things. It'll make the wolf lie down for a bit."

"The dock?"

Rainer pointed to the back of the house. "Go out that door. You can't miss it."

"Oh, all right." I guessed I hadn't thought about the back of the house at all. This place was old and about to crumble. "Thanks for the phone, Preston. Are you... late for work? Will you get in trouble?"

"Naw." He gave me a grin that I supposed would be charming if I didn't notice right away that it was fake. His real smiles were different. "I won't."

Jarret followed Rainer through the door. "He owns the place. Swamp tours. Maybe fifty boats now. Lots of different sizes. A crew of about thirty. My big brother has really done something pretty extraordinary. He might be the richest guy in town."

Preston's cheeks reddened, and I looked up at him through the tops of my lashes. "That's incredible. Own your own place. Wow."

He cleared his throat. "Thanks, Jarret. I didn't know you knew that much about it."

"Of course I do. I'm really proud of you."

This wasn't the first time I'd felt like an intruder on

someone's private moments. Anytime a friend's parents would fight in front of me, or I'd watch them get dressed down for doing something that might have been better handled in private, I'd felt like a voyeur on humanity. This was different. They had taken me, and I was getting to witness the Lejeunes on display in a way I imagined few did.

I wouldn't talk about them, and watching them now, I wasn't sure what the fascination with them was. They just seemed like a normal family with problems like the rest of us. All of the Louisiana families were held in high regard as though they were werewolf royalty. And none of that made any sense since we were trying to kill the wolf sides of ourselves. Shouldn't that have meant we let this all go?

I took the phone and stepped into the other room. Anton watched me go. I wasn't sure how to read his expression, but I smiled at him, and he did the same for me.

The blanket Anton had discarded the night before lay on the floor by the wall, and I sunk down on it before I dialed my mother's number. It went to voicemail, and I waited for the beep to record it. "Hi, Mom, it's me. I'm okay. Maybe you know already? You can reach me at this number. Gus Lejeune rescued me. I'm not really clear yet on what happened. I shifted." A tear leaked from my eye, and I pushed it away. I had to be strong. "I'm sorry. It was... unavoidable. I know you said never, ever. But... I couldn't control it. Please call me. I miss you. I love you."

I tried each of my dads and got nowhere. It was weird that none of them were home. My mom worked mornings, and she had to turn off her phone when she was in with patients' families at the nursing home. But the rest of them? Bernie should have been there. He worked nights, and I didn't remember him ever not answering.

I tried each of my brothers and got the same response.

As I got to my feet, Anton appeared in the doorway. He extended his hand, and I was glad to take it.

"I couldn't reach them. That's... off putting." He put his hand on the small of my back and led me forward. I stopped moving. "Anton, when you touch me, it feels... it feels too good. I don't know if you're feeling that, too, but it scares me a little bit because my wolf is so close to the surface, and it has to go away. Do you feel it too or are you just being nice to me and feel nothing? I have to acknowledge this because I don't want to accidentally stumble into something here or find myself... feeling something alone. If we're both feeling like this, we have to be careful and somehow... not."

He took my hand and placed it on his heart again. I sighed. "You do that and I think that it means you have feelings. And I realize that, for whatever reason, you don't like using that tablet. I appreciate that you used it last night. Am I reading this correctly or are you just being nice?"

Anton didn't respond so much as hold my gaze until I had to drop mine. He drew me to him, pressing my ear against his chest. I could hear his heartbeat. Maybe this was too complicated for yes or no. He knew what I did... we were treading on dangerous waters.

I stepped back. If I wanted to be careful, I couldn't be stupid. "Or maybe you do this with all the girls and I'm overthinking it."

This time he shook his head no.

We walked outside together. The sun was bright in the sky, and although I hated the humidity, the heat felt nice on my skin. I'd completely misunderstood this house. I'd had no idea it sat so close to the swamp. A short walk down to a dock and we were actually on the swamp.

I grinned, unable to keep the smile away at the surreality of this moment. "My mother will freak out when I tell her this. I'm on the bayou with the Lejeunes. You guys are kind of famous."

Jarret groaned. "Only because we never left. Families like yours, they'd packed up and left even before the Accords. They made a life. We've been stuck in a constant reminder of what we lost. The farthest we venture is three hours away to New Orleans."

"I think it's lovely here."

Anton waved at his head like he needed to fan himself. "Yes," I told him. "I bet it does get really hot."

I sunk down on the edge of the dock in between Jarret and Rainer. It seemed like they'd left that spot open for me. Anton plopped down behind us. The speech I'd given him? I could give to all of them, and I'd hardly spoken to Rainer. These men were dangerous to my well-being and conversely, I needed them to keep me away from whoever had gotten me. I was just going to have to tell this newly awakened sexual side of me to go back to sleep. I couldn't allow her out with male werewolves. There was too much on the line.

"Do you think my mom heard from Gus that I shifted and that's why no one is speaking to me?" I spoke aloud.

Rainer side-eyed me. "I doubt Gus told them anything more than Got Her. He's not big on sharing. He'd not have told them you shifted because he'd consider it your business and not there's. Gus still shifts. I think. I don't know for sure."

Now that was interesting. "Really? I didn't see him that way. He picked me up in his human form. Literally by the scruff of my neck."

Rainer laughed, throwing back his head. "I know that

feeling. He just kind of swings you along like you're not a creature that could take out his eyes like that."

"Sounds weird," Jarret threw a stick into the swamp.

The water was green tinged and still. The trees above our heads held moss, and it was all surrounded by what looked like twigs growing out of the water toward the bigger trees. Logs floated in the water but not much else. I stared at those moving logs. "Are those..."

"Gator." Rainer knocked his leg into mine. "Don't worry. I won't let them take your limbs off."

I shuddered. "Wow. In real life."

"You're a werewolf and you're wowing a gator."

Behind me, Anton made that laugh noise I'd heard before. He must have liked Jarret's joke. "So I know what Jarret and Preston do. How about you two? What do you do when you're not hiding me?"

I turned to look at Anton, and he winked at me. Clearly, the man was totally unconcerned with the staying away we were supposed to do.

Jarret pointed at him. "He's actually a writer. Published since he was eighteen. Fake name. Science fiction."

"Oh, that's really cool."

Anton nodded. Well, he was clearly in agreement about it. "I've never read science fiction, but I'm going to have to now. To read you."

"He's good. All of my brothers are really talented people." Jarret threw another stick.

"Hey, you're going to law school. That's hard. You're clearly very bright, too."

Jarret shrugged.

Rainer stared straight ahead. "I used to own a bunch of food trucks. But I haven't been doing that lately. That's partially why I was surprised Anton cooked. I'm usually the go-to for all things feeding."

"Used to?"

He sighed. "You might as well know. I spent a year in jail. It kind of... fucked up my life. Well, I should put that differently. The wolf fucked up my life, and now I have to figure out what to do next. I've been working as a handyman for the last few months. I like working with my hands. Maybe I'll ask Preston to let me fix this place up."

"Technically, we all own it."

Rainer laughed. "He'd say possession is nine tenths of the law. You'll have to tell me if that's true when you learn it. Louisiana has different laws than the rest of the country. Who knows if that's right?"

He'd dangled a huge piece of information out there, and I wasn't going to pretend I didn't hear it. "What happened?"

"I refused to not shift. Even after the Accords. I kept doing it. First rule of shifting? Don't do it alone. Preston and I used to do it together. I'm not sure what happened. But I woke up in a car that had crashed. I must have shifted because I had that haze in my head. Everyone else was dead. They were all human except one other werewolf. The madness took me. What they warned us happens with no Omegas, it happened to me. People died. We had to cover it up but there had to be... there had to be accountability. It was made to look like a terrible car crash, and I was charged with vehicular manslaughter. Lots of strings were pulled. I did a year, and I got off easy."

I wasn't even sure what to say to that. "Wow, Rainer, I..."

"You know we don't know what happened," Jarret spoke through clenched teeth. "And I never thought you did that. We saw you. Preston saw you. You didn't have the madness. You never did. It doesn't just come out of nowhere and rise up like that. There are warnings. You took the fall for something and you didn't even do it."

Rainer visibly swallowed. "I'm afraid that... the thing is I knew I shouldn't be shifting. Whatever happened. Ultimately it's my fault."

"Bullshit."

Anton pounded his fist on the dock. I could smell the anger again. It was at Rainer and also not...

Once again, I was watching their family. All sorts of layers unpeeling in front of me...

CHAPTER 4

MY HAND SHOOK, but I raised it to place it flat on Rainer's back. He'd told me something very personal but touching him made it more that way. Still, I could practically taste his pain on my tongue. I could certainly smell it and the other guys' anger had everything to do with what Rainer had told me. Whether he'd done what he thought he did or not, they believed in him and even hearing him talk about it made them mad. What would it be like if people outside of the family did?

I eyed Jarret for a second before I looked down. Some of what Rainer said to Preston earlier made sense. Jarret was carrying a lot of stuff.

I half expected Rainer to either move away or shoot me a look telling me that he didn't want my hand on him. Or he'd straight out tell me to let go.

Instead, he turned his head to look at me. I couldn't see his eyes, wouldn't let myself check, but I did feel his body sag a little bit. My hand felt warm like it had earlier with Jarret. The sensation was so startling I almost let go, but I didn't want to disrupt the peace that seemed to overcome the moment.

"Um." I cleared my throat. "How long should I expect to feel weird things until it stops and things return to normal?"

Rainer shook his head. "I spent a year in prison feeling like I had to detox the whole time. Like I was one second from going on a bender and that drug was becoming a wolf. Of course, I had been doing it for years and you've had one shift. So, I'm going to hold to what I said before and say a week. I think it'll be okay in a week."

I hoped he was right. The intense smells, the burning hands, the general feeling of just being off put, of not doing what I needed to be doing—the whole thing just needed to pass.

"I'm sorry that people died, that they were hurt, and that you had to go through what you did, too, Rainer. That must have been miserably hard on many, many levels."

He nodded. "Thanks for that."

The smell of anger seemed to lower and soon it was just the swamp around us that I could scent, which had in it the dullest scent of sulfur, like rotten eggs. I couldn't say that it would ever be my favorite scent, and yet I didn't find it repulsive either. Somewhere in the distance, someone was burning something, and a motor revved and stopped.

My hand cooled, and it was awkward the way I was rubbing Rainer's back. I dropped my hand and got to my feet. "I need a shower."

I was painfully aware of smells, and I really didn't want to stink. Could I tell if I smelled rank or was it one of those things that I was going to be nose blind about?

"There should be hot water." Jarret rose. "It works, despite the fact that this looks like the mansion of horrors."

I laughed, which made him smile broadly. Anton stayed on the dock, watching both of us, a piece of brown hair falling in his eyes, while Rainer didn't take his gaze off the swamp.

"I feel like it's not currently in its heyday, but it must have been beautiful. I love old things. I would like to be an interior designer someday. I'm about halfway through my degree. Working my way through, which makes me qualified for literally nothing, but I do like to pretend I have a good eye."

Jarret pointed at me. "See? It holds true. Werewolves are talented people. Artistic to go with our animalistic nature. Except for me. Not an artistic bone."

Rainer shook his head. "Oh, but Mom still has that drawing you did in third grade. So you are talented to her."

Jarret rolled his eyes and kicked his brother, who laughed. Anton joined, in that unique way that he did. I smiled at all of them.

"I... ah... I'm not talented. Just a dreamer. Listen, I'm not sure where Gus got these for me."

This made Rainer turn around. "When you shifted, you would have ripped away your clothes. So when you shifted back, I hate to tell you, but you would have been butt naked. Not to worry. Our wayward father is many things but pervy is not one of them. He's devoted to his mate... sorry, all this wolf talk threw me, wife. They don't see each other for huge amounts of time. She misses him to death, and he longs for her. Neither of them say it. And her other... husbands miss him, too. He feels their absence acutely. No one says it, and it's a big giant bit of pain."

I thought of the man who had brought me here with his abrupt ways and strange manners. My heart hurt for them all. "You say all that to assure me he would have quickly gotten me dressed and not looked at me more than he had to?"

He nodded. "Exactly."

"In any case, Preston said I could borrow his clothes but that doesn't solve the underwear problem."

I wasn't wearing any under the t-shirt and sweatpants I'd been dressed in. I hadn't thought about it before now, but all of my discomfort seemed to be coming back at once. I was small, only five foot two in my bare feet, which was now since I wasn't wearing shoes, but I was curvy, and I'd been wearing a bra during all my waking hours since I was twelve years old. I needed to do something about making myself presentable. I might feel more like myself if I was actually wearing clothes.

Rainer nodded. "Jarret will go to town and buy you what you need. Text him your sizes. You can find his number in Preston's phone."

Jarret seemed to pale. "You want me to go buy her underwear?"

Rainer nodded slowly. "I think you can handle it with your very high IQ."

"I've never bought women's clothing. Not even the kind that isn't worn under the clothes. Yes, sure I can do it. Sorry. I'm not... this pathetic."

Anton shook his head and patted Jarret on the shoulder.

I blinked. "You want to do it instead?"

He nodded again and held out his phone.

I understood. "Sure, I'll text it to you. Do you think you could grab me some regular clothes, too? I'm not sure how long I'll be imposing on all of you, but if I can manage to not have to wear Preston's clothes the whole time that might be better."

Jarret smiled. "We'll go together. I think between the two of us we can manage."

Rainer laughed. "Anton can show you where to go. That doesn't surprise me in the least that he knows how. The boy has the most girlfriends out of all of us."

Anton glared at Rainer, and their oldest brother threw his head back laughing. "Oh, you know it's true. They swarm you."

Anton stormed off the dock, and Jarret groaned. "He's going to be pissed the rest of the day. You know he never pays anyone any attention any more than you do. We have to figure out how to date humans. None of us have been very successful at it."

I one hundred percent understood that. I held up the phone. "I'll text you guys."

"Great."

Rainer stared at me from across the dock as Jarret left it. "You really do seem to understand Anton. Not everyone does. He won't use that tablet because he's just so used to communicating the way he does."

"Why don't any of you sign? I mean... I would think ASL would just make sense? Never mind. Not my business."

He winced. "When he was taken and injured... I was twelve. It was a terrible year. He came back a year later the way he is. Just two years old. No one had ever heard him talk. Our family broke apart. Joe was dead. Gus was wrecked. We don't know who our biological fathers are. Do you?"

I shook my head. "No, my brothers and I have no idea. They all seem to love us the same."

"Yes, for us, too. They were all destroyed. My mother announced we'd sign the Accords. And I think..." He winced again. "I think she still thinks in her deepest heart there was no need for ASL because he was going to get better."

That didn't make any sense. "The rumor was they took his vocal cords."

"It's a little more complicated than that. You can't exactly take his vocal cords. But, yes, they mutilated them. There won't be any getting better from that. But do you know a werewolf who stays injured or who even gets sick? Never, right? So she just refused to do anything for him. Homeschooled him. There were only werewolves pretending to be humans around. No one to notice. And Anton is so fucking smart... he just adapted. No, we never learned because she directed us not to as though learning it would somehow stop him from healing."

I swallowed. "You know, when people talk about the Lejeunes, it's like you guys are the perfect werewolf family. Exactly how we're supposed to behave, how we're supposed to be. Whatever you guys are suffering, you do a great job of hiding it from the outside."

"I know." He rocked back on his feet. "Every day is pretend. In so many ways."

━━━

Clean but still without clothes, since Jarret and Anton weren't back, I lay in one of Preston's t-shirts on the big bed in the room I'd been given. The shower had worked great, but the AC left something to be desired. The fan over the bed moved the hot air in the room so that it at least brushed against my face.

I'd just showered, but a dusting of sweat had already begun forming on my skin. It might not have been because of the humidity. I was hot, burning up. My gums ached and inside of me it really did feel like another creature wanted to burst through me from the inside out. I didn't remember my first shift except for the vaguest feeling that it happened all at once when I was terrified.

This was different. This was something...

A knock sounded, and I sat back on my elbows. "Come in." I tried to keep my voice pleasant. It was probably just Anton and Jarret with my clothes. Normalcy might help this whole mess. Those clothes would be the first step. Plus, I'd forgotten to tell the guys I'd pay them back.

Preston stood in the doorway. "I took a half day." He stepped into the room. "I like you in my LSU shirt. Maybe we'll even take you to a football game."

I shook my head. "Doesn't sound very hidden to me."

"After. When this is worked out. It'll be celebratory." He stepped further in. "I came home with pounds and pounds of live crawfish. We will be having a feast soon. Rainer got busy setting up the boil and when the other two boys get back with your underwear," he lifted his eyebrows, "we can eat."

I swallowed. "I've never had crawfish. How does one do that?"

"I'll show you." He walked closer. "You're sweating, and it's hot in here but not that hot. Ah... you're suffering. Why didn't you say anything?"

I didn't have it in me to lie. Not right then anyway. "You were handed me to hide with no choice in the matter. The last thing I want to be is difficult. So if I have to lie here and be silent about it until it stops, so be it."

He sighed. "My first week denying the wolf was right after Rainer went to jail. He told me he told you. I was twenty-eight years old. Old enough to know better than to shift. My parents are difficult but smart. I should have listened. I sweated for weeks and weeks. Months. And then one day it passed." He lay down next to me. "You're not alone."

"Thank you, Preston."

His presence should have made the room hotter, but it didn't. If anything, it made everything feel less lonely.

I turned to him. The looking but not making eye contact thing that I was doing had gotten easier. Preston stared up at the ceiling. "I hear that you want to design things. Want to help me with this stuff?"

"The house? Sure. I mean, I'm not a contractor."

"No, but I bet you can follow directions and my brothers—particularly Jarret even though he is so in denial about it—can wield a hammer with the best of them. We can all do it together, and then you can decorate it so it doesn't look like the set of a horror movie. Even if you've left, you can design over video conferencing or something."

I loved that idea. "Yes, I'd love to."

His smile was huge. "This place stayed empty so long. It would have been perfect for a werewolf family. Only my parents never lived here with us. We stayed down the ways a while. Visited this house. But no one has lived here since my great-grandparents. Empty too long. Maybe it's too much water. Maybe it's too much time. Maybe it's just too much... Maybe I should knock it over. Sell the land to the power companies and just let it go. But I can't."

"It means something to you. You really don't have to explain it more than that."

He side-eyed me. "Why am I telling you all of this?"

"People do tend to talk to me. My mother said it was my natural nature. Strangers on park benches."

Preston smiled. "Natural nature. I like that. Our natural

nature is to shift into four legs whenever the mood takes us. But we don't do that so I guess it's nice to have something left."

His sadness touched all my senses, and I squeezed his hand in mine just as my own heated up again. Damn it. What was happening?

"Does my hand feel hot to you?"

He shook his head. "Not particularly. Does it feel hot to you? I don't remember that being a thing that bothered me, but we're all different."

"It's on and off." I sighed. "I sound whiny to my own ears. How was work? Can you show me the swamp sometime?"

Preston lit up the room with a smile. "Yes, I'd love that. I almost never give tours myself anymore. I'm in the back room... dealing with things. But I'll show you myself after hours tomorrow when everyone else is gone. So you're safe. I'd love that."

That was something to look forward to. "And I'd like to help with the house like you suggested. I'd like to feel like I was giving back. Oh, and whatever money you're spending on me. The clothes. My food. Upkeep. If you could keep a log of it, I'll pay you back. I have a job. I work at a hair salon sweeping up, putting myself through school. It might take a while but I'll..."

He put his hand on my shoulder. "Sweet. You really are. I don't need your money. This thing we're doing? I'd never have anticipated it. I haven't wanted my family around for a long time. Watching over you? We're getting along for the first time in years. I like it. We've all suffered giving things up. Werewolves protect each other. I like that I get to do this. It does make something inside of me feel... right."

I leaned up on my elbow. "So which one of us is sweet? I think that would be you."

He held his finger to his mouth in the universal sign for shush. "Don't tell. I'm the mean one in the family."

Pain as though someone clawed at my insides wracked through me. I cried out before I covered my mouth to quiet the sound. I didn't like people knowing when I was in pain, not ever. From the time I was a little girl, I'd tried to manage these things on my own. Particularly because I healed fast, thanks to my unused werewolf genes. It always felt like an intrusion to force anyone to pay attention to me when I was just going to be fine.

Preston's face fell. He rolled toward me. "Okay if I touch you under your shirt on your back?"

I nodded. "Sure. I mean..." I couldn't really think right then.

He inserted his hand under the shirt that I was wearing and rubbed in circles. "Touch helps. It just always does. But if you hate this, I'll stop."

I closed my eyes. No, he was right. It helped. Preston made circles up and down my back, avoiding the lower areas where my butt was totally uncovered thanks to my lack of underwear. This was intimate but he was... respectful.

Eventually, the smell of spices drifted toward my nose, and I lifted my eyes. "What is that?" Preston had his own eyes closed, but he opened them. "What is what?"

"That smell. Um, garlic. Salt. Cayenne pepper." I sniffed the air. "Some other things."

His smile was huge. "Oh, those wolf senses. Nothing like them, right? Everything is going to feel kind of dulled after this. I don't smell it yet, but that's what it is. Rainer must be getting ready for the boil."

A second set of smells touched my nose. Cloves and the woods. I smiled. "Your brothers are back, too."

"You've got their scent as well." He tapped the end of my nose. "That's a good one. You might be even stronger than I was."

I shrugged. A knock sounded on the door, and I smiled. It was useful knowing all of these things a little ahead of time. I sat up slightly. "Come in."

Both Jarret and Anton strolled in holding bags. I gawked at the sight. I'd asked them for just a few things, but they really seemed to have gone shopping for a lot of stuff. Preston knocked his shoulder into mine. "Don't worry about the cost. We're rich. All the Louisiana wolves are. We're lucky that way. It's our pleasure to take care of you while you're here."

Jarret looked at Anton. "Yes, we didn't even think about it. We started to see stuff, and we just thought that she'd look really good in things and bought them."

My cheeks heated up. I didn't embarrass easily, but I took compliments about as well as I took gifts, which was a little bit awkwardly. "We're not rich in Colorado. In fact, most of the wolf community up there is living pretty much paycheck to paycheck. I've always had to be careful with money. I'm a little bit of a jeans and t-shirt kind of a girl mostly out of necessity."

Anton held up the bag and then pointed to the bathroom, obviously wanting me to change. I got out of the bed, pulling the shirt down so it didn't ride up around my legs on the way off the bed; otherwise they were all going to get a good look at my private parts.

And much as I wouldn't, for the first time in my life, mind that idea, it was forbidden. Some things I had to keep normal. Even if I had already fallen down the wolf rabbit hole. I had to keep my head about me. "Hey, Preston. Can you check your phone? I left it there by the side of the bed. I haven't heard back from my family... and that's really unusual."

He grabbed the phone. "Nothing from your family. Few texts from various people looking for me but nothing I'm going to deal with right now. It's all... nothing. You haven't heard from them?"

Jarret crossed his arms over his chest. "That was hours ago."

"Right." Preston got off the bed. He walked over to me. "I agree. It's weird you haven't heard. Unless..." his voice trailed off. "There might be a very good explanation for all of it. Gus. He brought you here to be protected. I bet he told your parents to go into hiding. If the Hunters got you, they could be in your area looking for them. He'll know where they are, or if they just took themselves into hiding and told no one, then he'll know how to find them. I'm going to call him."

I hoped that was the answer. My stomach tightened. It was impossible not to focus on what was happening to me. The whole new half of me suddenly rearing to life was taking all my attention since I was pretty sure if I gave into the feelings inside of me and just let go, I was going to shift again. I wasn't even sure how I'd done that the first time. Still, it might just be like breathing. No, I forced the thought out of my head. I could not, would not shift. Even if I had to Dr. Seuss-esque rhyme in my own head over and over for the next week. Somehow, I had to manage not to also be a total narcissist.

"I need to know my family is safe. And I'm sure they've been worrying about me."

Anton put his hand on my cheek. I leaned into it. For a

second, I just stood there before he placed the bag of clothes into my hands.

"Thank you. I will pay back every penny." I looked at all of them. "Rich or not... I've never not paid my way, and I don't intend to take advantage of your kindness just because you have big bank accounts."

Anton dropped his hand from my cheek and took mine in his own again. He placed it over his heart. I sighed and this time the warmth that went through me had nothing to do with the shift. "That's very sweet."

Jarret nodded. "I get how you're feeling. Lately, I feel like I take and take. But we really can do this and not give it another thought. How about if I promise to tell you if you somehow cross a line that's too much? That'll be a hell of an uncomfortable conversation, but I'll do it."

I laughed. "Well, that was honest. Thanks. Yes, tell me. We'll have one of those moments we can both pretend never happened, but I'll know I haven't gone too far."

Preston spoke into his phone. "Sir, it's Preston. Leaving you a message, obviously. Anyway, I don't talk on the phone much, and you don't text. So we need to know what's going on with Mac's parents. Can't reach them. Call us back. And she's fine." He met my gaze. "She'll stay that way. I promise."

CHAPTER 5

"SO I PULL the head off of it and suck the juice out of the head." I held the red body of the boiled crawfish in front of me. "And then pull the meat out of the body?"

Jarret had already eaten half a dozen while I stared at the one in my hand. Anton wasn't far behind him, and I was pretty sure Preston lapped the two of them and had consumed a full twelve on his own. Rainer watched me. He hadn't started eating yet.

"Yep. There's also corn, potatoes, and mushrooms, if you don't like the crawfish itself. Also, I kept it spicy but not too spicy because it's your first time."

I stared at it. "Thanks for being considerate about the fact that I'm a crawfish virgin."

I'd no sooner uttered the words than wished I hadn't. Joking with Anton was one thing, but Rainer seemed like he might be something else entirely. Still, when he cracked a smile, I was able to let out a breath. My senses were dulled, with the scents of all the food overwhelming all other smells in the area.

I sneezed as a good whiff of onion hit my nose. I laughed. I hadn't eaten much since the change except for my starved middle of the night bacon fest. I didn't know if that was normal or not, my lack of appetite, but I was finding the new influx of spice very intense to my senses. Nothing ventured nothing gained. I tore the head off the bugger's body.

The spices burned my lips but the flavor... I'd never tasted anything like it.

An hour later, I was stuffed on crawfish and feeling as happy as I could remember being. The sun set in the distance, casting shadows of orange over the swamp. "It's pretty here. I didn't expect the swamp to be so alive."

Rainer nodded. "People think the swamp is dead. They make that mistake. It's alive out here. Even if these days there aren't werewolves." He stepped toward the edge of the dock. "Even if they buy the cock and bull story about the disappearance of the red wolves."

I knew that one. "They think they were relocated to North Carolina." Anton tapped on the dock and pointed at me. I blinked. "That's right. Gus found me in North Carolina. Do we believe in coincidences?"

In the background, a radio Jarret had put on played country music. He'd kept the volume low so that it was never dominant enough for me to try to recognize the song but loud enough I knew there was music playing. Maybe none of them wanted to answer my question, maybe they thought it was hypothetical. Or maybe they didn't know any more than I did and there was nothing to do but sit with our bellies full and watch the sun go down.

Anton placed his head on my shoulder, the way I'd gotten used to him doing. If anyone found that odd, they didn't comment. I didn't know what had happened to my family. I had no idea why we hadn't heard back from Gus. Hunters had taken me, locked me up, and I'd been forced to shift, when I could have gone my whole life without doing so. I'd learned the sweetness of feeling more than I'd ever been, and I was going to have to give it up. So, for right then, I was going to indulge myself in a good dose of denial. I was going to pretend that Anton didn't do this with all the girls. I was going to act like it was perfectly okay for me to be sitting here with feelings developing for all four of these werewolves as though that was allowed. Thirty years ago it would have been. In fact, I could have considered the idea of mating the Lejeune brothers.

That wasn't an option anymore. For tonight, I was just going to pretend it was. I'd had enough reality for a while.

Preston dragged a mattress into the main room and then went back and dragged another one. They hadn't asked me if I wanted to spend another night downstairs. Yet, they'd been right in their assumption. I did. It had been nice to be surrounded the night before, and I wanted the same feeling again. I probably would until the shifting need fled.

I eyed Rainer. "Are you and Preston staying, too?"

He nodded. "If that's okay. Might have been just a little bit jealous last night."

Anton patted him on the shoulder, and Rainer grinned at him. They really were all wonderful at communicating with him when he didn't say a word. Rain pounded on the roof of the house. It sounded like small pings for a second before a deluge of rain replaced the gentle noise.

I stared up at the ceiling. "Wow, that's a lot of rain."

Preston came in carrying a bowl and scooped some ice cream into his mouth. "It'll pass." He lifted up his bowl. "Want some?"

I shook my head. "No, thank you."

The rain continued to pound, and I shivered, listening to the sound. Give me a good snowstorm any day. I didn't like the sound of the rain. It almost felt... ominous. I shook my head. Letting my imagination run wild wasn't helpful. I'd always been ridiculously able to get carried away. I turned my attention back to the moment at hand and tried to ignore the pounding on the roof. "Sorry." I rubbed the back of my neck. "Guess I don't like the sound of the rain on the roof."

"It's loud." Jarret agreed with me before he patted the mattress. "Come lie down. Once you get used to it, it's soothing. That's one of the few sounds that can lull me to sleep here."

Preston groaned. "Oh no, little brother. You and Anton are on the second mattress tonight. You got her last night. Rainer and I get to cuddle tonight. Scoot."

Jarret rolled his eyes, but he didn't argue. Instead, he got up and moved to the second mattress. Eventually, everyone settled down. It was late, and darkness filled the room as solidly as the guys did. I stared at the ceiling, listening to the rain. I kept thinking it had to stop soon but it didn't.

If the guys were sleeping, they were silent about it, but I suspected they were up.

"Thank you for keeping me here, treating me like family, and making me safe." I swallowed. "I was at work. Sweeping up hair in the salon where I've been working for five years. I woke up in the back of a van."

I swallowed away my tears. The memories had held off, but they were, alive, vibrant, all consuming. I wiped away the tears and snuggled down on the pillow. "Sorry." I rolled onto my stomach, hoping to hide my head in the pillow.

"It's okay. Things are starting to return to normal inside. Stands to reason you're going to start to have more regular human emotions and fewer controlled by the wolf." Preston rubbed my back, and Rainer put a hand in my hair.

On the mattress next to us, Jarret and Anton both shifted, the floor squeaking as they did. All four of them were worried. The acrid smell hit my nose, but they weren't angry. The upset from the day before seemed to have passed, and for that I was grateful. These were nice men. They shouldn't have been fighting.

I must have drifted off, because when I woke up, it was to the sounds of breathing all around me. Rainer snored lightly, a comforting sound. Preston was silent and, like the night before, Anton and Jarret were quiet. I sat up. Something was wrong.

Goosebumps broke out on my skin. It was dark—so terribly dark—in the room, and I couldn't really see. The storm outside continued to rage and there was no moonlight to help with my sight. My nose burned as I got to my knees. I could smell... werewolf.

But not the ones in the room.

Maybe it was my wolf senses that helped me see in the dark or maybe I just got lucky. Standing in the doorway, fully wolf even as he walked toward me on two legs, was the scariest sight I'd ever seen. For a second, my breath caught. This wasn't like Gus. This creature screamed out pack, but nothing about him spoke of home. No, the red eyes glaring at me as it loped toward me just made everything wrong.

My terror silenced me for two seconds before I screamed. I backed up into the wall as Rainer came awake, followed almost instantaneously by Preston.

"What's wrong?" The oldest asked, reaching for me, but by then I pointed at the door. The shifted-yet-not-shifted creature had made way for a second of its kind to come through. Anton and Jarett were by my side.

I pointed, still not able to find words and they all turned to look at where I indicated. Rainer was on his feet.

"Fuck me."

Preston threw his body in front of mine. "It's a Loup-Garou change. What in the ever-loving fuck?"

The second one howled before he snarled, throwing himself on the ground and advancing toward us.

"Okay." Rainer stepped forward. "I don't know what the fuck you two want, but you're not welcome here. Get out."

I knew instinctively they wouldn't listen. Not while he was in his human form. The two advancing on us were lost to human sensibilities. My nose screamed danger to my brain.

He swiped at Rainer who managed to duck out of the way. Preston charged forward, and the first Loup threw him aside. He hit the wall. My heart fell to my stomach. "Preston," I called out to him.

He groaned. "I'm okay, Mac. Don't worry."

That was a lie. He wasn't. I could smell it.

The Loups only had eyes for me. Like the first time this happened to me, I couldn't have controlled the shift even if I'd had a sense that it was coming, which I didn't. One second I was me and the next I was... more.

I fell forward, my body breaking, changing, reshaping itself. The pain was agony.

Jarret reached for me, but Anton grabbed him, his blue eyes seeming to glow as he stared at me. A second later, Jarret's did the same.

They were going to shift.

Inside, I smiled. My wolf longed for pack. This was what she wanted, what we both needed. Our pack. Our family. My brain changed, my thoughts shortening until impressions hit me more prominently than actual words. Pictures rather than anything else.

The Loup—not my friend—lunged for me, and Rainer shifted, catching the bad wolf mid-stride as he did. They growled, tearing at each other. I should have been worried, but I wasn't. My mouth watered. Alpha fought well. He just needed to wear his fur more.

Preston rose from the wall. He still wore two feet, and as he stared at his brothers, he tilted his head, his eyes glowing blue. Yes, he saw it, too. They were shifting. Anton hit the floor, his face matching the pain of his scent. I growled, hating the scent. Jarret changed first.

I knocked against him, and his wolf eyes met my own gaze. He didn't know what was going on right that second. He was in danger. So was Anton. No. The Loups couldn't get to my pack.

They wanted me. Fine, they could have me, but they wouldn't have my men. I ran hard for the door. Preston got in my way, growling as he once again put himself between me and the Loups. I growled back. I wouldn't have him hurt.

He tilted his head to regard me. Why? What was confusing him? The first Loup got away from Rainer and ran for me, forcing Preston to leap, grabbing onto his throat.

We still had the other one to deal with. That didn't matter. I would not let them get hurt. I would protect them, even from themselves. I rushed out the door. A quick glance behind me told me I had the Loups' attention. They wanted me. This wasn't just about a fight. This was about... madness.

Wrong. Yes, they were wrong. They were sick. Bad wolves. I ran hard, exiting the house and heading out toward the back. I couldn't launch myself into the swamp. Even a wolf as strong as me could find itself on the wrong end of an alligator. But the woods would do. I didn't know where I was going. I'd never left the house, but my nose wouldn't fail me. No one was in the direction I ran. I had to get away from this sick wolf or die trying. I couldn't fight him. He was too big.

I ran toward a new house. I couldn't smell anyone in it. The door hung open, swinging. I rushed through the front door. The rain pounded down outside, and I hoped the sick wolf lost my scent.

Behind me, wolves howled. It was my pack. They called to me. I wanted to howl back, but I wouldn't give away my location. I hated this. I didn't know all the things I should know. The wolves who should have taught me things hadn't done so. I had to... learn.

But in the meantime, I had to keep everyone alive. I rushed up the stairs. This house was in even worse shape than the one Preston lived in. There were balconies on the second floor. If I had to escape, I'd rush outside onto the roof from the balcony and jump down from there.

I could... I turned. Standing in the doorway was one of the Loups. My nose was strong, if nothing else, and I could scent it was the second one to come in. I stared at him, my nose itching and my paws burning.

He whined, falling down onto his front two paws. He

met my gaze and dropped his eyes. Why? He was bigger than I was, definitely up on the dominance chain from me. And yet... I walked toward him.

There was something he needed from me, and it was mine to provide. I walked toward him, rubbing my side against him. He whined again. Yes, he had the Loup madness. He had it because he hadn't had me around. That was a thought I couldn't shake. I could make the madness go away. That was part of what I did. That was my...

A growl sounded in the room, and Rainer charged through the door, taking the Loup to the ground. They faced off, the sick wolf looking less... something... right then. I couldn't focus on it. Rainer raised himself, growls sounding from him. The wolves were face-to-face; it would only take one of them to strike. My mouth watered. Yes, Rainer was strong. I loved seeing it. I could practically taste his victory on my tongue even as a feeling inside of me warred with the need to stop this immediately. That sick wolf needed... Well, damn, what did he need?

I could see pictures of it, but it didn't make sense. The moon. Touch. Fire. What did that mean?

Three bodies slammed into the Loup-Garou. Growling. They were huge, and they were mine. Their scents overwhelmed me, wanted to bring me to my knees with joy to have them there. Also, I longed to join in the fight. But that wasn't my job. I whimpered, catching the biggest wolf's attention. That was Jarret. His scent of cloves hit me. He tilted his head, backing away from their opponent. I approached slowly, my head lowered, my eyes down.

Rainer nipped at Preston, and they stopped, too. Anton was still in my way. He growled, and I rubbed against him as I approached the sick wolf. I tilted my head. He needed me, but the truth was I had no idea what I was supposed to do. He whimpered just as the other Loup rushed into the room. He growled, saliva spraying everywhere as he launched at the one on the ground. I reared back, Preston's body joining Anton's to block me from whatever was about to happen.

I met the new wolf's gaze in the darkness. Pain radiated toward me. I wanted to fix it. I whined. I just didn't know how. He grabbed onto his friend's scruff and threw both of them, using the weight of his own body to break through the glass and throw both of them through.

Rainer rushed to the window. Maybe he was going to follow him through, but Jarret grabbed him by the scruff and yanked him back. They tumbled backward.

They righted themselves, and all attention turned to me. I lowered my eyes, listening to the sounds of them breathing. We were all okay, but the Loups were still out there, and they wanted me. I just didn't know why.

Rainer padded over, bumping me in the side. I lifted and then dropped my gaze. He bumped into me with a low growl. Jarret strode over, nudging my face with his own. That was sweet. Rainer nudged me again. Okay, I understood. He wanted me to move, to leave here. I lowered my ears and trudged after him. We were going home. I liked home.

I'd run all the way here, but the walk back home, surrounded by four wolves who had literally chased me into danger, who were, unless my nose lied, my pack, seemed like it went faster. The rain continued to pound, but it didn't bother me. No, right then the only thing that could get to me was uncertainty. What did the sick wolves want from me? Why did getting the madness turn them from werewolves to the two-legged Garous? And what was I supposed to do with them?

A scent struck me as we arrived at the house. The rising sun gave light through the rain, enough that I could see Gus moments after I smelled him. He sat on the steps just under the canopy watching us as we approached. He rose to his feet, and Rainer ran ahead to him. In a heartbeat, he'd shifted back to his human form.

"As soon as I get them settled, you and I are going to have a talk about what you knew and when you knew it."

Gus nodded. "I knew all of it."

He knew all of what? Preston shifted behind Rainer. He patted his brother on the shoulder. "This is shift two for her and one for the boys. Let's make sure they're okay. Sir, you should make yourself at home."

Gus sighed. I tried to follow the conversation, but none of it made sense to me. This was home for Gus. He was family and that made him pack.

I called the shift to myself, bringing my human body back. A fog struck me hard, my thoughts thickening like I couldn't make my brain function. I knew this feeling. It had happened before, but I was aware of a few things all at once. Rainer and Preston were naked and now so was I. Anton and Jarret hadn't shifted back and I was so... tired.

Preston grabbed onto my arm, holding me gently, while Rainer ran up the stairs. When he came back, he was clothed below the waist. He had a t-shirt in his hand, and he quickly dressed me in it. Rainer was bigger than me by quite a bit, and it fell to my knees.

I nodded to him. "Thank you."

"You're welcome." He touched my cheek. "Are you thirsty?"

I wasn't, but our attention was quickly changed as Jarret

shifted back. He fell forward and would have landed on his face if Preston hadn't grabbed him. "Gotcha, little brother."

Jarret blinked rapidly. "Pres, what is going on?"

"Yep." Preston didn't respond to the question asked. Instead, he caught him as he fainted into his arms. "Got you. I'm going to put him to bed. Watch this one when he shifts, would you?"

Gus winced. "First one always comes with the fainting. You're holding on pretty well, little Omega."

Why did he call me that? The world tilted left, and Rainer held tighter. "Come on. We'll follow Preston. Don't shift back yet, Anton. Or if you do, do it next to Gus."

"I'm sorry about this, Rainer."

My Alpha blinked. "For what? Oh, it must be for running out of the room where I could protect you and leading two dangerous crazed Loup wolves out on your own to be some kind of... bait? It must be that."

I sighed. "I'm not clear on what I did, but if I did that, then I'm sure there was a good reason to do so. I want to protect you."

He shook his head, laying me down on the mattress next to Jarret. He stared at me for a second. "You're mine. You know that, right?"

I didn't get to answer him before Jarret closed his eyes. I was his. And I was Rainer's. And Preston's. And Anton's. They were all mine. And I was theirs. I didn't know how we were all going to give this up. The idea was so awful I couldn't even fathom it. Why had Gus called me an Omega? They were all gone.

Preston exited the room and returned a second later with an unconscious Anton. He laid him on the other side of me. "Go to sleep, Mac. You'll be better this time. Not as lost when you wake up. Clearer memory."

I knew he was right. I could already feel the fog lifting. "You're all going to suffer now. I didn't want you to. Or suffer more. You had to shift. You'll have to detox again."

Rainer stepped next to Preston. "We were already suffering and... MacKenzie, we may not have to give it up now. I don't know how this is going to go. I can tell you that I'm not going to go back to pretending, or contemplating how I can date human women, when there is a you in the world. I can't speak for Preston but that's how I feel."

Preston shook his head. "Just been waiting on you, brother. All these years. Yes, you're ours. Worst-case scenario, we hide in this swamp for the rest of our lives. But maybe it won't come to that. You might be here to save us all. We'll see."

Anton shifted, drawing me close to him in sleep just as Jarret rolled over and pressed closer to my side. Rainer and Preston looked at each other and the younger grinned. "Where was our beautiful mate when we had to learn how to shift? No one to hold. Just hours of loneliness."

Rainer shook his head. "I'm going to go check on Gus. Then we'll hash some of this out."

I swallowed. "I don't think I can save anyone. I'm not strong, and I'm so confused."

Preston bent down and squeezed my foot. "Worry about that later."

I wanted to but there were a million thoughts rushing through my too thick brain. "Where is my family?"

"We're going to find that out." Rainer nodded.

"Are the Loup coming back?"

Preston shook his head. "Not unless they want to lose their heads."

I stared at Rainer. "It's hard for me to imagine it, you

going mad like that. I look at you and you're strong, healthy. You don't smell like you were ever lost to that."

Rainer winced. "It's hard for me to imagine that, too. But people saw. Close those brown eyes."

He was my Alpha. I wanted to listen to him, only, first... I reached forward and grabbed onto Rainer's hand, which was hot, almost burning. "It's going to be okay. All of it."

I passed out.

CHAPTER 6

I PULLED myself to the surface of consciousness. I hadn't done what I needed to do, and I couldn't leave those men like that, not if I could fix them. Somehow, I recognized I was capable of such a feat. I stumbled off the mattress on the floor. Neither Jarret nor Anton moved or woke. Sweat broke out over my body.

I sniffed the air. I could find them. The werewolves who had succumbed to madness, who had become the Loup-Garou of legend, they needed me. I stumbled in the hall and someone in the kitchen rushed to me.

"Mac?" Preston grabbed me around my waist. "What's the matter? You've been asleep five minutes."

I shook my head. "Have to go. I didn't fix them."

I pushed at him. He was like a wall that I needed to get around. Rainer came out from the kitchen, followed by Gus. "What's going on?"

Preston didn't move despite my efforts to make him. In fact, he smirked at me. If I was in any other state, I might have found that either adorable or annoying. Right then, I just didn't care. "I need to go help those men."

Rainer walked over to me, touching the end of my hair. "MacKenzie, we don't have the slightest idea who those men are. They could be anywhere. I'm not even sure how they found you to begin with. But we can't just go wandering around the swamp looking for them."

He didn't understand. "I can find them. I can feel them. I just have to follow the... knowing."

Rainer looked at Gus. "Any advice with this? I can't believe she's up. Second shift, I didn't rouse for a full day."

Gus shook his head. "No advice. I've never seen this, but we know the Omegas are different. The last one I knew in our pack before she passed was always around her mates. They watched her like it was their job and... maybe there was something to it. Get too close without permission, and they'd lose it. I thought it was way overprotective. We wanted to keep your mother safe, but we didn't keep her from walking into rooms first. Now... I'm wondering if they just understood how things were with their mate. Your mother never made any moves to be her friend, so we lived very separately from them. I don't have any information."

Why were they having this conversation? "It's really important." I might have shouted. I wasn't entirely sure. I just needed them to *understand,* and they weren't.

Rainer ran a hand through his long hair. It had been down since the shift, the first time I'd seen it that way, out of the bun.

"Okay. I think we can all scent her distress."

Gus shook his head. "Not me. I haven't shifted in years."

"Really? We can talk about that later. Fine. Preston, go get her pants. We'll take her wherever she needs to go and hopefully not have to kill the fuckers since we managed to hold off doing that this time."

Had that been an option? "Were you strong enough to kill them?"

Preston nodded. "All Rainer would have had to do was indicate that was what he wanted."

"Don't... they're sick. And they need me."

I shivered. Much as I needed to do this, it wasn't bringing me any joy to do so. Preston let me go, and I stumbled backward into Rainer whose arms came around me. I was weaker than I could ever remember being, but I was going to accomplish this. There wouldn't be any rest until I did.

Gus shook his head. "I told them. If we did this... if we put away our wolves and denied what was true, then we'd never know if the Omegas came back. Only when they shift can they be scented."

Rainer tugged on the end of my hair. "I thought Omegas could be scented at birth."

"How are we supposed to know that if we can't smell anything at all? I only knew it was her because when she shifted, it hit me like a ton of bricks. I'd have to be dead to not know it. She also scented like family. I took a guess that at least one of you would belong to her."

Rainer pressed his nose against the back of my head, and I closed my eyes. That was nice. Really, ridiculously nice. "She smells like home. And..."

Gus held up his hand. "Trust me. I get it whenever I am around your mother. I don't need a description of just how much you guys all like the smell of her."

"Right." Rainer shifted his hand to hold me tighter just as Preston came into the room, carrying my pants. I stepped into them like I was a child who had to have help dressing, and even though I knew this should have been embarrassing right then, I didn't care at all.

I walked forward, and Preston grabbed my hand. "Shoes." He pointed at the ground, and I put them on. "And we're not walking. We'll drive."

That didn't sound right. "But they're out there. In the swamp. I can't... drive there."

"Well, you can't walk on water either, and I don't think the gators are giving rides. Come on. We'll take one of the boats."

Rainer nodded toward Gus. "Are you coming?"

"Nope. This is on the three of you. Whatever is happening, it's not my journey. I'm going to keep working on finding her family. That I can do. See you when you get back."

Rainer nodded. "Sir."

They were so formal with him. That thought swept through my mind as I followed Preston out toward the boat he'd spoken of. My family was easier than this. Sometimes we didn't get along but I'd never at any time called any of the males in my family sir. That would have been weird.

I shivered as we approached the airboat. I'd never been on one before, and it should have been exciting, but the unused power inside of me hurt. I rubbed my arms. They burned. Preston frowned at me while he helped me get on the boat. "You're pale."

I shrugged and pointed in the direction where the call was coming from. "That way."

Rainer shoved on his shirt as he boarded the boat behind me. "This is insanity."

"This is probably the new normal." Preston handed me a pair of ear protectors. I put them on, and he started up the airboat. It was loud. I could hear it even with the ear protection, and I was glad for them. Rainer had his on, too, but whereas I couldn't take my gaze off the trees as they rushed by us, he seemed preoccupied with staring at me.

I squirmed. "I know this is weird. I know that you just got home and shifted after the first time in years. I know how miserable this has to be. I'm sorry."

He shook his head. "I'm sorry this is happening to you. The need to do whatever it is that you're going to do is hurting you. I can smell it. Makes me want to growl, and I'm not in my wolf form right now. Weird sensation, disconcerting to say the least."

Preston nodded as he steered; he shouted over his shoulder. "Me, too. We'll probably get used to it."

"I hope not," Rainer shouted back. "I'm not even sure how this happened. The Loups could what... scent her? When we couldn't? And what is she going to do for them anyway."

"I'm going to fix them," I answered, even though he'd spoken to Preston instead of me, which was rude. But I'd worry about that later. I was loopy... I might not speak to me either in my current circumstances.

He must have realized what he'd done because Rainer winced. "Sorry."

Several broken down mansions that had seen better days appeared in the distance. One of them caught my attention, and I couldn't pull it away. It wasn't the house we'd been in when we'd been fighting but a different one. The Loups hadn't run far. I got to my feet, and Rainer tugged me back down.

"Don't stand up till he comes to a stop."

I pointed at the house. "That one."

Preston nodded. "Got it. It's one of the ones scheduled to come down. The town is getting rid of a lot of the really old ones."

That was sad. There seemed to be a lot of that going around. Just tearing down what didn't work anymore, letting things rot. Like the Loups. They were just being left to die, and I'd never given it a single thought. Why would I have? I was going to let my own wolf die. One way or another, I was expected to kill it, either with non-use after a shift or no shifting at all. We were all required to live these lives because of the Loups.

My parents had made it seem simple when they'd explained it. For whatever reason—whether it be a genetic flaw, fate, or some external issue we didn't understand because we couldn't afford to study it without risk of discovery—the Omegas died out. There weren't any born. It wasn't until after that happened that anyone realized just how much the Omegas did for the pack.

Everyone had understood they played an integral role, keeping an emotional balance of some kind. If a pack member was sad, they sought out an Omega and felt better afterward. But the problem with the Loup-Garou had been unexpected. There had always been Loups, but it had been a rare condition that mostly happened to lone, packless wolves. After the disappearance of the Omegas in the general population, the problem started popping out every-where, and since the Loups were senseless when they shifted, they'd exposed themselves to the humans in large amounts.

That's when the Hunters had gotten out of hand.

And hence the Accords. No more shifting, no more exposure, no more deaths from werewolf Hunters.

But here I was and what the fuck was I doing? I didn't have time to contemplate any of this very long as Preston smoothly stopped the airboat on the decrepit dock. He threw his own headphones on the ground and leaned over to tie his boat. Rainer tugged on my hand, and I let him help me up.

He strode ahead of me. "Stay behind. I'll go in first."

"No." I shook my head. "They're going to be afraid of you. I go in first."

He grabbed my arm. "I'm not compromising on this. I want to let you do what you want. I will always want that. It's... part of this. But I have to keep you safe. I don't know how any of this between the five of us can work, but if it's going to at all, then we have roles in this, and my job is to keep everyone safe. I go in first. If they freak out, they don't get to have your help. That's how this works."

I supposed I could have argued. I'd agreed to nothing. I could have told him that we hadn't settled that there was going to be anything between them and me. I swallowed. But that would have been lying, and they'd have known it the second I said it. Heck, maybe before I even said it. They'd smell the lie, taste it on their tongue. We all knew there was going to be *something*. Even if it was just the idea of a mating and the knowledge that we could have it in a kinder world.

Or however we were going to manage this now. The two of them... and the two we'd left unconscious on a mattress in the living room... we were all connected and not just because they were brothers. If we could live our truths, we should be mated.

I nodded to Rainer. "Okay. Keep me safe. Thank you."

He paused before he nodded back to me. "I'd love to know all the things you just thought about before you answered me."

"No, brother, you don't." Preston laughed. "We never want to know exactly what goes on in her mind any more than she should know your every thought and feeling. We're all better off leaving some things alone. Besides, you'd know that she preferred me if you could mind read."

Rainer glared at his brother. "Not the time and place for me to kick your ass or it would be happening, stat."

Preston nodded. "I'll take up the rear."

We lined up, and the closer I got to the house, the more my fingers burned. By the time we stepped inside, I wanted to scream from the pain. Still, I kept my mouth closed. Whatever this was I had to endure it and complaining about what couldn't be controlled would only make me feel weak.

The two men were face down in the living room when I came in. The house stunk of their sweat and pain. Part of me wanted to run. I'd never done well with illness, my own or other people's. Puke made me do the same. But I forced myself to walk over to them.

"I think I'm safe enough, Rainer."

He nodded. "For now."

I bent down over one of them and rolled him over. He breathed. I wasn't any kind of medical professional. That was going to have to be good enough as a medical diagnosis. Not dead would do.

I called the shift onto myself, which shred my clothes into pieces everywhere. This was the first time I'd ever done this purposefully, and it was easy, but it hurt like my bones didn't want to let my wolf out. I was tired. I didn't know how much people shifted or didn't, but twice in a matter of hours seemed like it was too much for me right now.

Preston widened his eyes, and I could smell both his and Rainer's shock tickle my nose.

"Can you shift right now?" Preston asked Rainer, and I ignored them. I had something to do, and it was going to be easier to do it as a wolf. How did I know that? No idea. I just did.

I rubbed up against the unconscious man. His eyes flew open and a ton of emotions hit me all at once.

He was terrified, sad, confused, and angry...

I ignored all of that. Right now, I needed to make his wolf okay again. Next to me his body reshaped, turning back into his sick wolf. I snorted before I growled. I hated the way he looked, the wrongness of his scent. He should never have gotten to this point. Someone should have helped him.

It couldn't all be me.

I pictured him healthy and sent all my energy—all of that burn—toward making him that way. He cried out on a whimper, and Rainer squatted down next to me, placing a hand on my scruff. "She's burning up."

Preston paced back and forth. "We don't know what is normal."

I tuned them out even though I loved their concern. I had to do this. Not just once but twice. The man's body reshaped again, breaking, reforming, his eyes clearing before he was finally a werewolf I could recognize again.

We stared into each other's eyes before he dropped his gaze and hit the floor, showing me his belly. I stepped back. No, I didn't want that. This wasn't about submission between us. This was who I was, what I did.

I backed away, turning to the other man and repeating the process. This time it was easier. I knew what I was doing. Still, he flung around the floor longer, like it was harder for him to fix himself. The knowledge hit me hard. That was all I was doing—helping him help himself.

Both of the men I'd helped shifted back, hitting the floor in their human forms. They gasped for breath, grabbing their heads and crying.

I turned to Rainer, wanting to be near him and Preston

more than anything. I called the shift, finding my human form even harder to get to than my wolf one had been. I might have fallen forward, but Preston caught me.

"Got you, Mac."

"I'm going to..." I never got to finish that thought. The world went black.

I woke up when Rainer laid me down in the bed. His worried gaze met my own. I couldn't even smell his emotions. Everything was just a big fog around my head. He brushed my hair off my forehead. "What you did... I've never seen anything like that before."

"I didn't know what I was doing. There had to have been an easier way. Someone to teach me. I... bumbled it. He got thrown around."

Rainer shook his head fast. "Stop. You saved them. They told me they've been Loups for years, losing their ability to function even as humans. You saved them. They tried to come home with us, but I sent them on. Told them they could thank you another day."

That was good news. I couldn't take people right now unless they were mine. "Thank you."

He shook his head. "Don't ever thank me."

I touched the side of his face. "They were always Loups. Once they were, they didn't change back and forth, right? They were human or they were Loups."

He nodded. "For years and years."

"Rainer, we don't know each other yet but don't you see... that means you can't have been a Loup. Ever. So whatever happened when those people died..."

He sucked in a breath. "MacKenzie," he looked away, "I know. I can't deny it. I know. Someone lied. Someone... I can't right now."

I nodded. I understood. Some things were just too much

sometimes. "Lie down with me. Please don't leave me here alone. I feel..." I swallowed. "Too many things." And one of them was empty inside, hollow. "Never mind. We don't know each other like that yet. I'm sorry. I'm not a needy person. I..."

He threw off his shirt and set it aside before lying down next to me. I was totally naked. They'd apparently foregone dressing me this time and just brought me home. Rainer scooted in next to me. His body was warm, and I was immediately calmer.

I managed to battle back my tears. "Sorry."

"Stop. No thank yous and no unnecessary apologies between us." He tugged me close to him. "I needed this, too. I wasn't going to presume, but I am going to accept your invitation graciously. Close your eyes. What you did. I'll say it again. It blew me away. First off, you shifted twice in just hours. Neither Preston nor I could do it. Then you fixed what is supposed to be unfixable. MacKenzie, that is... I don't have the words."

I swallowed. "Rainer, I feel empty inside. Like I'll never be filled again." I sucked in my breath. "I'm not tired. I'm wrecked."

He leaned over and kissed me. I closed my eyes. Rainer was warm, and even as much as it shocked me that he kissed me, I couldn't get enough of the sensation. He lifted his head. His eyes were huge. "I'm sorry. I know that was out of nowhere. I just suddenly felt like I had to kiss you."

I shook my head. "More. Please."

His mouth met mine again. I drew him closer, holding onto the back of his neck. There would be no such thing as too close to Rainer right then. He moved until he was entirely on top of me. The weight of his much bigger body pressed down on me, and the feeling of being surrounded by his strength took over. I couldn't get enough.

I squirmed beneath him.

We kissed and kissed. I let my hands roam the length of his back where I could reach. Rainer was hard, and he was covered in tattoos. I wanted time to go through them, to memorize what he'd chosen to permanently ink on his body. But right then I just wanted to feel more of him, as much as I could.

I was naked, but he was clothed from the waist down. I lifted my head to kiss all over his face. "Rainer." I needed to breathe. "Whatever is happening between us, you don't have to do this."

He blinked rapidly. "Do you think I feel forced?"

"You didn't ask for any of this. I'm throwing you into this situation. You didn't ask for any of this."

He pushed my hair off my forehead. "You are so beautiful, MacKenzie Harper. I'd want you if you were human walking down the street. I can't imagine a circumstance where I wouldn't want every inch of you. I don't want to rush you. It just feels like all I want to do is kiss you right now."

This man had spent time in prison. I wouldn't be the next thing in his life he had no choice about. I kissed his neck, and he shuddered. "MacKenzie."

"Rainer, you are a beautiful man. Tell me to stop." I kissed the same spot again, kissing down his neck until I reached his shoulders. He was warm, and I licked him, just to taste him more thoroughly.

He jerked his hips against me, and I cried out. I had no experience with this at all except for the one time I kissed a human in tenth grade. I'd tried to get into the idea of doing this with a human, but I'd never been able to muster up much enthusiasm for the subject.

I didn't know Rainer's sexual history, and right then I didn't care. We couldn't have STDs and unwanted pregnancies weren't a thing. We had to be mated to get pregnant, and we had to want it.

Rainer stared down at me. "You make me feel like I am who I'm supposed to be. You make everything suddenly make sense."

We didn't know each other yet. I wasn't going to pretend that I was suddenly a completely fulfilled person because I'd met my mates. Whatever this was, it was still developing. That was okay. I still wanted him. Forget that, it was more than that. I needed him. And I didn't know why it was so strong but oh, how I did.

He ran his hand down my body, pinching my nipple. I almost came off the bed. Rainer smiled down at me. His eyes were heated.

"More," my voice lowered. I hardly recognized the sound.

He nodded. "Anything you want."

Rainer replaced his fingers with his mouth and sucked hard on my nipple. I closed my eyes, a moan starting in the back of my throat and practically exploding out of me. He jerked his hips against me, brushing the cotton fabric of his pants against me when he did, reminding me that he was still partially dressed.

I opened my lids. "We need to get your pants off."

He lifted an eyebrow. "We don't have to do that. I can make this all about you. I want to. I need this, too."

I shook my head. "Both of us."

"I'm not going to say no." He winked at me. "But what I really want to do is make you come."

I had no experience with this other than with my own fingers. The idea of intimacy with humans had made me completely disinterested, but the words he spoke made my heart rate kick up. Yes, I wanted him to do just that.

I tugged on his boxers, and he took them off. His cock jutted forward, hard and catching my full attention. I didn't have much of a frame of reference, but he looked huge to me. Reaching out, I cupped the end of his cock.

He sucked in a breath. "Fuck. Your sweet hand."

I smiled at him. "Like that?"

"More than like it." He pressed his nose against my chest, taking a deep breath. "I'm never going to get enough of how you smell."

This was my Alpha and oh how I wanted him.

CHAPTER 7

"COME HERE." He pulled me up against him so that we were both on our knees. My breasts pressed against his chest. I'd always been curvy, and I didn't have to stretch hard to rub my nipples against the hard lines of his chest. A jolt of pleasure shot through me every time I did.

Rainer ran his hands down my back, stopping right over my ass before he squeezed my cheeks. He grinned at me. "I am a big fan of your ass. Just so you know. I may stare at it every time you walk past me."

I smiled back. "I didn't notice."

"Of course you didn't." He threw back his head, laughing. "Subtlety is not my strong suit so you must have been really unaware of it."

I'd always notice it now. I wrapped my arms around his neck and held on. He pressed our lips together, and I fell into the heat of the moment, letting myself just exist in the universe that was Rainer.

I'd never known this much heat could exist. He pulled back to stare at my face, and in that moment, his eyes were all wolf. Rainer winked at me, and then they changed back. He nuzzled my neck before he kissed me again.

I couldn't get enough of this and I... needed more. I scraped my fingers up his back, and he gripped me tighter before lowering us both down onto the bed again so that he was over me. I reached between us and stroked him from tip to balls. He hissed in his breath.

"You're a beautiful man." His long brown hair, his sculpted body, and his ink... I'd never known I had a thing for tattoos, but it turned out I really did on Rainer.

He shook his head. "Stop. Couldn't be further from the truth. You're the beauty in this bed." His gaze traveled over me. "Those eyes. Your hair. The shape of your body. Every bit of you... you're stunning."

My cheeks heated. I was naked underneath him, and I felt so much more exposed from the words he spoke than anything we'd done together so far. I touched his mouth. "Sweet words."

He stroked down my stomach, stopping right over my vagina, running his hands over my thighs. I shuddered. This was what I needed. "Touch me everywhere."

Rainer nodded. "I plan to."

He pressed his finger inside of me. Shivers ran through me. Yes, Rainer needed to put his hands on me, his mouth on me, his cock in me, anything to be filled up with him. I pulled his head down to mine and kissed him, hard. He smiled against my mouth, easing his finger out. He released my lips so that he sucked on the finger that had just been inside of me.

Rainer moaned, closing his eyes. My heart rate kicked up. I wouldn't have thought that was sexy but watching him like the way that I tasted, that was fucking hot. I swallowed. He opened his eyes again to stare down at me.

He was turned on. Even if I hadn't been able to see evidence of it from how hard he was, I could scent it. Rainer's desire for me was spicy, like cinnamon. I wanted to roll around in it. I kissed his chest. "You are going to show me all of your tattoos, tell me about them, another time."

Rainer nodded. "Can't... form words." I understood the sentiment. I kissed down his chest until I got to his cock. Where I'd gripped him before, I kissed him now, right on the tip. Where I was now, I could have taken him in my mouth, just wrapped my lips right around him and sucked. My mouth watered. That was just what I wanted. I opened my mouth, and he quickly shook his head.

"No. I need to be inside of you." His voice was scratchy. "We'll do it again, and trust me, I'll never say no again. Like a dream."

He'd formed words pretty well right there. I kissed him one more time. The smell of him was heady, male, and mine...

We had to squirm around to get back into position. It was funny. I giggled, and he kissed my chin. I'd expected more nerves than I had. I touched his cheek. "I've never done this before. But... I feel like it's the most natural thing in the world with you."

He kissed me, his mouth gentle. "It's the mating. I'll always take care of you, MacKenzie."

I loved how he said my name. He never shortened it. It almost sounded musical on his tongue. He pressed two fingers inside of me before pulling them out slightly, finding my clit.

I sucked in a breath. "Oh, right there."

"Good. I want to find all your spots. I want to know your body so well I can play it like an instrument. Plan on me learning everything."

I loved the thought of that. I cried out as he found a rhythm that moved through me. Pleasure surged from the tip of my chin all the way down to my pussy. I squirmed, drawing my knees closer to my chest. I couldn't find a position that was comfortable. Not when I had so much... need... inside of me. I had to... oh.

The world exploded. That was the only way I could describe what happened to me. Colors crossed in front of my eyes, and I shattered from the pleasure. I cried out. His mouth came down on mine, his tongue dancing against my own. He let go of me, but only to readjust so he could push inside of me.

My body adjusted but slowly. It took a moment as he pushed inch by inch. I opened my eyes and captured his gaze. He was inside of me. I'd never had this feeling before, and I wanted to remember it just like this; I wanted to imprint this moment on my brain.

And then he moved, and I couldn't think at all. I lifted my hips to take his thrusts deeper. We both cried out together. Shivers wracked through me, and I hadn't even come yet. I thought the orgasm from his fingers was intense, but it was nothing for what was going to happen. I could already tell.

My gums burned. The sensation caught me by surprise. I jerked in my movements, which caught Rainer's attention. He stared down at me, mid-thrust. "MacKenzie, are you okay?"

"I don't know what's happening. I..."

Fangs elongated in my mouth, and before I could overthink it, I bit down hard on his chest. I came hard as a taste of his blood coated my tongue. I moaned. This was heaven. The thought hit me even as horror threatened to overtake me. What had I just done? Rainer's cock thrust deeper inside of me as a jolt of pain took me by surprise. The place where my shoulder met my neck burned.

Rainer licked the spot where he'd bitten me, and I did the same for him. It was a heady sensation, and I shuddered, coming down as he spent inside of me. He lifted his head to stare at me, a smile in his eyes as his fangs receded, my own doing the same.

I tried to catch my breath, my heart racing. Pleasure still pulsed through my veins.

He grinned at me. "I forgot about the marking."

I panted as I spoke to him. "I didn't know. It was just... instinct. I'm sorry. I..."

He nuzzled against my neck. "Are you kidding? No apology. You just marked me first. It's what mates do. I'm probably going to want to keep that mark on you going all the time when it fades. You'll mark me again and again. I forgot that mates used to be covered like this all the time. It's normal. It's... sought after. A beautiful sign."

A wave of exhaustion rushed over me. I'd been so empty, and it had kept me awake, unsettled. Now, with him still inside of me, pleasure riding me, and his mark on my neck, I couldn't keep my eyes open. Rainer pushed the hair off my forehead. "You're so beautiful, MacKenzie."

I closed my eyes.

Light filtered into my consciousness. I was sore in the way that only came from lying in one position too long. I was half strewn over Rainer, who lay on his back with his eyes closed as he breathed deeply. His long brown hair covered the pillow. I lifted my head to get a better look, my gaze immediately drawn to the bite mark I'd left on him. It was red, and as I moved my own neck, I could feel where he'd probably left a similar looking mark on me. Not that I'd complain. That had been hot.

I reached out to stroke my hand over the evidence of what I'd done to him, and he shifted slightly, bringing his arm around me tighter but not waking up. I smiled down at him. He was hard like he'd been carved from rock, but right then he seemed soft. I turned my attention to the ink on his chest. He'd had quite a bit on his back, too, but I couldn't see it right then so instead I looked at the ink closest to where I'd bitten him.

It was a chain wrapped around a wrist. I stared at it for a second, hoping there wasn't some sort of symbiotic relationship between the bite I'd just given him and the placement of that picture.

"I got that one in prison."

I startled, and he placed his hand on my back, settling me. "Sorry, it's totally creepy to wake up and see someone staring at you. I guess. I've never had it happen."

"I like your eyes on me." He ran a finger over my skin where his hand had been. "That one I got in prison. It's meant to be a reminder to keep the beast chained up."

I shook my head. "And now you've had to shift again."

"No have about it. I loved it. Doing it with you... that was a whole different thing, too. The five of us together? Even though we were worried about you... afterward... that just felt right. Like how it was supposed to be."

I knew what he meant. There had been an ease about it. "Rainer, I won't be another prison for you. The Loups. All of these issues with what turned out to be my role in the pack. I won't have you chained up for it."

He stopped rubbing and laid his hand flat on me. "Mac-Kenzie, that is not a prison sentence. Being yours... while you do whatever this amazing thing that you are going to do is... that is what I was born for. It's like I can finally take a breath."

"We don't know what any of this will mean yet. What if there is a Loup breaking in every night? Are we all just going to stay here? Where is my family? What about the group that took me to that lab and locked me up in North Carolina? What about Hunters? What about..."

He leaned over and kissed me. I closed my eyes and let him. He wasn't shutting me up, it was more like he was sharing my anxiety with me, and that was nice.

"Whatever has to happen, I'll take care of you, and we'll do it together. As for your parents... let's go check in with Gus."

The door flung open, and Preston walked into the room. "Morning you two. Was just coming to make sure you're alive before I have to go to work. You both slept a full twenty-four hours. The younger two are up, drinking coffee after their knockouts. So I need you guys up to handle their confusion. Also, I just wanted to look at Mac before I left for the day. I'm selfish like that."

Rainer stretched his arms over his head. "Morning, Preston. You just spit out a whole bunch of information."

He pointed at my neck. "Oh, look at that. You marked her. Lucky fucking bastard."

Rainer grinned from ear-to-ear before he pointed to his chest. "Right over my heart. She marked me first."

My cheeks heated, and I groaned, embarrassment making me bury my head in the blankets. Preston walked over closer to the bed. I lifted my head to look at him. "I... I couldn't control myself."

"Nor should you have. It's called mating. And once, not so very long ago, none of us would have been embarrassed to talk about it. It's normal for us. We're not humans. You touch other wolves and transfer your healing energy to them because you're the most special wolf ever born. You're our Omega. Mark us. Please. I'll practically beg."

My whole body heated up. When I spoke, it was with a lower voice than I expected to hear coming out of my mouth. "You'll never have to beg me for anything."

He picked me up, pressing my naked body against his clothed one. "When I come home from work, I'm going to make you so happy. And when I'm done, I'm going to bite you some place the whole world can see."

The next time I went around humans they were going to think I was obsessed with hickeys. I didn't even mind the thought.

"Put her down." Rainer got up from the bed. "And go to work if you're going. I'm going to cook us something for breakfast."

"After I leave?" Preston kissed my cheek but did set me down. "All right. All of you stay here while I go work. I'll spend the day feeling resentful and annoyed. But you're going to be here when I get back so that part I'll look forward to."

I squeezed his hands. "When it's safe, can I please come see your business? When whatever this is, is finally done?"

He touched my cheek. "I'd love that."

Rainer put on his boxers and whistled as he walked out of the room. For a second, Preston just stared into my eyes. I wasn't sure what he saw there, but he nodded like he'd gotten some kind of answer. His scent was neutral but happy.

I kissed his chin. "I feel guilty. I shouldn't be this happy. My family is missing. There are Loups out there suffering. Our entire species is in massive pain, denying their nature.

But here I am in your house... happy. That seems wrong, somehow."

He kissed my lips, gently. "I've never known happiness like finding you. And... fuck the world, Mac. We're happy. I'm not going to suffer any guilt for that."

"Go." I stepped out of his arms. "Before I ask you not to."

I quickly dressed, and he didn't move, waiting for me to finish.

He extended his hand, and I took it, letting him lead me from the room. I loved how he said my name. What would it sound like coming out of his mouth in passion? I pushed away the thought. I'd had sex once. I couldn't instantly become an addict. Could I?

I separated from him at the bottom of the stairs. Anton came out of the kitchen and strode right to me. He took my hand and placed it on his chest. I could feel his heartbeat. His smile was slow but adoring.

I sighed, so glad to see him. "You know what happened?"

He nodded fast. Obviously, he could remember shifting. That was a plus. He pointed outside and then at me. "Yes, we left while you were sleeping. I had to save those men. I couldn't leave it. Like breathing..."

He pressed our foreheads together, grasping onto me tightly. I stayed like that for a second. "I wasn't at risk. I promise. I didn't go alone. And next time... if there is a next time... you'll come, too."

He nodded, brushing his cheek against mine. The slightest bite of stubble scratched me, and I didn't mind at all. Just to get to be this close to him was a gift.

"Anton, what am I going to do as the only living Omega?"

He pulled back to look at me. I didn't see any answers in his gaze.

"Hey." Jarret came toward us, handing me a bottle of water. "Rainer is actually cooking. A whole big thing of breakfast. I'm so excited. Kenzie, we all shifted together. I can't even believe it, and I did it. Feels like a dream. Thank you."

I shook my head, hugging him to me. "Thank me? No. This is all my fault. I don't know how this works, but you're going to have to go through withdrawal now, too. I... I should be apologizing. I mean, Omega or not, we can't do this. We're all bound by the Accords."

He hugged me tighter. "Right now I don't care about that. I always knew I was living a half-life, and I didn't think there was a thing I could do about it. You saved me. Something in me... it was dying. Now I feel me for the very first time. Thank you."

"Oh, Jarret... I..."

Sadness hit my nose; the scent overbearing, and I stepped away from Jarret. It wasn't him giving me that scent. No, I whirled around. Were there Loups at the door? Anger took over the smell of sadness and had me charging toward the door. Gus strode toward me from outside where he must have been by the swamp.

Preston was right behind him. I looked between the two of them. Had they been fighting? The guys had hostility toward Gus, that much would be obvious even if I couldn't smell it, but they'd never gotten really upset. I needed the whole story. We all hardly knew each other when it came down to it. Even if things had started to pick up in the feelings department.

"What's wrong?"

Gus lifted his brows. "You could smell it out there?"

"What's wrong?" I didn't want to talk about my nose. I'd repeat myself until I got answers. My hands burned. The energy trade that Preston spoke of earlier turned on. When something was wrong, I needed to fix it.

Preston came up next to me. "We're okay. You don't have to fix anything for us. No, honey. This is about you."

I steeled my spine. Rainer, Anton, and Jarret were behind me. "Somebody talk, now."

"I've been waiting for information on your family. It's what I feared. They've been taken. The same way you were. It seems like almost all the Colorado families were. I've sent trackers after them. We found you. We'll find them. They've shut the facility in North Carolina, but that means nothing. We'd already started to follow their money. They're Hunters. They should be killing wolves, but they're not. We don't know why, and they didn't have you long enough for you to even know, I don't think. Do you know what they wanted?"

My head spun. That was a valid question, an important one. It deserved an answer. I had to think. I had to... push through the nausea that made me want to puke. My family was taken. No, it was one thing for it to happen to me. Another to think of my brothers, my mom, my dads... none of them should be at risk.

Anton stroked his finger down my cheek. I blinked. They needed an answer. "Just vague impressions. A cage. Men in lab coats. Guns. Laughter. I shifted. I think I was drugged, and then I was a wolf. I'm sorry. I didn't know what was going to happen. You came. Like an avenging angel. And killed them."

He shook his head. "I killed one of them. You'd already taken down three all on your own. Don't worry. I always find my prey. Particularly the kind that takes what doesn't belong to them." His gaze quickly shot to Anton and then just as fast away.

My youngest mate rocked back on his feet. The quick glance hadn't been lost on him. I rubbed the back of my neck. "I knew I'd killed at least one. It's still blurry."

Jarret nodded. "Like my shift. I only have impressions of it."

Anton shook his head, and Jarret lifted his eyebrows. "You remember it? Clearly?"

He nodded in response.

Gus sighed. "I always remembered mine, too. Few do. It just is what it is. MacKenzie, I will get your family back. But now I have to go."

He had to go? "Where are you going? Can I help? I could come."

"No," he yelled over his shoulder as he headed for his dilapidated truck. "Stay here, Omega. Stay hidden. Every wolf matters, but for now you matter more. And my sons need you. They're all going to figure out how to pull their shit together. And how to take care of you. I have faith in them."

Preston groaned. Rainer rubbed my back. It was Jarret who spoke. "Come inside. It's humid out here. Let's go in. We can talk this out."

"Talk it out?" My temper flared, but I knew it wasn't fair to direct this at any of them. They hadn't caused this, and they'd been nothing but kind to me. I bit down on my lip before I could say something I'd regret. I'd never gotten mad particularly well. My anger was at these Hunters not at them. Certainly not at Jarret's sweet words.

I stepped away. I needed air, I needed space. I needed..." I don't suppose I can shift right now."

"Right now? In the middle of the day?" Preston looked around. "I..."

"Go to work," Rainer spoke to Preston. "No, you can't shift right now. Not even here with seemingly no one around. It's not safe. We'll shift when it's safe and when it's crisis. Otherwise we're going to be safe. Hidden. And that means not being flippant about when and how. I get it. You need some space. And your wolf wants to give that to you by running as far and as fast as you can. You want space, you can have it, but not like that."

I growled and then covered my mouth. Humiliation hit me, warring with the million other things I was feeling.

Rainer shook his head. "It's okay. I don't care if you growl at me. As long as you listen. I only want to keep you safe. Keep us all that way."

I shook my head. "I don't get mad well. I don't do... sad and angry well. I'm terrified. You must smell it. That's a very bad situation for me. I'm a grown up. I can learn to control myself. I'm working on it."

"So far all you've done is growl and not speak whatever you're thinking in anger." Jarret shrugged. "Last time I was terrified I was a lot more vocal than you. Don't worry about it. We're all terrible at this."

Rainer nodded toward the inside. "Come in. Let's eat something. You have to be starving."

I was. And coffee sounded like heaven. "They have my family. What am I going to do? How are they going to get through this? My mother..."

"Was once a shifting werewolf. Your fathers, too. Your brothers, if they have half your backbone, will be fine. It'll be okay. Trust Gus. He does what he says he'll do even when its obstinate and against whatever everyone else wants him to do. He says he's going to get your family, he will."

Preston delivered that speech and then kissed me on the cheek. Just like that, I believed him. Preston thought Gus would get this job done, and I had no reason to think Preston didn't know of what he spoke.

I nodded as my stomach grumbled. "Is there bacon?"

Rainer put his arm around my shoulder. "There will always be bacon."

Well, now that was a promise I could be excited about. "When we get my mother back, she's going to freak out that I'm living the way I am. With you guys. Shifting. I was always the best at pretending to be human."

Even if every day had felt a little bit like death. My family would be fine. They had to be. I couldn't accept any other outcome.

CHAPTER 8

I WAS SO full I couldn't move but that didn't mean I couldn't think. My family was missing. Most of the pack in Colorado was, too, and I needed to stay hidden like some kind of princess locked in a swamp. I had no illusions about why this was. Sure, I was the mate to the Lejeune brothers, but it was also because I'd turned out to be an Omega. I'm sure they would have wanted me safe if I'd been just a regular werewolf, but they were really not going to let me out of their sight since I had to keep the entire werewolf community from becoming Loup Garous.

Jarret bumped me slightly. "What can we do today to make things a little easier? Short of chasing after my father to go kill werewolf Hunters."

I chewed on my lip. "Maybe it would help them if I could come up with memories of what happened, of how they took me. It's such a fog."

He nodded at me. "It might. I'm not sure how we do that. My memories of last night are so all over the place. I'm not sure how to get that back. I can't advise you on how to get your own back."

Anton held up his tablet. Jarret sucked in a long breath. "Are you actually going to use that thing?"

With a smirk, Anton rolled his eyes at Jarret. "I think it's not helpful to get yourself upset over something you can't control. You're not going to get those memories back. It'll be like beating your head against a brick wall."

The low mechanical voice of the tablet spoke for Anton. He was right. I sighed. This wasn't going to get any easier.

Jarret pointed at him. "How is it that you have your memories? Why aren't you afflicted? You and Gus. By the way, I think that settles the question as to whether you're his or not."

Rainer snorted as he walked in the room. "Was there any question about that? Same shade of brownish, grayish eyes. Yes, he belongs to Gus. And you're Brian's. You look just like him."

Jarret nodded. "Not that any of us are ever supposed to speculate about that. We all belong to everyone. Six fathers. One mother. You're very obviously Kevin's." He looked up at me. "Although I've never been clear on Preston."

Rainer nodded. "That's because you don't have clear memories of Joe. He looks and acts just like him."

Their father who had died rescuing Anton. I'd forgotten his name was Joe. That was a famous story, and what had pushed the family into signing the Accords and giving up shifting.

Jarret cleared his throat, and Anton put his hand on his brother's back. He typed on the tablet as he shook his head. "That's never been your fault."

I looked between them. "Why would it be?"

"Because I was watching him. When he got taken out of the crib. My mother had left me in there, and she'd said stay here with your brother while I run dinner next door." Jarret pointed down the swamp. "About ten miles that way. That's where our home was. This one's been empty forever but that was our childhood home. They rushed in the house. I ran, leaving him in the crib. And, well... yeah."

Anton slammed his tablet down and shook his head again, pointing at his brother.

I swallowed. "How old were you?"

"I was three."

Rainer growled. "Have you seriously been carrying that around? And neither of you told me? You were three. You shouldn't have been left with him to begin with, even for three seconds, alone in the house. She fucked up. The neighbors had pneumonia. Her heart was in the right place giving them dinner. It speaks to how well behaved you were to begin with that she could even do that. We're lucky they didn't get you, too. I wasn't there, but my understanding is that you ran for help. Remember that much?"

Jarret cracked his neck. "No. I don't. I know that the dads never forgave me. And I know that even that little, I loved the baby, and I shouldn't have left him alone. If they'd taken me, we could have gone together and maybe I'd be the one with the tablet."

Anton shoved him. He was angry. I could smell it, an acrid scent that was more fury than mad. Rainer leaned against the counter, seemingly relaxed. I didn't get anything from him except calmness in his scent.

He pointed at Jarret. "You think Anton would ask you to trade places with him? Fuck, no. He doesn't even remember what happened."

"Yeah... well, Joe died and sometimes I forget he ever existed so I'm really a piece of shit."

Rainer tugged Jarret into a tight hug. "You were just a baby, too. My little brother. And they were waiting for her to go from the house, like they knew she would. Like they had a role to play in that woman's pneumonia somehow, anticipated Mom would leave the babies. They wanted you, too."

Jarret didn't speak, but I smelled his sadness fading. "You know they all hate me."

"They don't. They hate me a little bit. They don't know what to make of Preston. He's an explosion they keep waiting to happen. Anton makes them sad because they've never seen him the way he actually is. They don't hate you. They don't know what to make of you. We're a little bit fucked up to them. That's okay. We get each other."

Jarret stepped back. "Yes. And now we get her."

He winked at me, and I hugged him like Rainer had done. "My parents hardly think of us at all. It's not a happy life, not shifting, always pretending. Maybe they're all just so consumed with their own suffering they can't think of us at all because they're too busy just getting through the pain."

Anton tugged Jarret away from me and then hugged me tightly.

Jarret groaned. "Yeah. Yeah. I forgive you for shoving me."

Rainer put his arm around me. "About time we had this conversation. This is because of you. We might have gone our entire lives never speaking about this. You came. We're going to be better. I know it."

I sighed. "Rainer, I'm just one woman. Don't pin too many hopes on me."

"We'll see."

I needed to get busy. "Do you think it would be useful for me to go room to room and make a list of what we should fix in each one? Would that be helpful or annoying to Preston?"

Jarret laughed. "I don't think there is much you could do that would piss Preston off. This is your house. I mean, assuming we want to stay here. Is that what we want?"

"Don't look at me." Rainer laughed. "I'm kind of lost in the world outside of this group. I'll go wherever you guys want. For now, this is the best place to keep you hidden."

I rubbed my arms. "I don't want to stay hidden forever. There has to be a time at which I don't have to be. I know, I've been here just a couple of days and things are nuts. We're all acting like this is normal. A person showing up on your door who you have to care for who turns out to be your mate and also an Omega? You're uprooting your lives. My family is missing and... yep. I can't even. I'm not going down this path. I'm going to go room to room and, I don't know, do something."

To their credit, they let me do as I wished. I appreciated that no one argued with my need to go do something, to simply be busy. They didn't know me, or how important it had always been to me to be busy.

Even on vacation, I wanted activity. Not that I'd had that many of those.

I stared at the living room. What was I doing? I didn't know what had to be done in every room. I didn't have the slightest idea.

I was...

"A couch, to start." Jarret came up behind me, leaning his chin on my shoulder. "A couple of chairs. A television. Some paint on the walls. I actually think we should rip the molding off the base and redo them."

I grinned, not that he could see that. "I'm clearly not the

one who should be going room-to-room. That is obviously you."

"I like house design. Always have. I have no background in it, but I do like it."

I wrapped his arms around me tighter. "Why not do that instead of law school? You never sound enthusiastic about that when you bring it up."

"I never thought about it as an actual option. Home repair wasn't something any of my dads did." He put his nose against my neck. "You smell so good."

I leaned against him. There was his woodsy scent. I closed my eyes. "You smell pretty great yourself."

He made a sound in the back of his throat that was half sigh, half moan. "A rug."

I opened my eyes. "What?"

"We need a better rug in here." He kissed my neck. "You wanted to be busy. And much as I would love to get you naked right here on this floor, I'm going to help you keep busy in ways that keep your clothes on. For now."

I laughed, throwing my head back against his shoulder. "Naked would be okay."

"Then we'll get there." He took my hand in his. "After we work out several other rooms."

Was Jarret... playing with me? I grinned. He was. This was playful. He teased. I'd yet to see this side of him. "That so? You're that invested in fixing this place up?"

"I'm that invested in making a comfortable home for you where we can keep you safe even when this current threat has passed. And also in drawing out my time with you. The second Gus brought you into the house I... I was struck with you. I know why that is now. I just can't imagine there'll ever be enough time in this lifetime to look at you. I could do it all day every day."

That had to be the best thing anyone had ever said to me. "Jarret..."

He brought my hand to his mouth. "Come on. Let's figure out how to make this old house smile. And I'll do it for you."

We ended up visiting every room in the house except Rainer, Anton, and Preston's bedrooms. They should get to do their own. Anton typed in what we'd decided to call the study. He'd barely looked up when we walked in. That might be normal for him when he was writing. I'd never lived with an author before.

"All consuming," was all that Jarret said to me when Anton had nodded his head to indicate where he wanted to put a couple of desks.

Now, we were on the back porch, staring at the swamp. Somewhere, someone used a chainsaw. The noise in the distance was a backdrop to the muggy afternoon, and although it was far away, drowned out the noisy ceiling fan that did nothing useful except move the hot air around the room. Holes in the screens let in the mosquitoes we were trying to keep out.

I reached out to touch one of those holes. "I can see why wolves settled here. It's a good defensive position. Hard to get at us from this side, and we can keep watch from the other."

He laughed. "In theory, except for those pesky little things called airboats created sometime around 1905, if I'm remembering my history. And before that there were canoes... probably around..."

I held up my hand. "Are you telling me you are one of

those people who can recall years things were invented? Like your brain actually works like that..."

He smirked at me. "Drives Preston crazy. But, yes."

"That's kind of awesome that you can do that. I don't have that ability." I loved how he blushed a little bit. "I don't know what I wanted to do for a living. I never did. School came second to survival, but I always assumed I'd make some kind of career in decorating or something. That's off now, right? Even when the Hunters are gone, I'm going to be a full time Omega, right?"

His smile fell. He opened and closed his mouth. "Probably."

I appreciated that he wasn't lying. "That's what I thought. And you will all have a second full time job to whatever you do to watch over me."

"You say that like it's a bad thing." He shook his head. "That's the job of the male werewolf. Not something I was supposed to get to do. The female is the center of the family, the males keep her and their home safe. Or try to. My fathers failed. But to get to do that? For you? Yes, please."

To me it sounded like we were all going to be wrapped up in a bubble that none of us might have chosen. Not the relationship part. That I would have picked anytime. He was correct. There was a rightness to all of this that settled inside of me, like picking up pieces that had been missing. But the rest of it? With the Accords, what we were doing was illegal, and not forgetting that if every werewolf alive decided they needed an Omega fix, I was going to be seriously in trouble.

Unless I wasn't. Maybe I was overthinking it.

Jarret kissed me, pressing our mouths together. It was a sweet, calm embrace, and it took my attention entirely from my own thoughts. I melted against him. Eventually, he lifted his mouth from mine.

"I love how you taste. I love how you smell. I could become obsessed with you, Kenzie."

I kissed his chin. "I want to make you happy. I want to know that your days are ones that make you... satisfied."

He lifted one half of his mouth in a half-smile. "I want that, too. And although I have no experience with this, I imagine I will be very satisfied."

I shoved at him lightly. "Dirty mind."

"Only for the last few days." He fit me against him. "I was thinking about the bedroom situation. Do you want to make a sixth room? Kind of a communal sleeping area... like we all have our own space where we keep our stuff but one room to ah..."

The sound of an airboat tearing through the waters abruptly caught both of our attention. As most of the houses around us seemed to be abandoned homes that had basically become rundown shacks, there didn't seem to be a lot of traffic around here. This one, with three men on board, came to an abrupt stop in front of us.

"Hey, Preston." A man called out. "We need you."

Jarret looked at me for a second. "Wait here. Don't come out there, okay. Better yet. Call Rainer and get him to come stand here with you. Or Anton. Either."

Did he know these men? They thought he was Preston. I had a million questions, but they could wait. I sniffed the air. All I got was human and male. They were anxious but not angry and nothing about them was setting off any alarms my wolf might have. Not that I was any kind of expert in this.

I nodded, stepping away from Jarret as he headed toward the door from the screened porch.

"Hey there, Preston's at work. I'm his brother, Jarret."

"Oh," two of them seemed to say at the same time. And the third who had done the shouting spoke again. "I forgot he had brothers."

I turned and headed inside. "Hey, anyone who can hear me. Jarret said to come here. There are men on airboats outside that he's talking to."

Jarret had increased his accent, thickened it when he spoke to the men on the boat. Had that been purposeful or just something he'd done on accident? His southern sounding drawl had been lightweight when he spoke to his brothers and me. Now, as he conversed on the dock, he sounded more like Preston.

Rainer came down the hall with a wide stride and nearly collided with Anton on his way out of the study.

"Humans," Rainer pointed. "Stay inside."

"Jarret is talking to them. Told me to get you."

Rainer took me by the shoulders, putting himself between me and the door. "That's good. It's complicated. I'm sure you're not at risk for anything. But if they're looking for Preston, then we have to be careful. He does things to keep himself in the loop with people who may not be who you should be around."

I blinked. "What does that mean?"

"I'll explain when they're gone."

I hated waiting, but I was also not an idiot. If Rainer wanted to wait and was putting himself between me and the door, then they weren't men I wanted anything to do with. One kidnapping was more than enough for me. My gums burned. It was a different feeling than when it happened to my hands. I didn't want to fix anything. I wanted to fight.

Anton put his hand on my chin and turned my head to

look at him. I could see what he wanted in his eyes. I needed to calm down. I couldn't shift right then. I took a deep breath and nodded. His small smile told me what I needed to know... he was glad I was listening.

Jarret turned and came back in the house, the sound of the boat engine filling the air as it drove away going wherever the men were taking it.

He closed the door and locked it.

"Well?" Rainer asked him. "Do I need to call Preston?"

"I don't know. The thing is that I'm not sure Preston knows if they're Hunters or not. There hasn't been activity in this area for a long time."

I choked. "Hunters."

Rainer nodded. "One of the reasons Preston stays here is because he keeps an eye on things. Obviously before we left there was a huge problem. Not this house, but this area is where they took Anton. There were so many local legends about the Loups that the word had become synonymous with werewolf. There were attacks. We had to go. But there were Hunters. When Preston came back, he tried to sort of infiltrate them."

What? I sucked in my breath and almost inhaled a fly that buzzed right by me at the most inopportune moment. That would have been just my luck. Eating a fly. I swatted it away. "A werewolf infiltrated the Hunters?"

"Tried." Rainer nodded. "I don't know that he's actually succeeded. But the locals do seem to like him. He's never been invited to a meeting or anything."

"Do they have meetings?" I asked the question, and Anton grinned at me. I shook my head. "It's a reasonable question."

Jarret sighed, running a hand through his hair. "They

must have meetings. How else do they plan things like kidnapping gorgeous brunettes and taking them hostage?"

None of this was funny and yet there was still the element of the ridiculous to it. "Email. Facebook groups. Maybe there are Twitter hashtags."

Rainer groaned but it made Jarret smile. "What would it be? Hashtag Get The Werewolves?"

"We've lost the point." Rainer strode back to the kitchen. "We had a Loup attack and then these guys show up looking for Preston. They don't necessarily know the Loups were here but maybe just that they were in the area. Or maybe it's nothing at all. Maybe it's beer and poker. I don't really care. I just know Preston needs to speak to them. And you need to be kept away. If they're Hunters, and I know that's a big *if*, then we have a situation because they'll probably have the kind of resources to learn that they lost you and their people were killed. I don't want them putting two and two together."

A feeling of dread moved through me. It wasn't fear of being taken; it was more like being trapped. "Does that mean I can't go outside at all?"

"No, that would be excessive at our current situation. But it might get that way. We'll keep an eye on it. Unlike years ago, we are aware of the risk. We'll keep looking, but if any of them come up to the house, go in while they're still too far away for them to get a good look at you."

That made sense. I took a deep breath. I wasn't trapped yet. I put my hands on my knees. "Maybe I should dye my hair."

Rainer and Jarret both made a sound of distress, and Anton shook his head. I guessed they didn't like that idea. I lifted my head to look at them. "It's hair. The color can be changed. It grows back."

Rainer tugged on the end of mine. "We like you like this. But maybe for safety that makes sense."

"I'll text Preston about the guys and get him to pick up some hair dye while he's out. They know that his brothers are here. That should at least buy us some leeway to move around for a bit."

Anton held up his tablet, and we all waited while he typed. "Let's not get too paranoid. This isn't the kind of situation where everyone is watching our every move. I doubt they have satellites. These are idiots with a monster agenda."

Jarret shook his head fast. "Much as I hate to disagree when you are finally using the tablet, I'm going to. When they took you over two decades ago, they were idiots with a gun. They didn't kill you or want to. They wanted to hurt you. That's what they did. But when they took our mate, it was to a research facility where they were going to do who knew what to her."

He made a good point. "Maybe they've gained sophistication and money."

"I agree with Jarret." Rainer strode toward the kitchen. "We can't be too careful. That's all there is to it."

I was suddenly so tired I could almost not deal with it. "You know not shifting was supposed to keep us safe. I never shifted. Not once. And someone got me anyway. That means there was betrayal from someone who knew. The only people who would know that are other werewolves."

Rainer stopped walking and turned to look at me. "That's true."

"They took almost all the werewolves in Colorado. I'd love to know who they didn't take, but I suppose that is neither here nor there since there are conspiracies everywhere. The woman with pneumonia, who may or may not have lured your mother from the house over two decades ago. The people who blamed you for killing those people, Rainer, when you could never have been a Loup, never lost to the madness because you shift like a werewolf now."

Anton's tablet spoke for him. "Conspiracies fill me with nausea."

"Me too." I touched his arm. "So many things kept hidden and I'm not talking about me. I'm talking about all the things we never discuss. Like what happened to the Omegas. How did this happen? Why don't they tell us anything except not to do what we were born to do? What are all the things they all wanted to bury in that swamp or in the mountains of Colorado or in the snow in Alaska? What is so bad that we're all being lied to all the time?"

Jarret wrapped me in his arms. "Whatever it all is, I promise you, our sweet Omega, that we'll be okay. They won't get you a second time."

I wanted to believe him. But I'd already spent time in a cage, and as the lies, not of our creation, continued to build, I wasn't sure I could trust the universe to be that kind.

CHAPTER 9

JARRET LEFT to go buy some tools he wanted to start fixing up the house. That seemed like the perfect time to take a shower since I was running out of things to do. The guys were really good at cleaning up after themselves, and in any case, I wasn't going to start being the housekeeper since I pretty much hated having to do those kinds of chores as much as I hated doing anything. I'd always clean up after myself, but I wasn't going to start folding laundry just to make the time pass.

I walked into my bedroom and stopped at the sight of a book on my pillow. What was that? I walked over and picked up the paperback. I hadn't read on anything but an e-reader for the last year, but I did love the way a book felt in my hands. I stared down at the cover. It was a man by himself, staring off in the distance at a fog surrounding him. It was the author's name who caught my attention.

I grinned. This was Anton's book. Well... I'd just been given something to do. I set the book down. This was Jarret's doing. Anton would never have handed me his own book. Jarret was so proud of Anton it had actually become a scent, like cinnamon, that I could identify. I sniffed the book. Yes, the woods and cinnamon. Jarret had brought me the book.

Downstairs, the smell of shrimp cooking in butter traveled up to me. Rainer had been in the kitchen most of the day. When we weren't worrying about conspiracies, he hummed to himself while he cooked. Happiness wafted off of him.

I grinned. Last night had made me pretty happy, as well. It was just too bad I couldn't stay that way. Life infected all of my joy. My family was taken. And everything might just go to hell.

I took a deep breath. I had come up to take a shower, and I was going to stick to the plan. Preston had put me in here because the bathroom worked, and I was glad for it. I did like hot showers, the kind that practically scalded my skin. The hot water here lived up to my hopes. Before long I was clean.

Still, I wasn't ready to be done with the water. I'd once made a joke about wolves liking water that no one in my family had laughed at. I filled the tub up with hot water, trying really hard not to drip all over the floor while I did so. I was really wasting water and right then I didn't care. At home we tried to be careful with our environmental footprint. We'd never discussed it, but it was probably the wolves in us. Even when we didn't discuss it, we were aware of the environment all of the time.

Thinking of them all made me tear up, and I grabbed one of the towels and placed it over my head before I sunk into the hot water. At home, one of the few things I splurged on was lavender bubble baths. I loved the smell.

I took the towel off my head to stare at the peeling paint on the door. We'd have to fix that.

I rolled over onto my stomach and leaned on the other edge of the tub. A creak in the bedroom caught my attention and a second later Preston poked his head through the open door.

"Oh, I'm sorry." He quickly looked away. "Came to check in. Rainer said a lot of things were thrown out today that may have made you anxious. Coupled with your family. I wanted to see if you were okay, but I'm not going to invade your privacy. I thought maybe you were asleep. I was just going to peek. Anyway, sorry."

Preston was actually rambling. It was sort of adorable. "You've seen me naked a few times now."

"Right." He looked down at the floor. "But this is different, right? This isn't shifting. This isn't you with my brother. It's just the two of us alone."

"Oh, I see." My stomach grumbled. I'd skipped lunch while I'd wandered from room-to-room. It was catching up with me now. I smiled at Preston. "If you get me a towel, we can talk and..."

The smell hit us at the same time. There were humans at the front door. I'd not heard a car come back but then again, I'd not been listening for it.

Preston scowled. "Fuck me. They're back. I already talked to them at work. Those three are jumpy tonight. Stay here. Okay?"

I nodded. "Sure. I'll wait. I get it. I'm not to be seen."

He winced. "And I get that you don't like it. I wouldn't either. Wolves don't like to be caged. Thanks for not being stupid about it."

I waved my hand. "I'll just stay in this bathtub and do nothing."

Preston groaned. "I have to go talk to humans while you're naked in the tub. Life is so unfair."

His words warmed me as much as the water. I flipped around. Rainer appeared where Preston had been.

"Same three as earlier. They're here to talk to Preston, and Jarret's going to go out with him. I'm not sure what has them so worked up. But it can't be good. I don't want you lying in the tub just in case." He held out a towel. "Here."

Well, there went that great plan. "Really? I was thinking of living in this tub. Maybe permanently."

"That would be a shame." He winked at me. "You'd become a giant prune."

I couldn't believe how amazingly at ease I was with the four of them. Oh sure, I'd had sex with Rainer, but even that shouldn't have brought on the constant feeling of self-confidence. I'd never felt so comfortable in my own skin before. Was that the wolf or was it these guys? Or was it something else entirely?

I pulled myself out of the tub, and he passed me the towel. I didn't suppose it was realistic to live in the tub. I quickly dried myself off, not missing the way his gaze followed my every move. My heart rate kicked up. It would be impossible to be naked around Rainer and not want him. Even when the timing was totally off.

I passed him heading into the room and changed quickly into clothes. If Rainer was worried, I didn't want to be caught mostly naked.

"Are we okay?"

He nodded. "I think so. For now. They're really adamantly talking."

I met Anton in the hall, who stood back in the shadows watching the exchange through the window at the front of the house. "How's it going?"

He put his arm around me and tugged me to him. His scent was stressed, and I leaned into him. "You didn't want to go out there, either?"

He shook his head fast and rolled his eyes. I didn't blame him. I didn't want anything to do with them either. Why did they keep coming by? Was this just some sort of buddy buddy thing? I'd always found it hard to make real friendships with humans, and what was more was that I was pretty sure that even though they didn't know why, the humans were sort of off put when they were around me.

"How do they not think you guys are werewolves? They kidnapped you as a baby."

Rainer took a step toward us, coming from the shadows on the other side of the window. "Anyone who took Anton is dead. And there was no shifting involved. We went in as humans. Went out that way, too."

"We?" I asked Rainer. "You were there."

"I was." He nodded. "They didn't bring Preston, but I was old enough to defend our family. I was there."

Anton's sudden intake of breath told me he hadn't known that. Rainer didn't react. He continued to look out the window. "Anton didn't shift when they hurt him. How could he have? We don't do that as babies, but they didn't know that. And then when we rescued him, we were humans. If anything, we confirmed our human status to them. That is if somehow anyone who was there lived through the experience. No one was left alive."

They'd lost Joe, but we didn't need to bring that up right now. "Who knows what they know now."

"Exactly the problem. Those three? They might have been teenagers. Aware of their family's proclivities. Not quite yet involved. That would be my guess."

Anton shook his head and pointed at Rainer. I followed his thinking. "You went. They might have gone, too."

"Maybe. But then they'd just think we were violent humans." He stepped away. "I should..."

My hands burned a second before the scent hit my nose. There was a Loup coming.

"Fucking timing," Rainer spoke through clenched teeth. "We need to get them out of here."

I didn't even know if we had that kind of time. Loups were out of their mind. They couldn't be counted on to not engage in front of humans. Particularly if they were trying to get to me.

Rainer tore out the door. Surely Jarret and Preston must have smelled them, too.

I rushed forward, but Anton grabbed me, keeping me back. I whirled to stare at his face, his grasp not lessening on me. He shook his head, his meaning clear. He didn't want me to go out there.

I hissed. My hands were outright burning and my need to shift rode me hard. There was a Loup coming, and he needed me.

Anton pulled me closer. His touch was gentle but firm. I wasn't getting out of his hold unless I wrenched myself away. We both knew I could do that and that he could go even further to stop me. What I had to assume was he wanted me to resist the need to get away from him. He needed me to think through this. I didn't know how I understood him so well. I'd never be able to explain it except that I did. I was either crazy to think I was right, or I simply understood most of what Anton would say were he able to do so.

I'd try to figure out our connection another time.

For now, I'd started to shake. He put his head down,

pressing his mouth on that place where my shoulder met my neck, that was solely his. Rainer had bitten me on the other side. Somehow, even in just days, this side had become Anton's spot. He breathed heavily. This was hard on him, too.

If I shifted, he would. I closed my eyes. I had to resist. I wouldn't only risk myself. It would be all of them. For them, I'd hold on.

A roar sounded outside. It was the Loup. I winced. Rainer must not have been able to get the humans away or lead the Loup somewhere else. I really didn't know what he'd meant to do.

"Get the guns." One of the humans shouted, and I growled. No, they couldn't hurt him. He'd come here for me. He was mine to fix.

"We're going to get one. Yes. I'm going to kill another fucking werewolf."

Another one? No.

Anton let go of me, nodding. He understood it. His eyes turned wolf. My own were probably the same.

I would protect that Loup until I could save him. I shifted mid-way out the door. The colors of the world changed, becoming less intense as the scents threatened to overwhelm me. No matter how good my nose was in my human form, it would never be as good as when I ran on four legs.

Words became pictures, how I understood life changing. What did I know right away? There were shouts. Not just because I'd come out as a wolf. No, because the Loup was there and because Rainer, Jarret, and Preston had shifted as well.

Gunpowder. It reeked. A loud sound. Someone had fired. No. I growled loudly, menacingly, and I attacked.

Humans had threatened us, and the humans would be dealt with. Blood filled my mouth as I tore into the man's neck. I wasn't alone. Behind me, Anton knocked into the man I had, digging his mouth into his arm.

The human couldn't scream. I had his neck. It didn't matter. I tasted his fear. He should know that before death.

Still, the need to protect the Loup overrode my need for death. I let go of the one who would hurt us and turned instead to the snarling sick one. My heart broke for him. Why were so many of us sick?

The madness brought the physical change. I knew that even though I shouldn't. I rushed toward him. This was going to hurt. It always would. But it was my job to save them until there were no more to save.

I pushed my energy into him. He was sicker than the other two I'd saved. His bones were brittle, his mind practically gone. I closed my eyes, and a whine escaped from my throat. I might not be strong enough for this one. No, there was something else. I sniffed. I was more than tough enough to heal any Loup. What was wrong?

I jumped back as awareness overtook me. One of mine was hurt. The humans were all dead, but someone was hurt. Jarret. I rushed over to him. They'd gotten a shot off. Rainer stood over him as Jarret whined, staring up at me. He was sorry. The Loup needed me. I brushed against Jarret. The Loup would wait. Mine came first. Always. I nudged at him. Emotional healing was hard but physical was harder. Still, my energy could fix this. He wasn't too far gone to bring back.

I threw everything I had into those moments, knowing he was getting better. I could smell the metal as the bullet hit the ground, taste the smell of the healing on my tongue. His scent improved.

I couldn't let go until he was all right. Sounds eventually traveled into my consciousness. Jarret was okay. He licked my face, the whining a different sound than before. I blinked. Yes, he was fixed. I panted. Okay. There was something else...

I could hardly think as I remembered the Loup. I limped toward him. Rainer growled at me, getting in my way. My Alpha didn't want me to do this. I understood, but I was doing it anyway. There wouldn't be any rest, any fixing anything, until this was done. I pressed my head against the side of the sick Loup, and I gave him everything I had left. I really hoped it was enough.

―――

Sometime later with the sun officially gone, I collapsed. It was like my back legs simply gave up on me. I couldn't support myself on them. The Loup was fixed. That much I knew. Rainer, already shifted into his human form, stared down at me. He squatted. "Shift back, MacKenzie. It's enough."

I did as he asked, staring up at him. My head pounded, and it tasted like I had cotton in my mouth. "Is Jarret okay?"

He limped over next to Rainer. "I'm going to be okay, Kenzie. You didn't have to do that. It wasn't life threatening. It could have waited."

I shook my head. "The four of you will never wait."

"I'm sorry he got me."

Rainer put his hand on Jarret's back. "It's your second shift. You don't even have your instincts intact yet. You did fine. They had guns, and they wanted to kill werewolves. They didn't get us thanks to our Omega."

Preston walked over and scooped me up. "She's spent.

There has to be a way to stop this from happening. To control it." The former Loup groaned. Preston stepped over him. "One of you deal with him. Get him away. He's already had all he's going to have from her. We can make a thank you day, but it isn't going to be today."

Anton squeezed my foot as we passed by him.

Rainer shook his head. "Sure. I'll deal with him. I've got to call Gus. They used to have a place where they dumped bodies in this swamp. I need to know where it is."

Anton pointed at the boat, and Rainer turned around. "You know where it is?" Anton nodded.

I pressed my head against Preston's chest. "You're okay?"

He laughed. "Am I okay? Yes. I can't believe how this went down. They were Hunters. I knew it. But to have them come after us when they'd been coming to my house to bullshit about the Saints for years... it was something else. I'm wondering how we cover this up. But you don't need to worry about that. Gus and the other dads were experts on this. They'll tell us what to do."

He skipped taking me upstairs and instead went to the living room that still seemed to be working as a makeshift bedroom. I held onto his hand when he would have left. I knew this feeling. I didn't need sleep. It was the emptiness that hurt like a wound, like someone had taken off my arm. "Preston... I'm aching inside. Empty."

He blinked. I hated having to explain this, detested the neediness. He pressed himself over me like he was doing a pushup but stopped before he went back up. His mouth met mine. It was warm, and I breathed him in. Still, I halted, putting my hand on his chest to stop him.

"You don't have to." I hated him feeling obligated. "I'm sorry. I hated asking Rainer, and I won't force you to do something you might not want to because I have some kind of need. I'll figure it out."

He lifted one eyebrow and smirked at me. "You think I don't want to? Have I not made myself clear about this?"

"Yes, but..."

He kissed me. "There's no but. I want you however I can have you. If that helps you to be better, then even better. This isn't an obligation. It's a privilege. You're mine." He put his nose on my neck. "And I need my mark on you. It would fill me up inside."

Now it was my turn to smirk. "Way to turn that around."

Preston laughed, it was a low sound, and it moved right through me. He lifted his head and looked over his shoulder, the sound of the retreating airboat filling the room. "They're all leaving. Even the Loup."

I followed where he'd indicated. "How do you know?"

"About the Loup? I can smell it. Want me to take you upstairs?"

I poked at his chin. "If they're all leaving, then we can stay right here."

He kissed my chin in response. My body tingled, and I closed my eyes. I just wanted to let Preston bring me pleasure and give it to him in return. I didn't want to think or face a crisis. I just wanted him.

I ran my hands across his abs. "The shifting made it so much easier. We don't have to undress each other. I get to see all the... goods right away."

"The goods?" He grinned, and I decided that Preston's smile was the best thing I'd ever seen. "No, I'm the one who's going to see the goods."

He kissed down my chest toward my stomach and down farther. I didn't have a shy bone in my body and spread my knees apart. If he was going to go for it there, then I was going to let him. Preston kissed my pussy. His breath was warm, and it sent a jolt up my spine. I moaned before I placed my hands in his hair. It was soft. The blond tips shone out, illuminated by the one light coming from the kitchen.

He replaced his lips with his tongue. It was even warmer. I squirmed and giggled. He lifted his head to meet my gaze. "None of that. This is a very serious matter."

I loved his fake tone. "Sorry. Guess I'm ticklish tonight."

I'd no sooner said it than it passed. I couldn't be laughing and silly when his mouth found my clit. I bit down on my lip. Oh yes, that was what I wanted. He moaned, and I could smell his desire. The only problem was that I couldn't touch him in return. I raised my hips; I couldn't have stopped if I'd wanted to. Pleasure rode through me, and I was close. Still, he didn't let up with his tongue. It was almost too much. I might have asked him to slow down if I could have formed words, but soon that second of needing him to back off passed, and I exploded in his mouth.

I cried out, and he continued to stroke me until the wave passed. I panted, couldn't catch my breath and wasn't sure I ever would again.

Preston lifted his head. "Hey, beautiful. You coming... that's the best thing ever."

I smiled at him and crooked my finger. "Get over here."

He scooted up fast. I put my hand over his heart, and it pounded fast and strong beneath the pads of my fingertips. He kissed my chin and then all over my face. "How are you real, Mac? I keep thinking I'm going to wake up and you're going to never have existed. Like I made you up."

I kissed his lips gently. "The more we get to know each other, the more you will see that there isn't a piece of me in existence that is perfect. You'd never have dreamed up someone who is going to drive you as crazy as I am bound to do."

He shook his head. "I highly doubt that."

I wasn't going to argue with him about this right now while his cock was hard and finally right where I could reach it. I stroked him, a long hard swipe from his balls to his tip. He jerked against me, and I smiled up at him. "Think you like that."

"I can't get enough of you touching me. Even if you brush against me accidentally in the kitchen. You can't fucking believe how much I like it when you touch me there."

Actually, I could, but he kissed me before I could tell him. I stroked him hard, finding a rhythm and keeping it up as I kissed him. Preston pushed his tongue into my mouth, dancing against my own.

He moaned, a low, almost pained sound, and stopped my hand with his. "I want to be inside of you, and I'm going to be honest... I'm close."

I nodded. "Come inside of me, Preston. I want that, too. I want to be connected with you that way right now."

He shifted his hips slightly, lining up so that his cock was on the edge of my core. A moment later, he pushed inside of me. I cried out, my body stretching to fit him. He moved slowly, his hand on my forehead while his fingers traced my face. He pressed our noses together for a second before he kissed me with such tenderness I teared up from the intensity of his care.

The heat built between us. His hips jerked in motions that moved his cock right over my clit. It didn't take long. I came on a sigh, a noise I'd never heard myself make before escaped from my lips. My fangs elongated. Without giving it another thought, I bit down on his neck. His whole body jerked while he emptied himself inside of me. His own mouth pressed down on my skin, right above my heart. I cried out, coming again. He marked me as I licked his blood.

I smiled.

CHAPTER 10

I HAD TO PEE, which gave me the opportunity to put on a shirt. When I came back, Preston had managed to dress himself from the waist down. He put out his hand, and I took it, letting him draw me down onto the mattress. We wrapped each other up like a pretzel. Who needed covers? These werewolf men were like heating blankets.

I ran my hands through his hair when he spoke. "I promise that I'm going to make you so happy. You're going to be happy here. I promise you."

I rubbed my cheek against the slight growth of hair on his cheeks. The stubble burned and I loved it. "I don't need promises. I'm actually a pretty simple person. I might be wrong to be the first Omega born in who knows how long. I should be spiritual and all knowing. The only thing I can think about right now is how many clothes we go through with the shifting. Put them on, tear them off."

He snorted. "We should go get a whole bunch of cheap clothes in bulk. We can all match. And just tear them to bits without caring about them."

"Do you think the Loups will just keep coming? How

are they finding me? There can't be so many around that they can smell me."

Preston kissed me. "I don't know. All things that we will figure out. I'd promise but you said no promises."

My hands burned, and I looked around. There was no scent in the air, no indication that anyone was coming. I didn't have the nervous energy that would usually indicate something approaching. No, all of my attention turned to Preston.

He tilted his head. "What's going on?"

"My healing is on and only you are here. Maybe I should ask you that. What's going on?" I stroked his back, slowly letting the heat move into him.

He shook his head. "There's no need for that, you amazing Omega. I'm okay, Mac. I'd just had a sad thought. It'll pass."

It wasn't a small one. That was for sure. A small thought wouldn't have brought my powers online. It was weird to think like that as though it was normal. Powers. I continued to rub his back, and he sighed. "Seriously, don't waste your powers on me."

I didn't respond to that. This wasn't much of a power drain. This was more like a hug, and he clearly needed it. "What made you sad? Or am I prying? I realize we just shared... well, what we just shared. But you're totally entitled to not tell me. We don't know each other yet."

He shook his head. "We do know each other. I feel like we know each other's souls. We're mated." He placed his hand on my shirt over the mark he'd made on my chest. "We have to work out the details, but we *know* each other."

Maybe there was some truth to that. "I'll accept that answer."

He smiled. "That thing you're doing, it's like a hot bath.

Fuck. I was thinking about Rainer and how when he went off to jail, after he signed the Accords, that it seemed like all the light went out of the world. Like I was going to live forever with half of my soul dead. Maybe I thought about it because you brought all the light back."

I snuggled closer to him, keeping my warm hand flat on his back. He closed his eyes. "I can't tell you how nice all of this feels."

Whoever had done that to Rainer had really destroyed the whole family. A family that had been through enough with the kidnapping of Anton. I knew very little about werewolf politics other than the names of famous families talked about by my mother and others. The Lejeunes had been one of them, but they were very different than the rumor mill portrayed them.

The door swung open, and my other three mates entered. I lifted my head the same time Preston seemed to rouse to look at them. Jarret leaned on Rainer. My powers, which had dimmed, surged to life.

"You're hurt."

Anton nodded, pointing at Jarret when he must have realized I was already moving. He got out of the way. I rushed to Jarret. "What happened?"

"I think my joint is just stiff from the shot. I've never been shot before, so I don't really know and—" He stopped talking when I placed my hand right on his hip. He sighed.

Anton pulled off his own shirt and headed for the mattresses. I watched out of the corner of my eye. They'd both just had their second shift. They had to be exhausted. "You guys held out a long time."

"They helped me get rid of the bodies and send the Loup—Seth—on his way. He's not from anywhere around here, by the way. And he doesn't know how he got here, just that he felt compelled to come." Rainer shook his head. "Which doesn't make me happy at all."

"Thank you."

Rainer sniffed the air. "You mated. Excellent. That will be great for all of us. A true mating is supposed to make us all stronger."

I pulled my hand off Jarret, and he nearly fell over. Rainer grabbed him. "Okay, brother. Come lie down. She fixed you. Let's be done for the night. Hopefully."

Unless another Loup showed up. Or somehow the humans instantly knew we'd killed three of them and came for our heads. I dropped my gaze. Rainer had given an order, and I wanted to follow it. The submissiveness of the first day struck me out of nowhere.

"Hey." Preston touched my arm. "None of that. He's not mad at you."

"I feel like I've done something wrong." It was hard to speak the words. "Like all of this is happening because of me. Jarret got shot tonight. That's..."

Jarret looked at me from over Rainer's shoulder. "My fault. Not yours."

Preston took my hand. "I think we're going to have to work on the idea that you aren't dooming us to anything. We want this, Mac. We want it more than anything. If you left or something happened to you, we'd never get over it. Bring on every Loup in the world. They'll all get handled. Along with any Hunter who shows up."

I let his words warm me, even though I knew they had to be more bravado than truth. For now, I'd just let myself be the kind of woman who believed that all things could just work out in the end. I'd do that for tonight.

Jarret lay down on the mattress with Anton. "This is becoming the norm. Me crashing next to him. We haven't shared a bedroom since he got taken from the other house."

I walked over to him, leaning over to kiss his mouth. "Get some rest. You'll not pass out after the third. I'm totally energized."

"Good to know." His head hit the pillow, and he was out. I walked to the other side of the mattress and covered Anton up. Rainer patted the mattress next to him, and I walked over, placing myself in the middle of Preston and Rainer.

My powers had officially shut off, and I wasn't feeling empty or sick. That was a nice change. I settled between them. Rainer kicked off his shoes, and by the time he'd done that, Preston was snoring.

Rainer and I grinned at each other. "Does he snore regularly?" I kept my voice down.

My Alpha nodded. "Yes, but if you nudge him gently so he turns his head, he'll stop. For a little bit. Then hopefully you can be so out cold you won't notice it."

I was in the mood to be lied to, to be told half-truths that couldn't possibly be true. Preston had started with the promises of a happy life that I knew he thought he could provide but couldn't guarantee. Then he'd continued with the "we'll keep you safe" promise. Now, I wanted Rainer to continue. "My family will be okay, right?"

He turned his head to look at me. In the near complete darkness I could see his eyes. He linked our fingers together. "Yes. They're absolutely going to be fine. This time next year we'll all be together. My family, too. Everyone will be happy, safe and sound. Even Gus will have come back home and for the first time in twenty plus years, my mother will smile even in her eyes."

I smiled. He'd read me correctly. "That's what I

thought." I kissed his cheek. "Goodnight, Rainer. Thanks for knowing where to hide all the bodies."

"Well, I didn't know, but I learned." He tugged on the end of my hair.

"Then thanks for being willing to find that out."

He rolled onto his side, placing his leg over mine. In the process, he pushed lightly on Preston who rolled over, putting his other leg over me. He quit snoring, and I smiled. They'd effectively pinned me to the bed.

I guessed I wasn't going anywhere without one of them waking.

"I'll bury as many bodies as it takes for us to be safe. We will have this family. I promise you that."

It was a night for the little lies. I'd take them.

I woke up to the sound of hammering in the other room. I sat up, glad that my two oldest mates had moved enough for me to do that now that it was daylight. Preston covered his head with the pillow. "It's my day off and that fucker always got up with the dawn."

As Anton still slept, it had to be Jarret. I got off the mattress and followed the sound to where he was making his racket. I stared at him through the doorway. He wasn't so much hammering as banging the molding off the walls in the study.

He looked up when I came in. "Oh, sorry. I thought I was far enough away this wouldn't wake you."

I walked over to him, squatting down. "You're making your brothers nuts, but I had enough sleep. No coffee yet so don't expect me to have great thoughts or ideas."

He grinned at me. "You are so pretty all the time. How

can anyone look so good when they first wake up in the morning?"

I waved my hand at him. "That's the mating talking. Why did you pick this room to start with? Just the location?"

He shook his head. "I thought if I screwed up this room, no one would mind. I'm probably not doing it the right way. I should watch a video on doing this, but I'm sort of making this up as I go along."

I didn't have the slightest idea either way. I smiled. This morning was kind of normal for the way things had gone lately. House projects. Lack of coffee. "Got another hammer? I can do it wrong with you."

He reached past me and picked one up. "They're all going to end up in here mad. Even Anton will glare. Although if it's you, they probably won't. So, yes, by all means, bang away."

I took the hammer. "Maybe we should wait an hour. Come on. I'll burn breakfast."

"Fair enough."

———

I'd no sooner put on pants than I heard the trucks pulling up in front of the house. I stopped and looked out the window. Gus stepped out of the car, but he wasn't alone. No, with him were four other men and a woman. I stared for a second, knowing instantly this was my mates' family. The Lejeunes had arrived. This didn't surprise me. Rainer had called needing to bury bodies. For sure they'd come to check on things. I stared down at myself. I had on a white t-shirt and a pair of jeans. This was pretty much what I always looked like.

Still, I sort of wished that I could have been a little better dressed right at this moment. Anton walked in the door. He pointed at the window, and I nodded.

"Your mom and fathers." I rocked back on my heels. "I hadn't thought about meeting them, and suddenly, I'm nervous." He shook his head and then shrugged.

"Yeah... well, it might not matter to you, but it does to me. Meeting your family is not a small thing. Wait and see how you feel when you meet mine."

He visibly swallowed and then grinned at me. I pointed at him. "And don't think you're getting out of that by not speaking to them. I'll lock you in a room with my Will, one of my dads. He gets everyone communicating."

When he paled, I nodded fast. "Yep. Not so much fun when it's on the other foot. Come on. Introduce me to your family."

He nodded but stopped me at the door, backing me into the doorframe. Anton pressed his body to mine before he placed my hand over his heart.

I swallowed, my throat suddenly thick. I had to find the words. "Don't you think it's too fast? Like isn't it? Is it just the mating? Or am I thinking too much like a human because I never got to see what this looked like for our people. My parents wouldn't talk about their relationship. We all spent so much time hiding."

He kissed my knuckles. Maybe it didn't matter. The feelings were there, and they were what they were. Why did it matter how and when they came?

We walked downstairs together, and I was halfway there when I realized I wasn't wearing any shoes. Great. I was going to meet my mates' mother and fathers barefoot. Internally, I sighed. I supposed it didn't matter.

The smells coming from the living room were not joyful

happiness. No, there was nothing but tension in that room. Still, my powers didn't react, and I took a second to observe the people I was about to meet.

It was obvious who their mother was. She was the only female there except for me. I shouldn't have been surprised that she was gorgeous. I'd heard that about her. Yet, still, I stared at her in awe. My mother was lovely. Strong bones, beautiful eyes. But Aurora Lejeune was stunning. Her blonde hair fell just past her ears where it curled toward her chin. Her face was long, her cheekbones high. She was slender and fit. Dressed in a long pink skirt with a white V-neck blouse to match, she was flawlessly put together. She'd matched the whole thing with a pair of white-heeled shoes and pearl earrings.

I stared quickly at my bare feet. There wasn't much I could do about that now. I was going to meet their high-heeled mother without even having a pedicure.

I needed to wait for introductions to know who was who and that was going to require me to actually step foot in the room. Anton nodded, and I stepped inside. My three guys had to know I was there with their alive and working wolf noses. They hadn't indicated my presence, which I appreciated.

"Hi, everyone," I smiled. "I'm sorry I wasn't downstairs and that I'm not really dressed for visitors. I didn't know you were coming. But then again family is always welcome, right?"

I had the full force of everyone's gazes on me immediately. I'd never been good at this. There was a reason I'd done so well at my second job sweeping up at the hair salon where everyone's focus was mostly on themselves. I liked being behind the scenes.

But I was the Omega, and even more so. I was the mate

to the children of the people in this room. They had every right to stare at me as I disrupted their chosen way of life.

"MacKenzie." Gus smiled at me. "Always so brave. And in a room with a bunch of wolves who are angry and most of them don't know why." He smiled at Aurora. "Let me present my mate, Aurora Lejeune."

She shook her head. "Gus, we talk and talk about this, my love. It's wife. You have to say wife, and if you want to be technical, it looks on paper that I'm Kevin's legal wife."

He shook his head. "This is your sons' mate. She's an Omega. I've told you all of this, but you are standing here in her presence now. Surely, it must seem real at last."

She turned her blue gaze to mine. "MacKenzie." She lifted her brow as she spoke. Her accent was beautiful, like listening to someone speak music. "It is lovely to meet you." She extended her hand, and I took it, shaking her soft fingers.

"It's nice to meet you, too."

Her smile seemed genuine, but her eyes were sad. Still, my powers stayed where they'd been, shut off. Whatever bothered her, at the moment, she didn't need my help.

"May I present the boys' other fathers? You know Gus. This is Kevin." She indicated the man that Jarret had said was Rainer's father. I could see the resemblance right away. Rainer really did look like a younger version of his bio dad except his brown hair was more auburn than his father's.

Kevin nodded to me before he shook my hand. Aurora continued the introductions. "This is Brian."

I smiled, and he returned the grin. Yes, he was Jarret's father. I wondered if anyone did this to us. I didn't have the slightest idea who my biological father was.

She went on, motioning toward the last two men. "Stanley. And Cristian."

Everyone shook, and Preston walked over to place his hands on my shoulders. "Okay, we've done the getting to know you. It's great to see you. All that. But I have to say that your timing isn't wonderful. We're trying to keep our girl hidden around here. Plus, you may not remember the getting to know you stage since yours was a million years ago, but we're in that. So, much as we love to see you, you could get out. That would be fine, too."

Wow. I swung around to slightly glare at Preston. The first time I met his mother I didn't need to throw her out of the house. I smiled at her. "Can I offer you some coffee? We don't have much in the way of food at this point, but I could certainly make some up. Or Rainer could, since he, as you know, is a gem in the kitchen. I do tend to burn water."

He laughed. "I can make coffee. Or we do have enough food for me to throw something simple together. Who's hungry?"

His mother shook her head. "We're not here to eat."

Brian shrugged. "I could eat."

She shot him the same look I'd sent to Preston, who still had his hands on my shoulders. He was obviously not intimidated by my glare.

"We didn't come for food. We came—"

Kevin interrupted. "If Rainer is back to cooking then I am not going to say no. How can we help?"

"You can't." Rainer waved his hand. "Just come on down to the kitchen. I'm going to whip up some eggs. We'll all eat those. And then you can tell us all the reasons you came, Mom. Bad news is much better given on a full stomach."

Preston sighed. Apparently, he'd really thought he could get his family gone within minutes of their arrival. We all followed Rainer. It was the longest, most awkward standing around a kitchen and watching someone cook, ever. No one said a word. How long had the Lejeunes been like this? Was it a new thing? Just my presence making things weird or was this long term? Rainer's prison sentence? I wanted answers, but I wasn't going to outright ask them in front of everyone.

"So I'm renovating the house." Jarret started pouring coffee. I'd had my usual allotment, but given the circumstances, I was willing to have too much.

Cristian cleared his throat. "Really? You've never shown any interest in that. How are you learning how to do that?"

"Trial and error." Jarret shrugged. "I figure if I can do this in our house then I can officially learn the trade after. But just to see if I have any natural talent."

Cristian rocked back on his feet. "So no law school?

Jarret cleared his throat. "That was never really for me, and I think we all knew that."

Aurora put her head in her hands. "Focus has never been your strong suit."

I opened and closed my mouth before I found the right words. "Maybe it's not a lack of focus but just seeking his true path. It's hard to find that when we're living half lives."

"Well, there it is," Aurora raised her voice. "Let's talk about it. Enough with this awkward delay. We have to talk about what has happened."

Rainer flipped an egg. "Eggs are still cooking, Mom. No misery until after they're done."

She huffed, and I imagined I could see steam coming right out of her ears. Jarret met my gaze and mouthed the words *thank you* to me. I gave him the slightest nod. I didn't like how she'd talked about him, and I might not have known all the details, but I was always going to have his back when it came to, well... anything.

Finally, the eggs were done, and Rainer passed them out. I really couldn't fathom eating again so soon, but I managed to chew and swallow just the same. It tasted wonderful. Aurora eventually set down her fork.

"Now, I am going to speak my mind."

I didn't suppose Rainer could put her off any further. The woman had something to say, and she was going to get to it.

She looked between all of us. "You think we don't understand, but we do. I certainly remember what it was when I met your fathers. They were suddenly all just there. In our case they were strangers, not already family, but it was instant. It felt like the whole world had opened up. But I have to beg you to please do not continue down this road."

Preston's scent changed to utter fury. I placed my hand on his. "We aren't giving up Mac because it screws up some plan you had."

She held up her hand. "I don't blame you nor would I ask you to do that. Would I have preferred that all of you, including Mac, as you call her, met humans? Yes."

Rainer shook his head. "I don't call her Mac. Only Pres does that. Please don't call her that. She has a full name. Let's use it. MacKenzie."

"Her friends call her Kenzie," Jarret supplied. "But I guess you're not going to be that."

She ignored their quips and continued. "Stop shifting. Live like we do. You can all be together. Pick one to make it official and just get on with it. Don't separate."

"That's not going to happen." Rainer practically growled. "We're not going back to living like that. We have our mate. She is an Omega. We are going to live like shifters. We will keep her safe. End of story. I don't care if you like it or not."

"It's not a question as to whether I like it," Aurora officially shouted now. "You signed an Accord. After you went crazy and hurt people. You agreed."

I had to interrupt. "You don't understand. He can't have ever been a Loup. That's a lie. Once they turn, they never turn back without help. He's a werewolf. A normal, healthy, happy werewolf."

Rainer winked at me. "Well, happy now. Wasn't so happy last week but now? Yes."

Aurora sighed loudly. This was not going well. I still wished I had my shoes on.

CHAPTER 11

"YOU AGREED NOT TO SHIFT. One or two slip-ups the Council will forgive. This? They're going to punish you," Aurora pleaded with Rainer.

"They've already punished him. Weren't you listening, Mom?" Preston shook his head. "He was never a Loup. He went to jail for something he *didn't* do."

Brian answered. "That is... I mean, how can that be?"

"It just is. They destroyed our family because we wouldn't comply. I'm not playing anymore. Our not shifting is not an option."

Rainer nodded. "I'll go deal with the Council if they find out. Otherwise, I say what they don't know can't hurt them."

Kevin laughed. "Do you think you can hide an Omega? From what you told Gus, they're coming for her with no advertising her at all. I assure you that Loups turning back into wolves is going to get their attention. They will come for you, son. They will be angry you didn't come to them."

Rainer winced. I think we could all smell the truth in

his words. My oldest mate spoke through gritted teeth. "I'll go."

"You can't go without me," I added. "I'll have to go present myself, too. But not until my family is found. I'm not dealing with any bureaucracy until then."

Gus smiled, a wolfish grin. "I like you so much."

Aurora must have had enough. Her scent changed all of a sudden to such sadness my Omega powers pulsed. My hands burned.

"You have to stop shifting." She covered her ears with her hands as though she couldn't tolerate the sound of her own voice. "You don't know what it is. You had three Hunters. We had... more than we could count. And they came, and they took my baby, and they broke him." She shouted now. "You can all judge and talk about half lives, but we weren't the only family. And now they have MacKenzie's. You don't know how they'll come back. They broke my baby."

I walked toward her, taking her hands off her ears. I wanted her to hear me. "Listen to me. Anton is not broken. It's important you understand that. There isn't a thing about him I would change. He's brilliant, and kind, and... perfect just as he is. Do you want to know how I know he doesn't need fixing? My powers. They fix what is broken. And never, not once, have they reacted to him. I wouldn't care if they did. I'd gladly give all I have to all four of them. But he doesn't need it. Not yet, anyway. Right now, the only person broken here is you. When they came and took Anton, they broke the rest of you but never him."

I didn't need to look at Anton to feel his reaction to my words. I could smell his love like a warm bath of lavender. Right then what I needed to do was give this woman a hug. She was stiff in my embrace and annoyance permeated her scent, but still I hung on, sending her all of my healing energy.

She closed her eyes. "Oh, MacKenzie." Her voice shook. "I'm so sorry about your family."

I sucked in my own tears. "They're going to be okay." Maybe if I kept saying it, I'd believe it.

She nodded. "Gus and Cristian are going out to join everyone else looking. He found you. He finds everyone. And with Cristian, they can't lose. We've been lucky. Except for when they hurt my baby and killed Joe."

There it was. I could practically feel her wolf pressing against mine. Nothing was going to get better if she didn't let that wolf out. There would be nothing but pain and the idea that she deserved it because of what happened in the past. I'd only had my four mates for days and I couldn't imagine losing one.

I let go of her. She was going to have to deal with this herself. I couldn't fix this for her. The heat in my palms cooled. I blinked. This was the first time I'd had any control over how and what they did, ever.

"You could shift." I stepped away. "I think this way we're all living, it isn't going to fix anything. You need that half of you."

She sighed. "Not until it's safe. Maybe you being the Omega is a sign that things will get better." I didn't particularly believe in signs, but I left it alone. That wouldn't help anything at all. "But until I can be sure, I won't do it. We delayed following what the Council wanted. And look what happened? Anton lost his voice. Rainer went to jail. Preston stays away from all of us, and Jarret is lost."

Sometimes people needed to have things repeated several times before they heard it. "Or... Anton is stronger than he'd ever have been and makes himself understood just fine. Rainer was framed, and yet he came out whole. Preston created a huge business all on his own. And Jarret is looking for his path, and he's so smart he has many options, most of which people never get."

She nodded and headed for the door. "We need to leave. I'm not helping anything here. I'm sorry, boys, once again, your mother is making things worse."

"Mom." It was surprisingly Preston who spoke. "You don't make things worse."

She leaned up and kissed him on the cheek. "Well, you know us Lejeunes. We do things in big ways."

Rainer took the next kiss. "Hate to tell you this, but we're not Lejeunes anymore. You know what happens when we mate. It's the female's last name. We're Harpers now."

I gasped. I hadn't even thought about that. Thinking I was going to have a human life had made me think about last names differently. But he was right. In the werewolf world, the males took the last name of their mate.

Kevin whistled through his teeth. "That's right. They're not Lejeunes anymore. I left my last name and took yours. We all did. Still plenty of time to try for that girl, honey."

She groaned and stormed away. We could have babies a lot longer than humans could as we lived about fifty years longer. That was one of the reasons we'd had to avoid humans in the past. I shook my head. I didn't know a single werewolf who had successfully dated and married a human. It just wasn't going to work. But if it had been that hard to get through to my mother-in-law, then it was going to be twice as hard to make anyone else listen.

Each of the dads patted the boys on the back and nodded to me, even Gus, who winked at me when he left. It was Kevin who held back.

He stared at Rainer when he spoke. "Two things." He held up that many fingers. "If I recall correctly, the last time I checked, the furniture we left in the other swamp house is still there. You guys need to put some in here. If you don't want to drive out and buy some because you're keeping MacKenzie hidden, then go get some of that. It's nice to be able to sit down."

Rainer laughed. "Okay. Good point. Thank you, sir. Something else? Number Two?"

"The last Omega in our pack. Do you remember her name?" He lifted his eyebrows as he spoke.

Rainer scratched his head. "No, actually. She was just the Omega."

Preston cut in. "Tyra Garretty."

Rainer nodded. "Thanks. Why?"

"Ms. Tyra had three daughters. We all hoped they'd be Omegas, considering their mother was one. Not that there was ever a biological component about who got to be an Omega and who didn't. It seemed random. Obviously, they weren't. But maybe they could help. Maybe they remember what their mother did to protect herself, what her mates did to secure her. How she kept every Loup in existence from coming out to them every night. There were always Loups. Not like now. I could be wrong, but I don't think they were bothered nightly. If it were me, I'd go find them. Just a suggestion."

Rainer nodded fast. "That's a great idea. Thanks. Did they move to New Orleans with everyone else?"

"No. I'm afraid we didn't know them well. I don't know where they are. But I think there is this amazing thing called the Internet."

Preston threw his head back, laughing. "I'll get on that."

"You'll have to come to New Orleans, whether you

want to or not, maybe even before she's secure. So bring her home to us in New Orleans. We can keep her safe while you handle your business. Even if I have to shift to do that. I would never let anything happen to your mate."

Even if I couldn't have smelled it, I'd have known that was love. I'd had it my whole life, too. Things weren't perfect. Everyone suffered. But at the end of the day, we'd always been family.

———

I'd no sooner walked away from the door than Anton pushed me up against the wall again. He breathed hard, and I smiled at him before I rubbed my hand down the side of his face. "I meant every word. I just want you to know that. You're not broken. And screw anyone who thinks so. Even if she's your mother."

Rainer walked past us. "I'm going to take Preston and Jarret and go check out that furniture. See you two later."

My body burned in the places where Rainer and Preston had bitten me. I wanted Jarret's. And right then I really wanted Anton to bite me with everything that came with it.

He didn't even wait for the others to leave to kiss me, hard. Anton's lips were soft, but his face wasn't shaven. His whiskers burned me, and I loved the contrast. He was going to leave red marks on me. I rubbed my cheek against his. He jerked his hips, and I smiled.

Anton dropped his head, kissing me along my neck, stopping right on my collarbone. Goosebumps broke out on my body. I didn't know that I had that spot, but apparently, I did. He touched me everywhere I had bare skin, running his finger down the slope of my nose. His eyes met my own, and for a second, I could barely breathe.

He looked around, and I blinked. Was he searching for the tablet?

I turned his chin so he'd look at me. "I don't need it. I swear, Anton, it's like I can hear you in my heart. From the first time you held me when I was still groggy and confused. I... I can hear what you want to say. If you want to find it, that's fine. But I'm... hearing you just fine."

He put his hand over my heart the way that he tended to do. I smiled at him while he took his own hand and placed it over mine.

I didn't know why I whispered, we were alone, except that sometimes the things we said were so important they were only for the ears of the two people speaking them. Even the wind shouldn't hear me. Only him. "I love you, too."

He kissed down my chest, stopping where my shirt covered me. The wall pressed into my back. He pulled my shirt over my head. Anyone could show up just now. The door could fly open and I'd be naked from the waist up except for my bra. I didn't even care. Sexy was a real feeling I'd recently discovered. Right then, I was bathed in that sense, as though it was a light inside of me.

Anton bit down on my lower lip before he kissed down my face. He quickly unhooked my bra and threw it aside. I watched him, transfixed. He stopped above my breast, lifting his head to replace his hand with his mouth. He squeezed my nipple, and I jerked, hitting the wall behind me. He lifted an eyebrow, this time dipping his head to do it again. He quickly pulled off and lifted my whole body instead so that I wrapped my legs around his waist. I sucked in a long breath, and his mouth came down on my nipple again. Pleasure zoomed through my body, stealing my thoughts. I had to hold onto Anton so that I didn't fall, which limited how much I could touch him.

I kissed the top of his head. "Let's move someplace else."

He nodded but didn't put me down, instead, he shifted me slightly into his arms so that we were more face-to-face as he carried me upstairs. I grinned. So he wanted to make love against a wall in the living room but now he wanted upstairs. Whatever, all of it worked for me however it happened.

Anton brought me into his own room. I was immediately struck by the smell of soap from his bathroom. He smelled like the woods back home and some of it had to be coming from that aroma. Not all of it. I breathed him in which he must have liked because he hardened against me before he set me down on the bed.

He came over me, staring into my eyes.

"I want your shirt off." I tugged on it. "Skin-to-skin. That's what I want."

He nodded and took it off. I ran my hands over his muscles. Anton was thin but built, with defined muscles that twitched under my fingers as I stroked my hand over him. He shuddered before he went back to kissing my nipple. I arched against him.

That was hot but I wanted more. I squirmed until I could unzip his pants. We twisted against each other, undressing the rest of the way. His cock was warm, and I ran my hand over him, from his balls to his tip. He winced, but I didn't see pain on his face as heat consumed his gaze. I did it again, and he tilted his head to the side, giving me a sideways grin.

"Close?" I asked him, and he nodded.

I was plenty turned on, and I had a feeling I would be that way every second of my life when I was around him. We weren't going to have trouble in that regard.

"I guess the question is, do you want to come here in my hand, which would be hot, or do you want to come inside of me, which would be equally as hot?"

He smiled, pointing at me.

"Inside of me."

He pressed a finger in my core, which I hadn't expected. I gasped while he found my clit. He swirled his thumb over it, and I bit down on my lip. "Yes. Right there."

He continued what he was doing. "That rhythm. Just like that. Yes."

It didn't seem like he needed the direction. This was our first time together, but he was reading me like he understood my body already. I held onto his shoulders. I breathed hard, pleasure coming but not quite there yet.

I shook my head. I loved this, but it wasn't enough, not nearly. It wasn't what I wanted. "Inside of me. I'm not going to come otherwise."

He tilted his head to the side, and I laughed. "I'm not kidding. I need you in me. I need you completely."

Anton smiled and nodded. He pressed inside of me, and I sighed. Yes, that was what I needed more than anything—this connection. "Stay just like this for a few moments. I just want to remember this forever."

He met my gaze, both of us remaining still. Anton flexed a muscle in his neck. It wasn't lost on me. This was hard on him. I rubbed the back of his neck. "Okay. Please, Anton. Make me come."

He pushed himself deeper, and I wrapped my legs around him, drawing him closer. I shifted my hips so his thrusts pressed against my clit. I was already swollen and ready, and I cried out. He pressed his nose into the spot on my neck that was already his. I held onto his shoulders. We moved together like we danced in a rhythm that was just our own.

The pleasure I'd chased earlier overtook me. I came slowly, on a sigh that was so sweet it brought tears to my eyes. He thrust once, twice, a third time, until he emptied inside of me. My gums burned, and I knew what that meant. I didn't rush for the bite. It would come any second, and we'd never get a first time together again. He bit down, right in his spot that seemed like it had been his from the second we'd laid eyes on each other.

I cried out again as I found the same spot on him, I tasted his blood, loving the copper as it touched my tongue. The wolf and I both loved this completely unbroken man.

———

Anton moved the oars through the swamp with an ease that surprised me. We'd had the idea to meet everyone at the house, but it had been his idea to travel there in the canoe. It had seemed sort of romantic. Now, of course, I couldn't stop thinking about the possibility that I would have no idea how to handle the canoe if something happened to him.

I'd been raised doing outdoorsy things in the woods and the mountains, but it had never included handling a boat of any kind. Not to mention, this water was quite different. It must have been harder.

I leaned back and pretended I wasn't a worrywart. "Did you decide that we should do this in the canoe as a means of getting me outside, but seeing to it that I was less likely to be spotted this way?"

He nodded and gave me that half smile I'd learned

meant I'd caught him in a devious thought. He'd thought he was being sneaky.

The sun shone through the moss on the trees, reflecting off the water. I'd almost gotten used to the faint smell of sulfur and the way the floating logs might or might not be trees.

I looked at the houses as we floated by them. Some of them had residents, some of them were vacation homes, some of them were mansions that had become so dilapidated they were practically shacks, and others had been shacks in the first place. Silence with Anton wasn't uncomfortable, and eventually, we reached the house they'd lived in when they were kids. Well, Anton hadn't lived in it very long.

I stared at it as we approached. "Why did you guys have two houses?"

He shrugged. Maybe he didn't know. He'd been a baby. I'd ask Rainer when I saw him. That would be the kind of thing he'd remember. Not that it particularly mattered. We pulled up to the dock. This house was bigger. Maybe they'd meant to have a huge family. I looked at the house next to it, where the woman had been sick and Aurora had left to help, leaving her kids unattended.

She was a sad, flawed woman but no one deserved what happened to her family. Jarret came down the dock. "When you texted to say that you were coming, we thought the driveway."

Anton shrugged again, and Jarret grinned. "Smart thinking."

"Yep." I let Jarret help me up on the dock. "Why did you guys have two houses?"

"Uh... I think our house, the one we're living in was the

guest house for other werewolves or something. Like when delegations came down."

He put his arm around me while Anton tied up the canoe. Jarret kissed my cheek. "I see you have another mark. Looks good on you. Still have room on there for me?"

"Count on it." He nodded. It was a funny thing, it hadn't occurred to me that he might worry about it, but this was Jarret who was always being told he did things wrong. "Don't take it like it was some kind of order. It just worked the way it worked. You have just as much a place in my heart as they do."

He kissed my cheek again. "Let me do something special for you, okay? Let me... make you feel how I feel about you."

I blinked, my heart swelling and tears coming to my eyes. "You already do."

"Hey there." Leaning in the doorway was Preston. "Look who's out of the house! I noticed when Anton texted to say this was happening, it was just to inform us that it was and not to ask what we thought about you leaving the house."

I winked at him. "I guess Anton doesn't do decisions by committee."

Preston touched the edge of his mark on my chest, visible just at the top of the vee in my t-shirt. "So this is where you lived? Why did you pick the ah—guest house— when you decided to move here?"

"Bad juju in this house." He thickened his accent when he said that. "I thought it might be better to not live where the Hunters came for us and screwed up our family."

Rainer called from inside. "If you guys are here, I'd really appreciate the help. We've got most of the things that are salvageable into the truck—and the few things that aren't but that Jarret wants to try to save—in there, too. Just need some chairs loaded up."

I followed the sound inside as the guys went to help Rainer. The place was huge and not in the same way that our house was. This one had ceilings so high I could barely see the top of them. This house had been designed for royalty. Werewolf royalty.

My sneakers squeaked as I walked through the center hallway. How had Aurora decorated things?

"Did Gus get dressed up for your mom? When he hung around? Before the shifting stopped? I mean, this is the swamp but was it a dress up swamp house or a casual one?"

Preston looked over his shoulder at me. "My mother isn't from a dress up, fancy background; her parents were farmers. Well, farmer werewolves. The Lejeune name was famous from her uncle. He never mated or had kids. So when he died, the famous part of it passed to her. A few years later, she mated our dads. The dress up part? She does it because she thinks she should. Like an obligation since she inherited the obligation of the name."

I supposed that made sense. "Hard to imagine werewolf society as being a thing when mostly now it's a hush hush truth."

"Gus keeps my mom connected to her roots. Joe was like that, too. And Cristian to a degree. Kevin is who you go to when you want to put on a show. That being said, Brian is the one to tell everyone to get over the nonsense, and Stan doesn't care what anyone thinks. But to answer your question? Gus would put on a tie and smile if it would make her happy. He only leaves because she supports him in needing it. If not, he'd try not to need it, which is an impossible thing. But he'd try. They're many things. Connected.

Loving. Even if it doesn't make sense when you break it down to its pieces, it works as a whole."

I supposed that made total sense. "All family is like that. I can see it, the way you describe it."

"That being said? Keep me far away. They all make me nuts. I don't want anything to do with anyone's rules, obligations, or pasts anymore."

"Really?" I smiled. "Anyone's?"

Preston smiled. "Well, yours is a different matter. Give me all your problems, honey. I'll solve them all."

I rolled my eyes and laughed. "Well, I'll just get on that."

This was my family now. Even as my own was missing, absent, and a constant worry on the edge of my mind, I could feel with each bite as their family became mine.

CHAPTER 12

I DIDN'T KNOW if I'd expected the ghosts of the past to come and introduce themselves to me just because I stepped into their childhood home. It had been such a very long time since anyone had been here that I couldn't even smell the scents of anyone having lived in it. The house didn't scream neglect. Someone, as in from the other house, had been coming here and at least keeping the place from falling completely into disrepair. The decorations weren't to my liking—I'd never liked wallpaper as much as I did paint but that was a personal preference.

Preston turned the corner, staring at me. "Amazing you found just the room."

I lifted my eyebrows. "Sorry?"

"This was the nursery where Anton was in his crib and where Jarret escaped and ran for help."

I looked around. "Funny, I was just thinking I had no sense of anything, but it looks like I stumbled upon the right room."

Preston held out his hand. "Come on. Let's get out of here."

I linked our fingers. "Who keeps this place up?"

"My father Stan. He comes up every so often and cleans and fixes things. He did the other house, too, until I took it over."

Well, that answered that question. "I'm sorry that this place holds those kinds of memories for you guys."

"That's okay. I've never felt particularly invested in living in the past. I wasn't there when they took my brother. I didn't get to go on the fight to get him back. All of that was done without me even around. I was pretty useless to Anton then. But I've tried to have his back ever since. I can't do anything about then. Just now."

I touched his cheek. "Let's go home."

It was funny how fast that place had become home. I didn't know what the humans knew about us, what they didn't know, but I knew that they thought of us as monsters most of the time. Well, my monster heart swelled every day as I discovered this world I never expected to have.

He nodded. "Sounds like a plan."

Rainer sat and placed his phone at the center of the table. He'd made everyone chicken. "Gus says there might be a lead."

I looked up. "A lead?"

"On your family. North Carolina is a dead end. But it looks like they're headed to Texas. He didn't have a lot of details yet, but they're headed there."

I tapped my fork so fast that it made a clinking noise on the table. "I don't suppose we could go."

Preston tilted his head. "I won't lose you, Mac. Do you understand? We take you there and there is every chance they take you again. I get it. You don't want to be a damsel in distress, staying in one place doing nothing. So I'll tell you what. I found the sisters. The ones related to the Omega. We can go there tomorrow when I get done with work."

Rainer nodded. "That sounds like a plan. Let's find out more about what it means that you're the Omega."

I yawned, which took me by surprise. I hadn't realized I was so tired. "Do you think we're going to get another Loup visitor tonight?"

Jarret kissed my cheek. "I hope not. We could try to patrol and keep them away, but I don't know about the rest of you, but as far as dealing with them, there isn't any putting them off. They want her, and they're determined to get to her."

Rainer sighed. "At least so far it hasn't been full on daylight in the center of town."

"Or you know... in front of someone with their cell phone out." Jarret sighed.

I looked at Anton. "What do you think?"

He shook his head and met my eyes. Anton didn't think we were getting through this night without a Loup. I sighed. "Well, if that is the case, then I want to do something fun. Can we get some decent Wi-Fi in here? Some television? So we can do something with our evenings."

Preston sighed. "I was basically working all the time. I'd come home, drink beer, and not think of shifting. Yes, I'll get us better Wi-Fi and some television in here. We're going to all start helping Jarret fix this place up. Under Jarret's direction, of course, since I don't have the sense of it."

Jarret leaned forward. "We took out those three Hunters. Do you think it might be safe enough to shift just for the fun of it? Not because we're in any dire circumstances?"

Rainer tilted his head. "Well... it's risky. Or maybe it's not. I have no way of knowing. When they were attacking us and the Loup, they didn't, as far as I can tell, call for help. I think we might be clear. But I'll tell you what... you want to go shifting and running around with our girl, stay close for now. I'll stay nearby so that if something bad comes near, we can all help."

Preston looked between us. "They get to go out alone?"

Rainer hit him in the shoulder. "Jarret's turn."

"Aha." Preston grinned at Jarret. "Well, have a great shift and whatever else while I am trying to double check the address of the missing daughters of the Omega with my very slow Internet." He shrugged. "You know what? This is exciting. Doing the mundane with this family here is wonderful."

I shook my head and leaned over to kiss him. "There is nothing mundane. Hunters running around. My family missing. Missing daughters. Come on, Pres, it's high excitement here."

Anton grinned at me, and Rainer shook his head. "The mundane will not seem so bad when we have furniture, so I am going to start unloading the truck."

Anton pointed behind him and mimicked typing. He was going to work.

Jarret took my hand. I'd never shifted for fun, and my heart skipped a beat. "Where are we going to go?"

"I think we'll figure that out when we do it." He looked at Rainer. "That's how it works, right?"

Our Alpha nodded. "That's how it works and someday soon I'll know it again, too. For tonight, you two have fun."

I patted him on the back before I leaned over to kiss

him. "I feel very hopeful tonight, as though things are finally turning around. They're going to find my family. We're all going to be together. Sort out the Loups. Look at me. I'm an optimist."

"You weren't already an optimist?" Rainer lifted an eyebrow. "I smell optimist all over you. I think the dive into pessimism was a temporary problem."

Joy filled me from the inside out. He was wrong. I'd always been... fine. Sort of neutral. This kind of happy? No, this was new for me. I wanted to roll around in it.

Jarret stared at me in the setting sun. "It's funny. I don't know how to call the shift without crisis." He ran a hand through his hair. "The last two times were just instinct."

That was true for me, too. I'd never done it just to do it. "How hard can it be? Maybe we just need to concentrate?"

Rainer paused in unloading the car to look at us. "Try picturing the woods. That used to help me. Eventually, the shift will just happen. Like right this second I could shift."

I closed my eyes. The woods? That was easy. I'd grown up around woods. Cool woods, where sometimes it could even snow in the middle of June. The altitude was different than here.

I could feel Jarret shift, clearly the mind trick worked for him, and I was glad for him, but I stayed on my two feet. Picturing the woods wasn't getting it done. But then, to be fair, I'd never been a wolf in Colorado. My only experience being a wolf was here in the swamp. Just in the days that I'd been here it had become home.

I pictured the deserted mansions and shacks, the way the gators floated in the water, the way the sense of rightness had filled me up when we'd all been together. Goose-bumps broke out all over me, and a second later, I shifted, my bones breaking, my muscles reshaping, fur bursting out on my skin.

I looked around. Yes, I'd done it. Jarret rubbed against me. He was the biggest in wolf form of all my mates. I sniffed the air. There was something to eat nearby. There was no danger, no Loups, none who needed anything from me other than to just let me be me for a change. Jarret tilted his head, amusement in his wolf eyes. There was no way he didn't smell it, too.

I took off running, knowing he would follow me. Rabbit. I wanted it. And it would be mine.

━━

I lay on the ground, looking up at the stars, Jarret next to me. We'd both shifted back, and with my belly full, I stared at the sky, my head on his shoulder. We were both naked. If someone came upon us right now, we'd be hauled in and arrested for public indecency. I smiled. That would be funny as hell.

Jarret nudged me. "How great was that?"

"I feel so alive right now."

He nodded. "Me, too. Like I can finally be me for the first time in my life."

We were on the dirt and in our human forms. If we made love here, then we would be a mess, but I didn't care, and I suspected the same was true for him. He grabbed onto my waist and then traveled his hands down to my hips. I kissed him, hard. Jarret was gentle, he met my embrace but easier than I'd done it. I smiled against his mouth.

"Jarret Lejeune, I want to make love to you right here."

He sucked in his breath. "Okay, but you've got to get the last name right... I've got yours now."

I nodded. "Sometimes I forget how things are supposed to be because to me they never were."

He cupped my chin. "For me, too, beautiful. And yes I want to make love to you on this ground."

I climbed fully on top of him. He moaned as I connected our mouths again. He drew my head even closer, his hand on the back of my neck. He fisted my hair, and I loved the pinch of pain. Otherwise, he kept his movements easy, loving. Every stroke of his hand, every move of his mouth spoke of his love for me.

Jarret let me lead this. Whatever I wanted, it seemed he did, too. I kissed all over his face. The long slope of his nose, the slight cleft in his chin. The high cheekbones that could have put him on the cover of magazines if he'd been so inclined. I kissed by his ears, down to his neck.

He shuddered when my mouth touched the skin on his neck. I did it again. "I think I found your spot."

"My whole body is a spot where you are concerned. There is nowhere you touch me that doesn't make me want to come."

I ran my hand down his abs. He was lean but strong. Jarret reached out and stroked his finger over my breast. My nipples hardened. Yes, I wanted more of that. A lot more.

"Put my nipple in your mouth." I knew I could tell him what I wanted. He smelled like mine. From the moment I'd met him, he'd been the one to give me what I needed. Within seconds of us seeing each other. I'd never not been able to meet his eyes. We were equals in whatever this strange dance of dominance and submissiveness that wolves did. Right then, I could have all of him and that was just what I wanted.

He did just as I'd instructed. Jarret sucked hard on my nipple and this time it was my turn to moan. My insides were on fire. I squirmed against him. Jarret lifted his knee, and I rubbed against it, bringing myself jolts of pleasure.

I ground against his knee, rubbing my clit as I did. He moaned, jerking his hips, and his cock grew. It was too good a sight to ignore. I stroked him from his balls to his tip. Moisture met my fingers.

I pulled my hand back to lick the pre-cum off of them. He let go of my breast and stared up at me with wide eyes. I winked at him. "You taste incredible. I can't wait for more."

"Kenzie." He breathed heavily. "Too much more of that and I'll never get inside of you."

I shook my head. "Okay. But soon. After we've taken the edge off."

I took him fully in my hand, loving the feeling of his hardness in my palm. I scooted forward before I took him inside of me. I rubbed against him one more time just to hear him moan. I grinned down at him. Jarret was so handsome, beautiful really.

He ground his hips, and I took the chance to push down on him, filling me up all the way on the inside. I closed my eyes to hold onto the moment, wishing I could stop time. He pressed his hands on my thighs, and I opened my lids to hold his eye contact.

We stared at each other for a long moment. Without speaking a word, I rode upward on his cock. I squeezed my thighs together to hold onto him tighter as I moved. He cried out, the muscles in his neck visibly clenching. I smiled. Jarret was holding on by a thin thread. I moved faster. I wanted to be there with him, and it was just going to take a little bit more to get there. The friction was fantastic, and I bit down on my lip. I wanted this and I was close. I knew I could get there. Jarret would bring it to me, and I would make him feel great in return.

My gums burned, and I knew by now what that meant. I was going to bite him; I was going to claim him. He was *mine*.

He arched his back, and I could see his own fangs. As pleasure rushed through me, I bent over, finding the place right on his neck that I'd be able to see just on his shirt line. If he moved, I'd get glimpses of my mark on him. I bit down.

―――

The house was a lot farther away on two feet than when we'd been running on four. The sun still hadn't come up, but a light from the house beckoned us home.

"You know what?" Jarret spoke for the first time in a while, squeezing my hand. "Now that you've been found and you're the Omega, if we can get the Council to get rid of the Accords, we could build this area back up for were-wolves. I could do the houses. People could come back."

I liked that idea. We could put my family next door. The thought stuttered in my mind. Maybe a few doors down. I loved them, but I didn't want my brothers visiting unannounced at really inopportune times. I liked thinking about them like that, made me believe such a thing was possible. They'd be saved.

Rainer leaned against the door, watching us approach. I smelled him before I saw him. *Alpha.* My senses were really heightened after a shift. It was even more intense than usual. The bite on my neck burned, but it didn't bother me, just reminded me of the new one there. Maybe that was why the scents were so intense. I had all of my mates now and the biting made it all... official. I was complete in a way I'd never been before.

Rainer stepped forward. He had two bathrobes in his hands, and Jarret and I each took one. I smiled at my robe-holding Alpha. "Thanks."

"You're welcome. I didn't sense any issues. Did you have any out there?"

I shook my head. "Not a thing."

Jarret kissed my cheek. "I'm going to go get a shower. I have dirt in some pretty uncomfortable places."

I should have been blushing from the implication, but the memory was too fresh, and I loved it. I wasn't embarrassed we'd had sex on the ground. Not even a little bit.

We walked inside together just in time to see Preston jump to his feet. "I've confirmed their address. It took all night with this shitty Internet, but I confirmed it. They still live in Louisiana. Just outside of New Orleans. We could go there tomorrow after work."

Anton nodded at his brother. He must have thought it was a good idea. He had a beer in his hand that he passed to me.

Jarret spoke as he ran up the stairs. "After I get eight hours of sleep, I'll go wherever you want. Assuming we think it's safe to take her out of here."

"I think if we keep her in the car, and maybe with her head down, it's safe enough." Rainer sighed. "I mean, we killed the three Hunters. At some point we have to be able to let her out of this little sphere of life. I'd feel better if we had her family back, but here to there and back again? Sure. I think it's probably okay. We'll pick you up from work and go from there."

Preston shut his computer. "Got it. That'll work. I'll take a boat to work, and I can leave it there overnight."

"Guys." I hated to interrupt their planning, and I actually loved the normalcy of it. Who was picking up who and how it was going to go. "Do you think we could all sleep together for whatever is left of the night?"

Rainer touched the side of my cheek. "Sure. We can do that."

"Great, I'm going to shower, and I'll meet you guys on the mattresses."

Jarret scratched his head. "I think that we should probably figure out how to make one of the bedrooms upstairs work for all of us to share. That way we can seriously live like we're slightly civilized instead of like we just rolled in out of the swamp."

This must have tickled Anton's funny bone because he threw his head back like he was laughing. I loved this life.

━━━

We woke up like a pile of puppies. I was half on top of Jarret who had his arm slung over his head. Rainer was curled up on me, his head on my stomach, his legs sort of hanging off the bed. Preston had his hands in my hair where he lay on his back next to Rainer. Anton was in a similar position on the other side of Jarret, his hand on my temple. They'd all managed to figure out how to touch me while I'd slept.

I couldn't remember ever feeling better. Light streamed in, and Preston groaned. "What was I thinking starting a business that was open seven days a week?"

I smiled at him even as Rainer elbowed him. "The rest of us don't have to be up. You could keep it down."

"Yes, I'm fully aware that only Anton and I are working

right now, and he gets to do it from his own computer whenever he wants to."

Anton smirked and rolled over. That was his body language equivalent of telling him that yes, he knew he was lucky, and Preston could shove it. Rainer lifted his head. "I've already been considering this problem. I'm going to get a job cooking again. If I can find someone who'll hire an ex-con."

Anton rolled back and then shot Rainer a look before lifting his eyebrows. Rainer shook his head. "I don't want to take money from my brothers."

"But we'd like to do it," Preston said. "I'd set Jarret up too doing houses if this works out."

They bickered back and forth, and I zoned out. Their talk made my stomach twist. They all at least had some semblance of a plan for their lives. I didn't have a clue and much as I loved this moment, lying between all of them, this wasn't what I could do with my life. I wasn't going to just be an Omega, hanging around enjoying her mates with no job. I had to have some kind of purpose on my own.

What did I want to do? I didn't know any more today than I had the week before.

Rainer got off the mattress. "I'm going to make us all breakfast so Pres can go to work with his blood sugar intact and not accidentally eat someone's head in his wolf form."

Preston laughed and rolled his eyes. "Oh come on, that only almost happened once." He paused. "I'm kidding, Mac. That didn't happen."

Breakfast sounded like a good idea. I needed coffee if I was going to consider big life decisions today. Maybe a lot of it.

I helped Jarret strip the paint in the study that was Anton's office. This only seemed to annoy Anton a little bit before he took his computer and went somewhere else to write. Jarret had started in the study; he seemed bound and determined to fix up this room before he went into any other rooms. Anton must have understood this.

"What do you think I should do with myself?" I stepped back to look at the mess we'd made. It was hard to picture what this was going to look like, but Jarret had a vision, and what was more, he was excited every step of the way.

He turned to me. "What do you want to do?"

"I don't have a clue." I stretched my hands over my head, letting my arms work out the kinks from the day's work. "I'm sort of... without ideas."

He put his arm around my shoulder. "You'll figure it out. I just suddenly knew, and actually, I credit you and your super Omega powers for helping me get some clarity. I wish I could do the same for you."

Had Omegas had support groups? If there was another one, could we get together and help support each other? Give each other clarity?

Could I have gone to see an Omega and have her suddenly show me my path in life? And how did I do that anyway? I didn't set out to show Jarret what he should do for a living. I didn't have any idea how that happened.

"I didn't do that."

Jarret turned to look at me full on. "Sorry, what?"

"I didn't tell you or help you with what to do with your life. I think you're giving me too much credit there. I removed your bullet, Jarret. I didn't fix things."

He tugged me to him even closer until we were so close he could kiss me on the forehead. "I think you're not giving yourself enough credit. The thing about you... that you have to understand above all things... is that we were lost. We were here, and I guess it was you who needed rescue... but you saved us. I can't even remember a day I was happy before we found you. Our Omega. Our mate. You did give me direction because you made it okay to be me, the one I always wanted to be. And fuck, maybe I won't be good at this. I'll find something else then. But when you're really ready, you'll figure it out and we'll help you. There's no rush for it. Everything is in upheaval. There is no need for you to announce how you see your world. Just know that even though this all was so unexpected... you are ours."

I wiped away my tears. "I'm... It's going to take a little bit of getting used to."

CHAPTER 13

WE PULLED up to Preston's work after following a long road that had a bunch of arrows with the words *Lejeune Swamp Tours* displayed on signs about every hundred feet. There weren't any turn offs so it was likely that a person turning down the road had meant to get to the swamp tours, but maybe it was just for effect.

The small highway we'd taken to get here had been modern, but the second we'd turned down the street it was as though we'd stepped into some kind of Cajun heaven. Pictures of alligators—both the real kind and the cartoon version—displayed along the road. I guessed it was something like branding, like setting the mood for the tour.

My sense of us being alone fled when we got to the parking lot. It was packed; vans with all kinds of hotel names and tour operators on the sides, as well as smaller cars and SUVs lined the area.

"Wow," I spoke aloud. "Busy."

Anton nodded, a grin on his face. I loved how he always seemed proud of Preston.

"He was really smart when he set this up. Well," Rainer laughed, "never mind. This is Pres. Despite his saying otherwise, he's always been very smart. Drove every teacher he ever had nuts. When you know you've got a kid with a gifted IQ but they won't do their homework? Yeah... drove them nuts. But, give him his own project? Yes, this is what happens. He's also pretty good with people. Managed to charm most of the hotels in New Orleans and Baton Rouge to send their guests here for this. I don't even know most of what he did."

I looked around. There was a cabin with the words Office displayed on a sign over it. It seemed like I'd have to walk through the cabin to get to wherever the swamp tours happened. "Can we go look? Is it safe?"

Rainer shook his head. "Sorry. Too many people here. I want to make sure that we're nice and safe for several days before we do full on public. Baby steps. I'm not going to let you get taken again."

I sat back in my seat and dropped my eyes to stare at my feet. Disappointment was a real thing, but I wasn't a child. I could see the smartness of his words, even if I hated the need for them. My family was still missing, and any time that I forgot that I should have it pointed back out to me. We weren't safe. Period.

Being out here, even in the car, was a risk. A Loup could show up, drawn to me, and hurt people. Or expose us.

Rainer took my hand in his. "I hate when you drop your gaze. I get it. But I want you to know that I always want your eyes on me. And that doesn't stop when we're wolves either. I want you to meet my gaze then, too."

I forced my gaze up. "Sorry. I... I can't seem to help it. There is part of you that is always going to be Alpha and make me want to look down when I'm nervous or if I've disappointed you."

He shook his head. "Always is a long time. We're new to this. You never need to be worried about disappointing me. No such thing from me when it comes to you." He smirked, looking over his shoulder at his younger brothers. "Now those two? Yeah... they could disappoint."

Jarret groaned, and Anton nudged Rainer in the shoulder. They never seemed to be particularly intimidated by him, even if they did seem to do what he wanted. Maybe I would eventually get over the eye thing.

Cars started pulling out of the parking lot, and Rainer sighed. "Preston is going to be a hot minute. They have to close up and deal with the money. Looks like they're running late. These people should have all been gone a long time ago."

Anton leaned forward and kissed me on the neck. I sucked in my breath. He held my gaze for a second before he leaned back and closed his eyes like he was going to nap, head pushed against the window.

Jarret had brought a notebook and was sketching something on one of the pages. I looked at Rainer. "If I were home, I'd have my phone to read on. I always had something to read."

My Alpha scrunched up his face. "We need to get you a phone." He sighed. "Do you want to go back to Colorado?"

I blinked. "Ah... I don't know. I love Colorado. I haven't spent that much time here yet... but you're all here and there is something about the swamp that calls to me, as though we're meant to be here. I don't know if that makes sense. Sometimes, I already think of this place as home. And then a second later, Colorado is home. I'm..." I sucked in a long breath. "Rainer, I am stuck between existences until it's safe. Right now I just have to do what I'm told and be careful. How can I possibly know what I do and don't want? Where I'm supposed to be."

He leaned over and kissed the end of my nose. "I can't argue with most of what you said. I'd do anything to snap my fingers and make you safe. But if you wanted Colorado, that is where we'd go. You're our mate. We'd go anywhere in the world to make you happy."

"That is so sweet of you." I kissed his cheek. "Look where we are. Not so easy for Preston to just uproot himself."

As though I'd conjured him, Preston walked fast from the cabin-slash-office and made his way over to us. He swung open the back door. Anton lifted his head, rubbing his eyes as the disturbance woke him from his nap. Jarret scooted over, making room. The guys were all a little bit big for the backseat but none of them were complaining, at least not so far. Preston shut the door and looked around at the rest of us.

"Hi there. I smell intensity in this car. One of these days we all have to learn how to be easygoing and relaxed."

Rainer put the car in drive. "When we have the time for relaxation and easy-goingness, I'm sure we will all be that way. Should you still be in there?"

"I delegated. If anything gets screwed up, I'll fix it tomorrow. It's pretty easy, and my staff knows what they're doing. Let's do this thing. Let's go find these women and see if they can teach us anything." He grinned at all of us and stopped on Jarret. "Hey, that looks really good."

Jarret lifted his gaze to Preston's. "Don't fuck with it."

"I'm not going to. Why do you always assume I'm here to mess with you?"

I had to turn around. If I kept staring backward in the car, I was going to get nauseated. I had to face forward. "How long is this going to take? How long am I sprung from hiding?"

"They live just outside of New Orleans, so about three hours. We may need to spend the night somewhere if it gets too late. Traditionally, werewolves offer each other shelter, but it's been a long time since any of us have lived like werewolves, and they aren't expecting us."

This was news to me. "You didn't contact them, Preston? When you found them?"

"And let them tell us no? I prefer to show up unexpectedly." He shrugged. "Worse comes to worst they shut the door in our face. But I doubt that. I can charm my way in most places."

Anton shook his head and mimed knocking then nothing. I nodded. "What if they're not there at all?"

"Then I guess we got you out of the house for a little road trip, Mac."

I watched the scenery change on the road as we went from a small two-lane highway to a much bigger one. The billboards disappeared and instead we were surrounded by trucks and cars, all of them racing somewhere at speeds over seventy miles per hour. I chewed on my lip. The guys were quiet. Even the sound of Jarret's sketching had stopped.

I looked at them through the rear view mirror. "Are you fine? One of you want to switch with me? I can sit in the back. Should have offered that to begin with."

Rainer shook his head. "I want you up here with me. Not just because I happen to like being this close to your scent, MacKenzie, but because I can keep you safer next to me. Or at least I like to think that I can. I'm not sure which part of the car is actually safest. It doesn't matter. We're not stopping unless it's an emergency. No one gets near you."

I lifted my eyebrow. "What if I had to pee?"

He side-eyed me. "Do you?"

"Well no, but what if?"

Rainer shook his head. "Then we'll stop somewhere, but I'd rather not if that is possible."

"Doing fine. Don't have to pee just yet, but I'll let you know."

We rode the rest of the way in relative silence, breaking it to discuss the radio here and there or whether or not Anton was deliberately infringing on Jarret's leg space. All of it seemed very normal. This was what it would be like if we took trips together in the car. I smiled at the thought.

Anton elbowed Jarret, and he grinned. "I smell it, too. She just got happy. First time in a bit. Was it the bumper sticker showing stick figures on the back of that semi or something else?"

"I was thinking about how much I liked this, the ease of it, the normalcy."

Preston laughed. "This is not the norm. We will take two cars."

Jarret shook his head. "Try three. And she'll ride with me."

Anton held up four fingers.

I laughed, throwing my head back. "Well, there goes my fantasy about road trips."

"You can still have them." Rainer smirked. "You'll just have to change cars every four miles."

We arrived at the sisters' house half an hour later. It was a small, tan, quaint house with a red door that was laid out over one story. Three small white columns broke up the front porch, and although I couldn't see the roof entirely, it looked mostly flat to me. There were two cars in the driveway that spoke of, hopefully, someone home. I looked at the clock in the car before Rainer turned it off. It was seven. We might very well be interrupting dinner.

My Alpha held up his hand, indicating he wanted me to wait in the car while he got out first. Preston jumped out after him, but Jarret and Anton remained. Was this something they'd discussed or was it just a natural thing, like they all knew who was going to do what in terms of my safety? I'd guess the latter. Rainer probably hadn't known how he'd feel until we got here.

He sniffed the air. It was a subtle move and one that anyone who wasn't a werewolf would probably miss. With a nod at Preston, he stepped away from the car while Pres opened the door to let me out. My second oldest mate crowded me for a second. "Missed you today. Pretty sure we're all on edge from being in a closed space with you and not able to touch you for hours, Mac."

I kissed his chin. "Try being overwhelmed with the smell of all four of you. My nipples might be permanently hard."

Deliberately leaving it at that, as a means of the best kind of torture, I slid past Preston and headed toward the house. I didn't miss the widening of his eyes or the way for just a second I could see his wolf reflected back at me. I winked at him, and he smirked. Anton put his arm around my shoulders. It was a sweet gesture, but if I had to guess, it was probably more about keeping me close.

I was out in public, and we were arriving unexpectedly at the home of unknown werewolves. Of course, I could shift as easily as any of them, and I didn't feel weak when I was in my wolf form. I could kick ass as well as they could.

Now was probably not the time to have this conversation. Still, I couldn't resist. "You know that if it came down to it, I could defend myself pretty well."

Anton nodded, but he didn't let go. Apparently, he agreed but that wasn't going to change a thing. Rainer rang the doorbell, looking once over his shoulder. "Back up just a little bit."

Anton did as he was told, which moved me with him. I swallowed. "If we're this worried about these women, should we be doing this at all?"

Jarret shook his head. "We're going to be really careful with all new werewolf meetings. Frankly, once the Hunter situation is handled, I can't imagine caring that much about the humans. They can't really hurt us if we don't expose ourselves."

That wasn't exactly true. We could get shot. Die in a car accident. Get trampled to death. But his point remained. The truth was they couldn't reach out and strangle me to death. Now that I had my shifting abilities, I was going to be stronger than they were in a one-to-one match. That would be the case as long as I kept shifting.

The door opened slowly. A woman with reddish-blonde hair stared at us. She was a wolf. I could smell it. But she didn't shift anymore. I could smell the wolf but not its current presence. Her eyes widened.

"Oh." She opened the door wider. "You're the Lejeunes. I remember you from when you were all so young."

I looked at Jarret. "Do you know her?"

"No. But you could count on two hands how many werewolves my parents have had around since the Accords. No more pack. Just families and lots of judgment. We do human behavior ten times worse than the humans do it."

Rainer smiled at her. "We were the Lejeunes, ma'am." I loved when they pulled out their fancy southern manners.

"Who's there, Justice?" Another woman, similarly aged to the one speaking to us, appeared at the door.

Justice opened and closed her mouth. "The boys who used to be the Lejeunes."

"I see that." She gaped. "Well, much as this is shocking and very unexpected, what are you doing here? How can we help you? I haven't seen your parents in a long time. We've broken no rules. We've kept her locked up. I can assure you."

I stepped forward. "Kept someone locked up?"

Rainer indicated me. "This is our mate. We have broken some rules. And as it is, maybe she can help all of us so that there aren't rules or the need to lock anyone up. You see, she's an Omega."

The second woman—not the one called Justice—covered her mouth, but I heard a little scream escape the same moment I scented her sadness. It was somehow a mix of elation and terror. In any case, I couldn't stay back any longer.

I rushed forward, but Jarret grabbed my arm. "Not until we understand that comment she made about locking someone up."

"Oh, I'm sorry. Please let me start again. I'm Raven. This is Justice. Are you really an Omega?"

Rainer held up his hand. "Who do you have locked up in there? My mate doesn't say another word until I'm certain of her safety."

"Our sister," Justice whispered. "I'm afraid she's not been right since we stopped shifting. Not okay."

Only men became Loups. Nothing was ever said about women having issues other than the general withdrawal of it all.

"I can help her." My hands burned, and I stared down

at them. Had they activated because I'd said that or was that going to happen anyway? "We're all... shifting. Can we maybe discuss this inside?" I looked at Rainer, and he nodded. "I'm not comfortable with all of the shifting-not shifting things where someone might overhear us."

I was good at hiding what we were. I'd spent my life doing this. It was familiar to me. We didn't shift but that hadn't meant we didn't sometimes discuss it. No talking about wolf things in front of humans. It was wolf life 101.

Raven stepped back. "Please come in. You can't know how glad I am that you exist. Our mother... it was her deepest wish that another Omega would come. And here you are. I'd given up hope."

"We'd like to talk to you about your mother." Rainer stepped in first with Preston and Anton right behind him. Jarret still hadn't let go of my arm. It was awkward to stand there waiting while everyone else was inside.

I shook my head. "Surely we could stand by the front door, inside."

"Nope. Not yet." He smiled at me. "Sorry."

"No you're not." I rolled my eyes. "This is how it goes. I get it. I don't want to be kidnapped. Surely, the two nice women aren't going to call the Hunters on me."

His smile could only be called sardonic. There was no mirth to it. "We never do know what people will do. They've locked up their sister. Let Rainer decide it's okay. Then you can go anywhere you want in there."

Preston came to the door. "We're good. And, yes, their sister is locked away. But she's not dangerous. Just lost. Come see."

Jarret let go of my arm, and I turned to him. "In the future, if you want me to stay somewhere, just tell me that's what you want. I'm not going to run or bolt, okay? I'm reasonable, I think. I don't think you need to hold me back like I'm going to run away."

He sighed. "Sorry, love. That wasn't well done."

"We're figuring this out. I'm not mad. This time."

"Got it."

The inside of the house was filled with stuff. Everywhere I turned, a picture covered a wall or a decoration of some kind. Books were piled but in artistic, interesting ways that told me that they'd been placed there purposefully, not strewn down in unthinking piles.

My hands still burned, and I studied Justice when she ushered us into the living room. "I need to see your sister."

She blinked fast and looked at Raven before she answered me. "Don't you want to eat something first?"

"No, I don't think I can wait that long. I'm being called to help. That is what I have to do."

The older woman bit her lip. "This is very new for you, isn't it? We never knew our mother when she was new to her gifts. She could always hold off doing what she did."

I smiled, or at least I hoped I did. I didn't have a lot of patience to spare with the need to heal rushing through me the way it was. "Nice to know that someday that can be the case."

Raven opened the door past the living room, and I walked through it. Rainer let me go first and followed me inside. The woman I'd been seeking appeared different than her sisters. They both had blondish hair. She was a brunette. Standing, she stared out the window, not turning when I entered the room to indicate she was aware of us at all.

"Why does she have to be locked up?"

Rainer answered me. "Justice says she sometimes bangs her head into things or speaks gibberish. They don't want to answer a lot of questions, so they keep her in the house. Not in a cage or anything terrible. One of them is always with her."

I walked toward her. "Why not just let her shift? Surely it would have to be better than this."

"The Accords are a real problem." Rainer sighed. "We are likely going to be in a lot of trouble. If you don't have family influence, they could really hurt you for breaking the rules."

I looked over my shoulder at him and nodded. That was a conversation we needed to have and soon. What kind of hurt was he talking about? It had never occurred to me to ask. I'd always intended to do just as my family told me to and not shift. Knowing the bad things that could befall me should I decide to break my oath had been something I'd not checked on.

"Shouldn't they have family influence? These are the daughters of the Omega."

Rainer walked toward me, placing his hand on my arm. "Sweetheart, the Omega is long dead. They're older, mateless. Seemingly never married. They don't run in the social circles my family does. No, they're not considered particularly important. I'm not saying it's right. Before we broke, they were our pack. It should be different. It's not."

Those weren't things I could fix now or maybe ever. But I could help this poor woman. "If I do this, she might shift. What will happen to her?"

"Nothing. I won't let anything happen, MacKenzie," Rainer spoke in my ear. "Not to you or to her. I promise you that."

I believed him. Come hell or high water, Rainer Harper would see to our safety. I took the final step toward the person who waited for me. I didn't know her, but I hugged her like we were old friends. My energy flowed through me until it wasn't just my hands that burned but my whole body. I wanted to shift, but she wasn't in wolf form and the same way I knew how to breathe in and out, I knew that I had to stay on two feet this time.

Someone gasped and a low voice spoke. It must have been Justice or Raven. I couldn't think about them right then. I held onto this third sister—whose name I hadn't been told—and did what only I could do. I fixed her.

She jerked in my arms and our gazes met, hers suddenly clear.

"Omega," her voice was low, like sandpaper, before she shifted. I let go, falling backward. I never hit the floor. Rainer caught me, holding me tight against him. We both watched while she shifted into a small, gray wolf. I'd never measured myself as a canine, but I guessed she was even tinier than I was in that form.

"Okay?" Rainer asked me quietly.

"I am." I didn't feel like I was going to pass out or as though I had to suddenly become a wolf. If fact, the burning in my body abruptly ceased, leaving me okay.

"We need someone to watch her. To let her shift and make sure she's okay." Rainer really did tend to think of things that escaped me. He called over his shoulder. "Jarret, take her outside. Let her run for a while. Shift with her and bring her back."

Rainer scooted us out of the way while the woman ran past us, heading for the door.

"Is it okay to let her out?" Justice asked. I could smell the mixture of excitement and worry in her voice. "Won't the neighbors notice?"

"Not if she has Jarret with her. You guys have a canal

back that way. I saw it on the way in. Stay low, out of sight, and by the water. No people. Got it?"

Jarret nodded once. "Got it."

My stomach grumbled. I hated to put them out, but suddenly, the thought of food was really appealing. "Do you think we could order a pizza?"

CHAPTER 14

WE DIDN'T ORDER pizza because Justice wanted to cook. My stomach grumbled, and Anton squeezed my hand. In an orange chair, Raven watched us while she drank sherry to calm her nerves.

None of us had spoken. Jarret was still gone, but I guessed he'd be back soon. If not, I suspected Rainer would go look for him. I couldn't worry that something had happened to Jarret. I had to believe everything was fine. I'd feel it if he was hurt. Everything was fine. I'd say that over and over until I talked myself into one hundred percent believing it.

"How did you do that with no food, just getting out of the car?"

I regarded her for a second while her sister cooked in the kitchen. The smell of chicken wafted toward me. Right then my wolf was so close to the surface I might have preferred it rare.

"What is your sister's name? The one I helped."

She took another sip of her sherry. "Mercedes. Mercy to most of her friends. Not that she has had too many of those in recent memory. Not since she slipped into the madness. And you brought her back. All she needed was to shift?"

"No." I shook my head. "Her wolf was lost. I found her. Then she shifted. But you know that. Or at least some of it because your mother was an Omega."

Raven set down her cup. "My mother never really discussed what she did with us as we weren't Omegas, and I think that was a huge disappointment to her."

I sighed. Parents weren't always reasonable. "It's not like you decided on your genes, opted to not be an Omega."

She tilted her head. "But we did. My mother always said Omegas aren't born, they're self-chosen. Like something you volunteer for. We had obviously not made that choice. It was disappointing to her. Of course, having seen what being the Omega did to her, I can't say as I'd do anything different. Nothing is worth the pain you're about to have."

My blood ran cold. Anton drew me back to him.

It was Preston who spoke. "What is about to happen to her? What pain? And how can someone choose to be any kind of wolf?"

"I don't really understand it myself. Only that she always said a person chose to be an Omega and we hadn't done that."

That was good and fine, but it sounded like her mother, the previous Omega, had been out of her mind. I'd made no such choice. I was going to leave that alone. I wanted concrete answers, explanations, and anything else that was fantastical could stay just that way.

"Pain?" Preston tried again. "I can assure you whatever pain she has will go away fast. We won't have it any other way."

I suspected Raven was feeling her sherry. She waved

her hand in the air when she spoke. I suppressed my grin but caught Rainer's gaze. He smiled in his eyes. Yes, we were on the same page about Raven at that moment. Maybe it would make her chattier.

"Have the nightmares started yet? My mother once said that they took her by surprise in the beginning. She and the other Omegas would talk about it. The inevitable nightmares."

I hadn't had any of those. "No, I'm sleeping great. Better than I ever have. I mean... when I first got to these guys, I had memories that hit me in sleep but not for days."

"Give it some time. You're going to have nightmares of those who need you, you won't even necessarily be able to help them. They could be in... Antarctica and there will be nothing you can do. In the last years when my mother was frail, after one of my fathers had died, she would wake up screaming."

Anton rubbed my back in gentle circles.

"Well, that sounds like it'll... suck."

She laughed. I was glad she could find some amusement in this. "You're only going to get so strong before you will not get any stronger. That doesn't make the needs of the pack any less. They always want more, and you're going to taper out. That's why my fathers were so protective. I can see that's already happened with you. And of all things, you got the Lejeunes."

Anton shook his head, and Preston spoke. "We have her last name now."

"That so?" She leaned forward. "What are you going to tell the Council? I wouldn't put it past them to kill the Omega just to keep the status quo. They can't have anyone bringing the packs back. Not when they went so far out of their way to all but destroy them."

I needed some of that sherry.

Jarret burst through the door, following the shifted-back Mercy. She was bright eyed, and when she saw me, tears leaked down her cheeks. I rose. I thought I liked it better when I didn't have to make conversation with the people I helped. There really was nothing to say. I was glad they were better, but I wasn't some kind of savior. Whatever this was... it wasn't that.

━━━

I lay in the dark in the hotel room we'd taken in New Orleans. We were in the area, and like it or not, Rainer had to speak to the Council. Better to rip the bandage off. Anton had booked the room online. We might have been hiding, but he'd spared no expense. We were in the French Quarter with a view of Jackson Square. It was dark but still noisy outside.

I hadn't asked why we didn't stay with their parents. I wasn't going to bring up the obvious trouble with the fact that I'd walked through a hotel lobby like I wasn't a were-wolf being hunted. I thought we were all a little turned around by the news we'd received.

Inevitable pain. For me, I had to endure it. For them, they had to watch me do it and try to protect me from what was going to happen whether we liked it or not. Choice? If that was somehow true, I was the stupidest werewolf to ever live. Who would volunteer for this?

We had two beds and another room attached with a sleeper sofa. Preston was on that bed in the main living room for safety. If someone tried to get through that door, they'd get to him first. Outside, someone played jazz music on a saxophone, a low, almost sad sound. I didn't know music that well, but I was pretty sure this one was called *Walkin' In New Orleans*. Only this musician had slowed it down, so rather than being upbeat, it almost sounded pained. The tone matched my mood.

The fan over my head whooshed, making the air in the room pass over my head in a circular motion. Jarret slept in the other bed next to Rainer, who lay on his back. I was pretty sure our Alpha was awake, but Jarret snored lightly. He'd shifted and run after a middle-aged woman for hours. I didn't blame him for needing his rest.

I wished I could have some. I'd used my powers, but adrenaline had me wide the fuck awake. Anton was awake next to me. He rolled over, placing his head on the spot on my shoulder where his mark was. I loved the feeling. That was where he belonged. I rubbed his back. The pain would be mine, but the worry was theirs. I wondered which one was worse.

Or if that even mattered.

"Why would someone pick it? Choose to be an Omega?"

Anton lifted his head. He didn't have his tablet and that was a question that went beyond my ability to infer what he thought. He looked over at Rainer.

"Let's assume that's a little hoo-ha mumbo jumbo, shall we?" He got up and walked over to the window. "Although, if anyone was going to volunteer for that sort of hell, it would be you. With your big heart? You'd want to do it just because someone should."

I shook my head. "Don't make me better than I am just because you love me."

I sucked in my breath almost as soon as I'd uttered the word. Love. We weren't really all saying that to each other. Well, maybe they did to each other. They were brothers after all. But I had just spoken it like it was a given.

He turned around, and I spoke fast. "Sorry. I mean... we're mated. Love eventually is supposed to come. This is early. I'm tired but I can't sleep. That was presumptuous and..."

Anton took my hand, placing it over his heart. He tapped it there, once, then twice. His meaning was clear. He loved me. Rainer walked from the window and over to me. He knelt down next to the bed. "We're all completely in love with you. You got that right, and we know it freaks you out because you were raised to think like a human, but you love us, too. We know that." He tapped his nose. "You know it, too. You can smell it, little, brave Omega. Our Omega. You love us and you know we're in love with you. Yes, I can speak for all of us." He kissed both my cheeks. "Use that nose. You can smell it. Anytime you get nervous about it, take a deep breath. It'll be right there. As for the rest of it, what you said, I'm not making you better than you are. I can feel your heart pressed right up against mine. Even now, there is a part of you wishing you could spare us from this, from the pain that might be coming. I'll say this as many times as you need to hear it. Okay? We were in a different kind of pain before you. Not one of us would go back. We'd pick you—and this—every time. Scoot over, Anton. We're both going to cuddle her." They moved fast, and I was pressed in between both of them. The queen-sized bed wasn't really big enough for this, but I wasn't going to complain. I did love the feeling of being smooshed in between my guys, like I couldn't move, couldn't adjust. I just had to be, because I was with them.

"Thank you," I whispered to them. "I'm going to do my best to see to it that it's not too hard."

"Stop it." Rainer answered while Anton pressed my head down on his chest. I could hear his heart beating strongly. I wasn't going to sleep but for now it was enough just to listen to it and to know that we were in this together.

I ran after the older woman. She moved very fast for a woman of her age. "Hey," I finally shouted. "If you want me to understand what we're doing here, you're going to have to slow down. I'm not able to keep up with you."

She turned around, her old wrinkled face scowling at me. "You have to keep up. And I don't know how you expect to ever understand anything if you don't open yourself up to do so."

Open myself up? "What does that mean?"

She pointed her finger at me. "I don't know how you can do this with two hands tied behind your back. You have to open up to the power, open up to the pain, take in the love. Be your wolf, MacKenzie Harper. It's a beautiful thing to be. You are the Omega. For now, the only one. And baby stepping it and talking to people who can't understand despite their best intentions about it won't solve anything. Be the Omega, MacKenzie or don't be. Open yourself up or shut it away forever."

I must have dozed off because I woke up when Jarret got out of his bed to go to the bathroom. The sun had risen in the sky, and the slow drift of jazz had been replaced with the sound of someone shouting at the top of his lungs and a car horn blaring. I was still pressed against Anton's chest. He had his hands tangled in my hair. I couldn't be sure, but I thought Rainer's head was on my back.

Jarret exited the bathroom and stopped next to the bed. I smiled at him, and he grinned at me. "You okay?" he asked me in a whisper.

I nodded. I felt great. I breathed in the scents in the room. I could even find Preston's in the other room. There it was ... that scent Rainer told me I'd always be able to find. They loved me. All four of them did.

Jarret tilted his head slightly. "Kenzie?"

"I'm okay." Even as I answered him, I could feel the knowledge those smells brought rushing through me. All I had to do was open up and take them... all that meant was that I had to let go of all of the years of trying to be something else. I was never human; I was never going to have that life.

And what was more was that my parents—hell, the entire werewolf community—were wrong to try to make me. Maybe they had the best intentions but, damn it, I was the fucking Omega. I'd always been. What kind of people denied the youth in their community any chance at happiness for fear of what? The kind of discovery that had always been a possibility but hadn't happened, not really, since the dawn of time.

It was like a train hit me. My whole body jolted, and I couldn't have stopped my eyes from going wolf if I'd wanted to. She was there, looking out my eyes at me.

Rainer lifted his head. "What just happened?"

Jarret crossed his arms over his chest. "She's going wolf. Sort of. In the eyes."

His own canine appeared, staring back at me. Jarret took two steps back, hitting the bed. He hadn't known that was going to happen. Anton lifted his head, his gaze sleepy like he'd just woken up. His wolf didn't take long to show himself. We stared at each other, practically breathing the same gasps of air, wolf-to-wolf, in our human bodies.

Preston charged in the room. His eyes were purely canine, and his smile was wickedly happy. I grinned back at him before turning to see Rainer waiting for his turn. Unlike the others, he hadn't turned his eyes wolf. Why not? He needed to understand the same way the rest of us had; he had to grasp what was happening here. We didn't have to be one or the other, we didn't have to hide, not from ourselves.

No, we had to be comfortable being all of it. I touched his cheek, my human hands on his human skin. He needed to shave. Or maybe not. I liked the five o'clock shadow at seven in the morning. It was sexy. I waited for him to catch up. He'd held on for so long. That long time in prison when he'd had to let the wolf go and not let any of the humans there know what had happened to him. He could shift, and he could lead but there was part of him that was always going to be afraid to lose control.

"You never could have been a Loup. I don't know much of anything but that I understand one hundred percent. You never lost control of yourself. I know it. They know it. Stop being afraid of him."

He sucked in his breath. "MacKenzie, if I lose control, you have to bring me back, okay? You can't let me be a monster."

"Rainer, you never were, and I'll never let it happen. I promise. We trust you, and you can trust us. I promise. You're mine."

He nodded, and his wolf rushed forward, staring at me. My own wolf wanted to howl, but we were in a hotel room. She understood the rules, she always had. There was a time and place when she got to be free. This wasn't that time. Even knowing that, none of us had ever been freer than we were right then. We could finally be what we always were—both beings—and something so beautifully unique that the humans who did know couldn't fathom our existence. That was why they wanted to destroy us, but they never would.

We were werewolves, and so help me, we would exist. We would *be*.

━━━

Preston had walked with his head down to one of the tourist places to buy us all sunglasses. I could have shifted my eyes back if I wanted to, but the problem was that I absolutely did not *want* to shift them back. Maybe wearing sunglasses everywhere I went, even inside, would be a new trend. Or perhaps people would think we were nuts. Or stoned. Or hung over. Whatever, I really didn't care.

My in-laws had a beautiful home. It was the kind of place I should have been afraid to touch anything for fear of breaking things, but I was too elated to really concern myself with that at the moment. I sat on Jarret's lap while his mother glared at all five of us like we'd just brought in a terminal disease from outside into her inner sanctum.

"You're all going to do that. Just sit there like that, eyes shifted, like you don't care at all that we are in the middle of a major city and anyone could see?" She shifted in her seat.

Anton nodded, and she groaned. He smirked at me. Maybe he never spoke back before or bothered to communicate with her at all.

"You can't see it. We're wearing the sunglasses for your comfort." Preston stretched out his legs so that his feet were on her coffee table. I had a feeling that was a big no-no. Partially shifted or not, Pres did love to push her buttons. He took off his glasses. "If you're not going to care about the effort we made, I'm happy to uncover them. There, is that better?"

A muscle ticked in her jaw. Kevin laughed, throwing back his head. "Oh, Preston, ever since you were a baby you've just charged into arguments. Like there is no softer touch. I would be deeply sorry if you ever tempered that. Put them on, take them off, I don't care and truthfully neither will your mother. But the Council? The ones on their way over here to see you based on the fact that you asked for them, they're going to care. Want a war? You can have one, and we'll fight for you, always have, always will, but just be sure you know exactly what that entails. Maybe try proceeding with caution."

He looked over his shoulder. "Rainer?"

"Dad's right. Turn them back."

Anton made a grunting noise. He didn't like that and neither did I. That didn't mean I wasn't going to obey. I leaned back on Jarret, and he squeezed my waist. I turned my eyes back human. Immediately, I missed the wolf.

With no need for them, I took the sunglasses off. "What will the Council want to know from me?"

My mother-in-law sighed. "Everything. They're very intrusive people. Be prepared to be probed about all aspects of your life. I do miss the swamp. It was so nice being there the other day."

That had been quite a shift from one topic to another. The woman dressed in silk missed the swamp? "Really?"

"Yes." She got to her feet. "We were so happy there. How were the James ladies? I haven't seen Mercy, Justice, or Raven in a long time. They used to visit us when we were first mated, on pack days. It was a big deal because they each had their own cars."

Rainer caught Kevin's gaze, and their Alpha father nodded. "Mom's been very nostalgic since she got back. I'm thinking our Omega daughter here may have done more than we realized. Any second we may all be moving back."

Aurora smiled. "I think I would love that idea."

"Really?" Horror enveloped Preston's face before he covered it. "You would go back to the swamp? After all these years of fancy."

She smirked at him. "Maybe. Who do you think raised you there?"

We didn't get to continue this conversation because the doorbell rang. Aurora steeled her features. I knew that they all had issues with their mother, but I would never make the mistake of underestimating her. She was tough. Her child had been brutally attacked, permanently injured, and she'd lost one of her mates. Even after all of that, she could pull herself together well enough to greet what had to be a little bit like the enemy at the door with a pleasant—even if it was fake—look on her face. That actually took a shit-ton of ability I wasn't sure that I had.

We all rose. Rainer stepped partially in front of me. All of the guys moved until I was all but surrounded in a circle of them. Their message was clear. The Council wasn't getting close.

Kevin nodded. "That's exactly right. I can't tell you how proud Joe would be right now. Out of all of us, he always had the most faith that the four of you were bound for greatness. I might have preferred safety and security. Although he would have choice words about those blond tips you keep dying in your hair, Pres."

"What?" Preston startled just as Aurora opened the

door. A smirk caught Kevin's face. Talk about making a moment less tense. Next to him, Brian shook his head and rolled his eyes. Actually, what he'd done had been brilliant. Now when the Council came through the door, they wouldn't scent anything but amusement and disbelief in the room. That was assuming they had any wolf abilities left at all. Maybe they wouldn't know the difference between terror and laughter anymore when it came to the aromas. I side-eyed Kevin. Unless he knew something we didn't.

The Council of Seven was famous. In the same way that my mom used to tell stories about the Lejeunes, she told tales about them. I knew their names, and I'd never met them. They were all about the ages of my mates' parents. That whole generation had been responsible for everything that had happened. Well, not the Omegas vanishing. They hadn't done that. But what had happened since? Yes, that was on them.

Cory Alaniz. Guy Boyce. Kayla Deelstra. Brennan Dew. Campbell Ealy. Ernest Juarez. The Council of Six. I didn't know who anyone was but Kayla since she was the only woman present, but there they all were.

They dressed like they'd all come from business meetings. Expensive suits, pristine ties, and their shoes polished.

We hadn't brought clothes to wear when we'd gone to the sisters so I now wore what I'd had on all day yesterday. It hadn't occurred to me to worry. My jean shorts and a white t-shirt were what I met the Council of Seven in.

"Is it true then? You're an Omega?" One of the men spoke.

It was Brian who answered him. "MacKenzie Harper, this is Brennan Dew. He's in charge of the Council. Apparently, he's forgotten it's polite to introduce himself to people who don't know him.

"My apologies. We've done so much research on you in the last hours that we feel like we know you. It doesn't follow that you automatically know us."

I should have had a lot of questions about that. The only problem was I couldn't think at all. The smells of the wolves who had entered the room overwhelmed me. My hands burned. These werewolves were cold, lost, empty inside. Dying from their souls outward. I caught my breath as my eyes turned wolf.

Anton grabbed my arm, steadying me. I lifted my gaze to face all of them. "How long have you all felt this... dead inside?"

CHAPTER 15

THE SILENCE that followed my question froze the room. Preston grinned at me. Leave it to him to like discomfort. I leaned on Anton. My knees threatened to give out. I'd had Loups appear in the middle of the night and not do what being in the presence of these seven were doing.

Rainer jumped into action. "Sit her down. Not sure what's happening. You okay?"

I shook my head. "I don't need to sit. I'm okay. Thanks, Anton."

Kayla stared at me, her eyes wide. "You really are an Omega."

She didn't have a bad taste to her, speaking to her didn't make my tongue feel like I'd just eaten metal. "I am."

She rushed forward, grabbing onto me. "It's like a miracle."

"Kayla, stop." Brennan snarled. For not having his wolf active, he could certainly do a great impression.

I didn't let the woman go. I could feel how she suffered, the same way my mother-in-law did. But there was something wrong. Not with her.

The air caught in my lungs. "Rainer, something in here... it's evil."

Kayla let me go. "What?"

"Not you. You're lovely. You'll be fine. No..." The world tilted. I wasn't going to survive the malice in here, not if I didn't protect myself.

"Sweetheart?" Rainer put his hand on my back. "Talk to me."

"Can't. Hurts." I had to get out of this form. It was the only way I could make this stop. My wolf couldn't be destroyed just from hatred; she wouldn't be brought down that way. I was too vulnerable as a human, too open to this kind of assault.

I shifted. There were gasps, but I didn't care. I needed this form.

"She's shifting." One of the men I hadn't met hollered. "This is an utter violation."

"Oh shove it, Guy," Aurora hollered. "My daughter-in-law never signed any Accords. She is entitled to shift, like it or not, and my sons, too, in order to protect her. The fact that we have an Omega all but negates the Accords."

Everyone shouted. I growled, getting low. I was going to kill Brennan. He shouldn't exist to cause the kind of pain someone like him would create. He had ill intentions for the world. I needed to save my pack from his existence.

"Rainer." Brennan backed up fast. "Call off your mate. I think she's going to kill me."

He looked between us before he laughed. "Call her off? I don't do that."

"You're her Alpha."

Rainer shook his head. "I'm not, really. For the moment, she's treating me that way, but Omegas don't have Alphas. Don't you remember your wolf hierarchy?"

What did that mean? He was my Alpha. I was sure of it. Right then I supposed it didn't matter. I wanted to kill Brennan.

"I do think she's going to kill you." Rainer smiled. "And if she wants to kill you, I'm sure she has a good reason for doing so."

"Rainer..." This time it was his mother. "You can't be serious."

Someone's phone rang, but I ignored it as Rainer bent over to stroke my head. "If you don't absolutely need to kill him, maybe hold off a second. I don't think doing so is going to endear us to this Council. They're already drooling over the fact that you're an Omega and you shifted."

I whined. He had to understand how bad Brennan was. Why couldn't anyone understand it? Why couldn't they scent it? Anton lifted his eyebrows, looking at Rainer and then back at me. I could scent his approval. He knew. That didn't surprise me. He often understood things that the others didn't. Maybe he could even smell how bad this man was.

"Why does she want to kill you?" Jarret asked the obvious question.

"How should I know? Maybe she's rabid. This is why we have the Accords." He backed up farther.

Kayla rounded on him. "One does not speak of the Omega that way."

I liked that he wanted to run, his fear tasted good. When he was gone, the pack would be healthier. I edged forward.

"That's not a real answer." Preston sighed. "And if you're going to lie, I say we let her kill you. She might anyway, even without our say so. Woman has a beautiful mind and she uses it. You'll have to excuse me, but if I remember the bullshit trial my brother went through, it was you who said you saw him as a Loup. I think you're a liar and maybe even worse. I think you probably deserve to die."

This was new information, and it steeled my resolve. I would taste his blood.

"Okay. Okay. I'll talk. I'll tell everyone everything."

Rainer patted my head. "Maybe shift back for the moment, sweetheart. If he needs to die, I'll kill him. I'm already a murderer to these people. What's one more death on my hands?"

The ironic part here was that Rainer had never killed anyone, and yet, I sensed no deception from him. He would kill Brennan simply because I wanted the man dead. The human part of my brain called me back, and I forced myself to return to my human form. Of course, now I was naked. I closed my eyes. Humiliation was going to be...

I never got to finish that thought. Anton's shirt was yanked over my head. He must have taken it off when I started the shift. He was much taller than me, and the shirt fell past my knees. I looked a little bit like a little girl tumbling out of her room in her nightgown to talk to the adults, but it was better than the nudity.

My mark on Anton was on full display, and I reached out to stroke my fingers over it. His eyes widened before he took my hand to his mouth, kissing my knuckles.

"Do you remember what that was like? What it used to be like?" one of the male Council members asked the room.

"More and more," Brian answered, looking at his wife.

I wrapped my arms around Anton, holding onto his chest before I placed my head on his skin. He was going to be cold without his shirt.

"You smell evil. You smell like you want to kill us all. It is my job to keep the pack in good condition. You are an enemy. It is taking every bit of my control to not kill you." I smelled the air. "I don't even think that anyone on the Council would care that much. I think they don't like you."

Brennan narrowed his eyes. "Okay. I'll talk. But everyone in here has to understand that—"

"Hold on," Kevin came in on the phone. That was right. Someone had phoned in the midst of my shifting. "Everyone stop. I have Gus on the line. He's found one of your brothers, Kenzie."

It wasn't lost on me that their father had just used the nickname my family, and Jarret, used for me. In other situations, I might have grinned.

"Which one? Is he okay? Whichever one it is." I couldn't speak fast enough.

"Agustin." Kevin met my gaze. "No, he isn't okay. Something is wrong." My stomach clenched. "What do you mean? Where is he? I'll come right now."

A bang sounded behind me, and I jumped. Brennan opened the front door with a loud thud and ran out of it like he was going to be chased. My mouth watered to do just that, but my brother took precedent, even against the threat to my pack. He could be dealt with later.

"My brother?" I pressed again.

"He's not himself, or at least not what we think he must have been like. He's rabid but not a Loup. Throwing himself against a cage, not making sense, threatening Gus with death. They have him restrained, and they're bringing him here. Gus wants me to check with you to make sure that isn't just what he's like."

"No, that's not what he's like."

Agustin was the sweetest out of all of us. Kind to a fault. My father used to say that when kindness was being doled out, Agustin had taken a double dose. He never had a bad word to say about anyone, and he certainly wouldn't be throwing himself against a cage.

"Why is he in a cage? Maybe if they took him out, he'd understand he's being rescued." I'd never been in a cage when Gus rescued me. Why was Agustin in one?

"To protect themselves from him. He tried to kill them."

Well, this was just ridiculous. Agustin wasn't harmful to anyone, and if there was something wrong, I'd fix it, end of story. "Bring him here. I'll take care of him. Whatever is wrong, I can make it better."

I was sure of it.

Kevin nodded. "Okay. But not here. We'll bring him to the swamp. Fewer human eyes. More control. We'll all go home."

That was fine by me. I wanted back in my swamp. Things were more in control there. If an enemy came, they could be more easily handled, destroyed. I blinked. Why had my thoughts gone so bloodthirsty? It was like one second I was myself, the next I was this creature ready to kill easily. Was this just who I was now?

"Ms. Harper," it was Kayla who spoke. "I don't know what has happened to Brennan or what you smelled, but you're an Omega, and you've come just when I didn't think such a thing was possible anymore. Perhaps you're here to save us all."

I held up my hand. "Do not make me some kind of savior. I'm never going to fulfill that role. I'm just me. However that works out."

She nodded. "Whatever you need, please, just ask. And... obviously you're all not in trouble for the shifting. We have to work out what to do. Brennan has been such an advocate for not shifting, such a strong voice, and you're telling us he smells wrong."

I shrugged. "Try shifting. Then tell me what you think. I need to go home. My brother is coming." I shivered. And somehow it felt like he brought the troubles of the world with him.

━━━━━

"They're going to flock to her like she's the second coming of wolfhood." Preston sipped a beer on the dock, staring out at the swamp. "And I thought she was going to kill Brennan." I stepped outside. There was no way that he didn't know I was there. That meant he wanted me to hear him even as he spoke to Jarret, who was drinking whiskey if I smelled it correctly.

"I wanted to. He felt like an affront to the pack. Like I had to save all of us from him. Would that have bothered you?"

He patted the dock next to him, and I sat down. "Not in the least. I'm more concerned with the way the Council was all ready to bow down to you. I don't want them coming here, demanding things. It'll be never ending for you."

"I don't think there is much we can do about that, and frankly I'd rather have them want me than want to kill me. I'm pretty sure Brennan wants to kill me."

"Mac." He kissed my cheek. "Brennan isn't getting anywhere near you. Did you see him begging Rainer to save him? He knows he's not as strong as us. I bet not even when he was younger."

Jarret threw a stick into the swamp. "I'm afraid of getting cocky. These were strong, powerful werewolves. He, and others, managed to convince an entire society of werewolves to give up shifting. He didn't do that by being weak.

We took him by surprise. Don't take that as powerless. He's regrouping."

Preston sighed. "Fuck. Couldn't let me have an hour of feeling glass half full?"

"Nope." Jarret sat down next to me.

I hoped we would have lots of times like this. Just our family sitting on the dock, staring at the swamp, in almost perfect silence. The thing about staring at the water in this unique part of the world that seemed almost entirely to belong to us, was that it really could make me feel like the rest of the world ceased to exist. Out here, as things floated by at a slow pace, hurried by nothing, I could simply be. My mind turned sideways; there was nothing but now.

"Do you two want to fuck me?" I used the f word purposefully. That was just the kind of sex I wanted to have. I hadn't had it yet, but I could imagine what it was like.

Preston lifted his eyebrows. "Is that a question?"

"Together?" I leaned back.

I never got an answer to that question. The sound of a truck pulling up caught all of our attention. Jarret jumped to his feet. "Your brother is here so we'll shelve that question until a more... quiet time."

Preston sighed. "And just as things were starting to get interesting. Guess it's time to meet your family."

I rushed through the back door toward the front of the house. Agustin was here. Aching for the wellbeing of my family had been a constant source of pain in the back of my mind. Having him here meant a small piece of rightness could finally fall into place.

I skidded to a stop, nearly colliding into Anton's back. He took my hand, stopping me from going forward.

"That's my brother," I spoke the obvious, but he wasn't

letting go. He held up a finger like he wanted me to wait.

Rainer strode toward Gus, meeting him as he opened the car door. Neither they nor Cristian said a word. Instead, they opened the lid on the bay of the truck, showing a cage. My brother lay flat in it.

I sucked in a breath before I shouted. "Why do you have him like that? No one could believe they were going to be okay if they're like that."

"MacKenzie." Gus shook his head. "Trust me I didn't want this. I can't explain it. I had to shift to subdue him. I haven't in all of these years. Not even to save you. And he's not right. My nose can't make sense of it.

My own was getting nothing this far back. I yanked my hand out of Anton's, who tried to grab me again. "That is my brother. I don't need to be saved from him. Not ever."

Rainer sniffed the air. "What is that?"

I could smell just what they meant. It was something metallic, and it felt like it coated my tongue as I got a whiff of it. What had they done to my brother? I rushed the cage, and he lifted his head. "Kenzie?"

Tears flooded my eyes. "Agustin. We've got you. All will be well." My hands burned so badly that I winced. I wasn't surprised. He must have needed a serious amount of healing. "I can help you. I'm good at it. I'm an Omega."

He furrowed his brow. "Omega?"

"Yes. Who would have thought it, right? Me. The one who can't really excel at anything is an Omega." I pulled on the latch. "Let's let you out of there, and we can talk about it."

"Sweetheart, maybe wait a second." Rainer touched my leg.

"This is my brother. He needs me. I fix what's broken. I'm not afraid of it."

Rainer sighed. "I fucking hate this."

I pulled open the cage. "I get that you've been scared, but it will be okay now, I promise."

In a million years, I wouldn't have expected my brother to shift into the scariest looking black wolf I'd ever seen and launch himself at my throat. In a million years, I wouldn't have believed I could ever have known the feeling of his teeth sinking into my human skin and tearing into it. The metallic scent that had coated my tongue overwhelmed me as I lost my ability to scream.

I'd forgotten... I was vulnerable.

I'd forgotten... bad things happened and rarely did happiness win out in the end.

I didn't know how long my blond-haired, blue-eyed brother hung onto my neck, trying to kill me. Maybe it wasn't very long. I didn't know how much blood I aspirated. I didn't know how hard I tried to breathe or for how long. There were six wolves there almost seemingly at once. My loves. Two of their fathers. It was all very vague.

Maybe it was endorphins that kept me from really knowing what happened. Maybe it was shock. Maybe it was disbelief that the brother I had worshiped and who had treated me like gold my whole life tried to kill me.

But that was all that I knew, all that I remembered. Everything faded gray before black. Then there was nothing.

━━━

The wind blew in her gray hair. She must never have gotten the memo that older women should cut their hair since my teacher's—and that was what she was—hair was well past her waist.

"You will live through this. And whatever comes next. Omegas are made of strong stuff. We survive. But I am sorry, MacKenzie. I wouldn't have wished this on anyone."

I took her hand. "Where are the others?"

She shook her head. "I wish that I knew."

━━━

"Stop," Rainer's voice filtered through the fog of nothingness, pulling me toward him. "You heard Cristian. She needs to sleep. I said *stop*."

Who was he talking to like that? I lifted my lids. Four very worried faces stared down at me. A second later, their individual scents mixed, mingled until the comforting sense of having mates around me almost dragged me back down to sleep again. I liked opening my eyes to see them there.

"Okay, see? You woke her!"

He had to be talking to Anton, who kissed my hand and not the others because they weren't doing or saying anything. If he wanted to be technical, it was Rainer who woke me.

"What's going on?" I sounded hoarse, like I'd been smoking packs of cigarettes one after the other. Or at least I assumed that was what it would sound like. I'd never smoked one. I didn't really know what would happen to me. This was just a guess.

"See?" Rainer let out a long breath. He visibly shuddered. "I told you there was nothing to worry about. She can talk. For obvious reasons, someone here has been really, really worried about that."

Anton brought my hand to his mouth again. This time he closed his eyes and held it there like he was never going to let my fingers go.

What was happening? The whole ordeal rushed back to me, and with my free hand, I grabbed at my throat. My brother had ripped at my throat with his fangs. He had... How in the hell was I still here?

No wonder my voice hurt. "How am I here? What happened?"

It was Jarret who spoke. "Somehow we managed to get you to shift. Do you not remember? You shifted and you healed. It was touch and go. Then you shifted back. That was... over a day ago. We weren't sure it would work. There are some things you can't heal from. Well, that's not true. You could probably heal us from those things, but you can't be healed. Fortunately, it was just your shifter genetics. They healed you up in the change. We weren't sure about permanent damage." He leaned over and kissed my cheek. "Cristian said you might sleep a long time. It's so nice to see those eyes open."

I took a long breath. "This is entirely my fault. I never thought that my brother would..." I swallowed, my throat burning. All right, there was nothing to it, I was going to cry. I let the tears go down my face. "I'm sorry."

Preston surged forward, his mouth on my other cheek. "You get hurt and you apologize? Stop that. You're okay. That's all that matters here. We love you. You need some more rest."

"Yes, she does. I need to speak to her for a minute. All of you out. I'll stay with her while she sleeps."

For a second, Preston's eyes flared wolf. He must not have liked that order from Rainer, but he quickly nodded and exited the room, Jarret right behind him, who turned before he left and stared at me for a long moment. Anton had still not let go of my hand.

"I get it, okay?" Rainer put his palm on Anton's back. "But she's going to be okay."

I squeezed my fingers in Anton's. "I'm sorry I scared you. The throat. That must have been... yeah. But you would have helped me if I lost my voice. We would have been okay."

He placed my hand over his heart in that way that only he did. He shook his head in long strokes before he touched the spot over my heart. I got what he was saying. If I had died, he wasn't sure his heart would have kept beating. The way I understood him was unique. Things would have quieted, and it would have been unbearable. I'd never heard him as fully as I was right then. It was like his words flowed straight into my head. Maybe it was a mating thing. I didn't care what the reason was. I lifted my lips to kiss his neck, and even though the movement hurt, I did it anyway. He pressed his to mine while he dropped my hand to support my neck. Finally, he let go.

With a nod to Rainer, he followed the path his brothers had taken from the room.

Rainer stared down at me. "I know you heard me at my parents' house when I said I'm not your Alpha. That there isn't really the same hierarchy with the Omega. Despite the fact that you sometimes drop your eyes when you look at me, I never smelled submission from you. Truth is, you have regularly ignored me when it comes to doing your Omega things, like with the Loups. You may not even realize it. The sisters confirmed what I knew. Their mother never submitted to their Alpha father."

I had heard him. "Rainer, half the time I have no idea what I'm doing."

"That's fine. Neither do I. But here's the truth. I made a terrible error in judgment letting you open that cage. I've gotten used to you being the miracle that you are. Watching you take down the Loups, bring back Mercedes, threaten Brennan... I forgot that you can't heal yourself. I had started to believe there was nothing you couldn't do."

I had clearly forgotten how vulnerable I could be as well. "I'm just as capable, obviously, of getting hurt as you are."

"Worse. Because you could heal me. If someone went for my throat, you'd fix it. I couldn't make you better. I had to just beg you to shift when you were all but dead and— once again—like a miracle, you did that."

I had no memory of doing so but what a relief I had. "I'll be more careful."

"I'm opening all doors. All cages. Or one of them is. You can save the world, but so help me, I will not lose you to make that happen."

I nodded, wiping away my tears. "I'm sorry."

"Don't apologize. The only one who should be saying sorry is your brother. I don't give a shit what they did to him. Attacking you? Un-fucking-forgivable."

I could see the cold in his eyes, the hatred as he'd lunged at me. "The dead don't say they're sorry." I choked up again. Oh, the tears. I hated to cry. And my throat was making this way worse.

Rainer lay down next to me, taking me in his arms. He smelled like home. "I guess it's a good thing he's not dead."

I lifted my head. Shock shook me to my core. "What?"

"He's your brother. I didn't kill him. Hurt him, yes. And you've not been around to heal him, so he's in a lot of pain. But he's alive. In a cage. In the living room. Being stared at by Gus and the other dads. I didn't kill your brother, Beautiful."

I loved this man. With every ounce of my being.

CHAPTER 16

THE REMARKABLE THING about how I healed was
that I didn't even have a mark on me. My mate marks
remained where they'd been. It was as though my body
knew what to heal and what to leave alone. I stared at
myself in the bathroom mirror, smelling the lavender soap
I'd used to wash up and the scent of the shampoo I'd put
into my hair.

My eyes were different. I'd never seen the lost expression I had in them right now. I blinked and tried to change
my look. Surely, I was in control of the story my gaze told to
the world. Nope. It stayed just the same. I leaned on the
sink. I was weak. If Rainer hadn't been sound asleep next to
me, I probably couldn't have sneaked into the bathroom to
take this shower to begin with. He hadn't budged when I
got up.

The whole house was quiet. I hoped everyone was
getting a little bit of rest. It was dark outside. My days and
nights were confused, and the truth was despite Jarret
telling me I'd been out for a day, I wasn't sure how long I'd

fallen back asleep for. I had completely lost track of...
everything.

The door opened slowly, and Rainer stood there, staring
at me. He was disheveled, and his eyes were still unfocused.
"You okay?"

"I'm clean." That seemed to be as good an answer as he
was going to get.

"That didn't really tell me anything. You're sad. I can
smell it. What's wrong?"

I covered my face with my hands. I was totally naked,
but Rainer had seen me that way a lot. I didn't have any
embarrassment when it came to nudity with him. "I don't
really know."

"You were attacked. It's going to take some time." He
wrapped me up against him, seeming to not care that I was
going to get him wet. He nuzzled his nose against his mark,
and I smiled. I loved when they did that. "And you should
have woken me up when you wanted to come in here. Your
shift saved you but damn, you lost a lot of blood."

I leaned against him. "Rainer, I can't stay in bed all day
and sleep next to you. I love it, but there are a million things
I could be doing. My brother. Figuring out Brennan
because I know it sounds cray cray, but I am here to tell you
that he is evil. I..."

"You haven't been in bed all day. I think you went back
to sleep about half an hour ago."

I stopped. I'd been in the shower for fifteen minutes.
That meant I really hadn't slept at all. At least that
explained why he hadn't woken when I got up. He'd just
fallen asleep. He wrapped me up in a towel. "Come on.
Back to bed."

"Rainer, I can't..."

"You can," he interrupted me, his eyes wolf. "You

almost died. Okay? It was close. You need to sleep. Come on." He pointed at the window. "When there is light in the sky, you can solve the problems. If anyone tries to infringe on you sleeping tonight, they have to go through me."

He pulled the towel off of me and wrapped me up in the sheets instead. I didn't usually sleep naked. But I wasn't going to argue. He was right. This was ridiculous. Why couldn't I settle? Rainer tucked himself in next to me, wrapping his leg over me, essentially pinning me to the bed.

I sighed. "Rainer, when I look in the mirror, I just see a lost girl who played with the idea that she could do something substantial and almost got killed for it. I'm not special. I have no business, as evidenced by how stupid I was, letting anyone pin any hopes on me."

He snuggled down so that we shared the same pillow. "Tonight you feel that way. Tomorrow will be a new day with new things to do well and new things to fuck up. Trust me. I get it. One morning I woke up and a girl died. Then one morning I was in jail. Then one morning I was an ex-con." He yawned. "Then one morning I was your mate. And trust me, you have already done great things. It was my fault you opened that cage. I should have stopped you. You've done nothing but trust in a mate who makes huge mistakes."

I shook my head. "I don't think you could have stopped me right then. I could only see Agustin. All of you were pointing out problems. I just did as I wanted."

"Mistakes made all over." He kissed my chin. "Rest, my love. We get this incredible redo every morning. We won't squander it."

I must have fallen asleep because I only became aware of anything again when the bed dipped. Preston's scent moved over me.

"She okay?" His voice was low.

"She's sleeping. Finally. Come in if you're going to. I don't want her waking."

The bed dipped farther, and then I had two hard bodies to snuggle me. Preston sighed against my shoulder, his hand caressing the mark on my chest that was his. "I will not lose her. Not ever."

"Not ever," Rainer spoke in a low voice.

I let them hold me in the dark night and drifted back into sleep.

———

When I woke up, the two who had been there were gone and in their place were my younger two mates. It took me a second to orient myself around the change. How and when had this happened and I'd slept through it?

Jarret winced in his sleep, and I ran my hand through his hair. It seemed to soothe him. Anton was restless, moving around a lot. They were both not sleeping well.

"Hey." I kissed Anton's cheek and then Jarret's. "You two. Time to wake up."

It took a second but they both eventually opened their eyes. I got two beautiful smiles from them. They didn't look that much alike, but in that moment, their smiles were almost identical. Anton stretched his arms over his head while Jarret leaned up on his elbow.

"So I know I went to sleep with two different mates in this bed. I'm not complaining. I would gladly sleep with any of you at any time. Did I miss something?"

Jarret laughed. "Preston wasn't sure you knew he'd been there. No, we may have bullied our way in around four am. Just didn't seem fair that they get you all to themselves the whole night. Rather than wake you, they relented."

Wow. I must really have been out of it. I pointed at the window. "Rainer said I was allowed to get up and handle the world when there was light in that window. I think I'm allowed."

Anton nodded, getting out of the bed to offer me his hand. I took it. Rainer had been right about one thing... life did feel better in the daylight.

The entire Lejeune family seemed to have gathered in the living room. Aurora looked the most casual I'd seen her so far. She wore jeans and a white t-shirt. If anything, the look made her seem younger, more vulnerable. Had she been hiding behind her fancy clothing? She had her head on Gus' shoulder. Everyone started talking when I walked in, but I couldn't take my eyes off the back of the room, directly next to the window, which had a makeshift curtain of a sheet pulled over it.

My brother was in human form, sitting in a cage. He looked at the floor with an expression I'd never seen on his face before. It was... brutal anger. I smelled the air. The metal taste returned to my mouth. I'd ignored it last time; I wouldn't make that mistake this time. What was that?

"Do you recognize that, Rainer?" Cristian asked my oldest mate as he walked out of the kitchen, holding a cup of coffee. He silently handed it to me. I could see where my mates got their thoughtful gestures.

Rainer sniffed the air. "It's familiar. When I get close to it, I want to throw up. How's that? This is what it smelled like in the place they took Anton. This is what it smelled like when they killed Joe. I'll never forget it. To me, it's the definition of the word... wrong."

I sighed. "Do we know why he smells like whatever that is?"

My brother's head shot up. "Omega."

"First thing he said since I've been here," Aurora said, not lifting up her head.

He'd said that yesterday, too. "Rainer, I need to get close to him. My hands are burning. My power wants on. How would you like to handle that so we all stay safe?"

Rainer pointed at the cage. "Preston, Jarret, Anton, you're with me. Sir," he spoke to Cristian. "Would you mind standing in front of my mate while we do this?"

"Certainly, Son."

I was a part of this family, and I'd do anything to protect them. But my family was in that cage, too. I had to do everything I could for him.

"Do you know who I am, Agustin?" He'd never been called Gus. He'd always had his full name. He was the baby of the boys but older than me, and I was pretty sure I'd worshiped him every day I'd been alive. He'd never been anything but kind to me.

He stared at me. "Omega."

I sighed. "Get the cage open, please. However everyone can be safe. I need to... touch him or I won't know what I'm dealing with, period."

I wasn't sure I'd know anyway but touch seemed pivotal. That was why my hands burned.

Anton stepped forward. He had his hand on the cage. I nodded to him, and he opened it. My brother launched forward, shifting. He didn't get to go for anyone's neck because Preston shifted at the same time, pinning my brother to the floor. There was an oomph, but Agustin didn't get away from Preston.

Jarret stepped near them. "I wouldn't try it, buddy. He used to pin me to the ground in his human form when we were kids. I assure you, I never got away."

Aurora smiled. "I remember that."

I walked toward my brother and the room fell quiet. Bending down, it was everything I could do not to wrap my arms around him and hold him close. Tears came to my eyes. "Why did they do whatever they did to you? They didn't do this to me. What do these people want anyway?"

No one was going to be able to answer my questions except Agustin himself. That meant I had to fix him. I placed my hand on his head, feeling his fur beneath my fingertips. My brother was all black. Blond in his human form and an entirely black wolf. The contrast struck me but didn't surprise me. The ladies loved him as a towhead. They'd probably love the midnight black fur in their wolf form, too. He inspired attention wherever he went.

My hands burned, and I closed my eyes, finding the sensation suddenly almost too much to bear. Anton and Jarret both placed their hands on my back, but I shook my head. "Thank you, but I think it's important you actually not touch me right now. I don't want my power confused." It would always choose my mates. If they were even tired it might try to fix that. They both let go.

I wished I'd drunk that coffee I'd set down somewhere or eaten anything. The last thing I needed was for my power to falter.

Pain struck me hard and brought me to my knees. My muscles ached; my bones felt like they might shatter. Shifting wasn't going to help. There was something so wrong inside of my brother. Tears flooded down my face.

What was this? It was like Brennan but different. I gagged as the metal taste threatened to overwhelm me. I didn't want to puke, but I might not have any choice. This was my burden to bear, and so help me, I would do it.

My brother shook. We were in this together. Whatever was going to happen was going to happen to both of us.

"Rainer? Your mate. What is happening?" Aurora cried out. "Stop this before this kills her."

"It won't. No one is stronger than MacKenzie." I was glad for his confidence. It actually helped. He was right. I was new to this, but I was fucking strong. I could do this. It helped to believe that.

I was on my knees, and I might even have doubled over, but I wouldn't let go. My brother cried out. It started as a howl but quickly he shifted into his human form, the sound changing to more of a bellowing pain.

My chest tightened. This was a new sensation. I was going to have to let go. Agustin stared up at my face. "Kenzie?"

That was improvement. For now, it would have to do.

I let go as my brother passed out on the floor. Sweat dripped down the sides of my face and my hands shook. Jarret rushed over, placing his hand on Agustin. "He has a pulse. He's just out. You fixed him."

Preston stepped away, shifting back into his human form. I wished I could agree with what Jarret had said. "No, I didn't. Unfortunately. But it's a start." I scrunched up my face. "I need to get that taste out of my mouth. Like metal. It's gross. I don't want to taste any more of that."

Rainer handed me the coffee I'd yet to drink, and I downed half the cup. I didn't know what was going on but this was different than the Loups. It was not the same as Mercedes. Their illnesses were based on things going wrong in the pack, in bad decisions forcing people to give up their wolves. This? It was something else entirely.

This was man made, Hunter driven, and I wasn't sure I could effectively pull my brother back from the brink. Only time would tell.

"Why would someone do this? Why not kill him? Why do this?"

Gus rose from the couch, Aurora with him. "It was a hard battle to get him. They always go for the guns, but they never catch me with their bullets. Cristian, too. We're good at getting what we want and getting away. I can tell you they didn't like that I had Agustin. That being said? They're not interested in killing the wolves they have. They want something else. I don't know what."

"What could it possibly be? For goodness sake, what do we have that the humans want?"

"Power," Agustin spoke before he opened his eyes. When he finally did, it was with exhaustion radiating from his pores. "They want our power. And they want me to kill you. That much I know. You were a problem for them, Sister. Whatever they did to me, didn't work on you. They said it was because you're the Omega. They want you dead. That was trained into me. Even now I'm having a hard time resisting the urge." His face fell. "I did hurt you, didn't I?"

I patted his shoulder. "Don't worry about that. I'm fine, as you see. Hard to kill me. I'm tough." And lucky. "Are you okay? Do you need anything?"

He put his palm on his forehead. "It feels like my thoughts aren't my own. They have this loud noise. When they play it, I can't think, can't do anything except what they say to make that stop. Eventually, it's like I can't think at all."

"Do you think it's safe to let him go sleep in one of the bedrooms?"

Rainer shook his head slowly. "Not yet."

My brother groaned. "Keep me from her. Whoever you all are. Please, keep me from her."

Preston pulled a shirt over his head. "I like him better already."

━━━

My brother slept fitfully in his cage. We tiptoed around, trying to be quiet. Rainer cooked lunch, but even the smell of chicken didn't rouse my brother. I'd taken one bite when the pain hit me. It was like I had my hands on Agustin again, as though I was right there. I managed to spit out my chicken before I hit the ground.

Jarret was closest to me and grabbed me into his arms. "Kenzie? What is it? What's going on?"

"I don't know..." I held onto him. "Pain. Like I'm healing Agustin but I'm not." The empty feeling was there, the one I'd had when I'd healed the Loup before the guys had marked me and filled me up inside. How could there be nothing next to so much pain?

I wasn't alone. I could see that they were with me so why was the agony taking them away from me? Stripping me of their presence inside of me?

"Talk to us," Jarret asked. It might have been the third or fourth time. I was losing track of things. "Honey? Please."

I swallowed even though it was hard. "It's like I'm... fixing him but I'm not. I'm not touching him. The pain is the same."

"Something about that smell?" Gus asked the room.

Someone knocked on the counter, and it took me a

second to realize it was Anton. He held up the tablet. Whatever he needed to say, he wanted everyone to understand.

"It's because she didn't finish," the tablet spoke for him. "It's not done. Her body... whatever she does... it fixes and then it expels. That's how this works. It's why she feels empty sometimes. She's not done and whatever this power is that she has, it's not finished, and it's punishing her for that. I don't think the Omega is supposed to fix in incremental steps."

I didn't know how he'd deduced that, but it sounded right to me. Anton sometimes just knew things. Maybe he should have been the Omega. I sniffed. "He's right."

"Fuck," Preston snarled. "But you're totally depleted. I can smell that. How are you supposed to finish like this?"

I didn't know if any other Omega had had to do exactly this before. This Hunter problem was a new thing. It wasn't like there were records anywhere to tell me of other Omegas' experiences. And the one who raised the Sisters I'd helped had told them nothing about her powers. Oh, it dawned on me fast, maybe this was the pain they'd meant.

"I've got to just do it." I forced myself to my feet. I didn't so much as walk as slump myself over toward my brother's cage. Shifting hadn't seemed to make sense before but now I was going to try it. I was stronger as a wolf.

"When this is over," I looked at Rainer, "I want a steak. Okay. Can I have a steak? A big, juicy, semi-raw steak."

He nodded. "Count on it. Don't die. We can't live without you. We love you. We can find a way to deal with the pain while you recoup. If you have to stop, stop."

"I love you guys, too."

I wasn't sure there was anything else to say. I had to do this. "Open the cage. I'm going in."

Anton's eyes were wolf when he did as I instructed. I

managed to speak through the ringing in my ears. "If this was something I somehow chose to do, to be this Omega, I must have been drunk when I agreed to it. Why would I have said yes to this? Why would I have done this to the four of you?"

I didn't want reassurances. They could tell me they'd pick me, pick this all day every day. There would never be a time I would really believe it. We couldn't even get through lunch without having an issue. Who in their right mind would raise their hand and say choose me?

I shifted and rushed through the cage door, throwing myself at my sleeping brother. His eyes opened fast and then wide, and I closed mine, letting my Omega power fill him. Even if it depleted me of my own. If I had to fix him all at once, then that was what I would do. He was my brother. He'd bandaged my knees when I scraped them, held me when I'd been sad, beat up a boy who hurt my feelings. When I'd needed money to pay to go to a concert and my own meager check hadn't covered it, he'd paid for it. This was a man who'd taken care of me even when he'd been nothing but a boy.

As my mind drifted away, scurrying from the pain, from every complicated feeling I had about what had to happen, I had to wonder if I'd be as apt to throw myself into potential life ending moments with a stranger? What if it wasn't my brother lying here? What if it was someone I didn't know?

━━━

I was sitting up in a chair in the living room. I looked around. How and when had I gotten here? My brother sipped a drink. He looked worse for wear, but he was upright. I rubbed at my eyes. "How long have I been in this chair?"

Agustin put his finger to his lips, indicating that I should be quiet. I looked where he pointed next and saw Preston was asleep in the chair next to me. Agustin smiled at me, and I answered with one in return. He was awake, his eyes were clear, and he was acting like himself. I'd obviously gotten the job done.

He got to his feet and headed toward me on quiet feet. It didn't seem to matter because Preston reared awake, jumping to his feet like he had to battle. I grabbed his arm. "Pres, it's okay."

He looked between Agustin and me before he sunk back down in his chair. "Sorry, I fell asleep."

I kissed his cheek. "How long have I been... in my human form and sitting here?"

Preston tugged on my hair. "Not long. Rainer went to go buy steaks. Jarret is patrolling around the exterior, looking for danger. Anton is writing. The rest of the family have gone to the other house. They'll all be back tonight. Then Agustin is going to give us what details he remembers, and we'll take it from there. You shifted back maybe half an hour ago. And we like him." Preston looked at Agustin. "A lot more now that he doesn't stink like death and isn't trying to hurt you. You were pretty out of it, and he seemed to care if you were okay."

Agustin finished walking toward me until he stood right in front of me. "Listen, I get it. You're a big tough wolf. You're her mate. All four of you have threatened me since I've been up. I hurt her although I don't remember it. So I'm going to say, Kenzie, I'm so sorry I hurt you, little sister. You know I wouldn't do it on purpose. You see..." He glared at Preston. "I've loved her a lot longer than the four of you

have, and I'd cut out my liver before I caused her any pain."
He stared back at me. "These guys had better be good to
you, or I'll be beating the shit out of them. I can speak for
the whole family on that end. And, wow, you're an Omega.
How did that happen? But then I think... of course it's you.
You're Kenzie. You take care of everyone. Always have."

Preston took my hand in his. "We won't hurt her. But
you'd be in for a rude awakening if you thought you could
fight me."

This was going to get old fast. I shot them both a
warning look. "Agustin, would you believe it looks like I
picked this? Somehow?"

My brother smirked at me. "Idiot."

Yep. That was pretty much how I felt. But there was
this other part. He was up and moving; he was going to be
okay. I'd done that. So as crazy as this was, I might as well
just embrace the ride. If such a thing was possible.

CHAPTER 17

RAINER LIVED up to his promise, and he cooked steak. It was delicious. Our kitchen table hardly fit everyone, but we squished chairs around it, and the entire Lejeune family plus the newly formed Harper family and my brother sat around it eating. Eventually, when his stomach was full, Agustin spoke.

"Can you guys help me with this wolf thing? I've only ever been one under the direction of the Hunters."

It was Gus who answered him. "I'm going to need a refresher course. We all are. Rainer? You prepared to give lessons?"

"I could, but I think Anton would be better at it."

As though that was the most ridiculous thing Anton had ever heard, he rolled his eyes.

"I'm serious. He's really good at it, and I think he was living with his wolf instincts intact even before he had an active wolf. That being said, if he doesn't want to, I will gladly do it. One of us can get you healthily shifting. That goes for all of you. Gus, I think you'll find it just comes back."

Gus smirked. "We're old, Rainer. I'm not sure anything comes back as quickly as it used to. Enjoy your youth while you have it."

They would probably feel bouncier after they shifted. Truth was, at their ages, they were pretty young for werewolves. I set down my fork, my belly full. "What happened with the Hunters? What did they do to you?"

My brother furrowed his brow. "I'm not sure how to describe it. They took you... as you know."

I nodded. "I don't remember being taken. I don't remember any of my time with them. Just the days before, the normal time, and then lapping up blood and seeing Gus. Even after that it gets blurry until just before I was here."

Jarret squeezed my hand. "Some of that is the shift blur."

"Right, but the stuff before? No." I hadn't given it much thought. Too many things had happened to make my head spin, but I needed those memories back and there was no sign that they were going to return, maybe ever. They likely would have by now.

"They took you from work. That was the most we could garner. We had to play it off like you were okay because we couldn't afford to have the humans investigating wolf business. Mom and the dads were frantic. We all were. There was a lot of discussion about whether or not it had just been a regular kidnapping. Like you were taken by some human psycho."

Rainer snorted. "She *was* taken by a human psycho."

"Right. But like one that had nothing to do with werewolves. You married some funny guys, Kenzie." Agustin rolled his eyes.

I patted his shoulder. "Mated. Not married. And yes, I find them very amusing." I winked at Rainer. He so infrequently made jokes. I wanted to encourage the instinct. It had to be a good sign that he was feeling very comfortable.

"Whatever. Same difference. We grew up with the human lingo." He groaned. "We were frantic. Didn't know what to do. One of our fathers, Ruben, he still had some wolf ability to smell things. I hadn't known that. No one did. But he confessed it. So he went to your work and smelled around. But all we could scent was humans."

Kevin shook his head. "I can't imagine the anxiety of not knowing what to do."

"We heard at that point that other wolves had been taken and knew then that it had to be wolf-related. So Mom reached out to you, Gus. We didn't know you, but you had that reputation for finding people, and she took a risk."

He nodded. "I was glad to get the call. Went searching. We had a little bit of intel on Hunter locations, and I went looking. Wasn't sure I'd find anything. They were old locations. However, since I've now found you and MacKenzie in old buildings, we think they've gone ahead and opened up all their old places. They must need the space. Anyway, go on. Yes, that was when I found Kenzie. You guys were already taken."

Agustin visibly swallowed. "We tried to be careful. Even considered going into hiding. We never got to make that decision. They came to our house. I mean... how did they know where we lived? How did they know where Kenzie worked?"

"Betrayal," Aurora whispered. "Someone on the inside gave them information. What else could it be? They emptied Colorado of werewolves."

"And yet whatever they did to Agustin didn't happen to me." Why had I managed to get away when he and no other member of my family had so far?

Agustin smirked. "Oh, they're worked up about that. I was in a lab with three others. Two of them I didn't know. A female and a man. Father and daughter. I never got their names in between screams. And Isaac." He paused for a beat as my heart tightened. "Our oldest brother. Anyway, they're fully aware you got away. They're fully aware that whatever it is that they do to us didn't work on you. And they're obsessed about it. They say Omega like it's a bad word. Apparently, that offers you some resistance to whatever they're doing. Then I can't really describe it. Such pain. In my ears. Loud noises I couldn't stand. Smells that were overwhelming. I shifted. Again and again. Then... I don't know. It was like my head wasn't my own. I couldn't control my thoughts. Isaac, I think he did better than me. They moved him. Somewhere else. In the end, they knew you were coming. They left me there for you to get me. Knowing I'd do what I did." He looked away. "I'm sorry, Kenzie."

"I know you are, and you've said it. I forgive you. No more sorrys. They took over your head. I really don't get it. Does anyone?"

No one answered, which only told me they didn't. How was it even possible to get taken over in that way? I'd fixed my brother. He was okay now. They'd taken Anton when he was a baby. What was it they wanted? "What's the point of any of this? Hunters... hunt. Okay. They think that we're monsters. That they need to kill us. Okay. Take gun. Point. Shoot me in the head. I'm dead. Why pick us up? Take us to labs? Kill us? That isn't what Hunters do."

"That isn't what Hunters used to do." Gus nodded. "It was the kind of thing that we used to deal with. I mean, my whole life." Cristian nodded, and Gus kept talking. "We always had Werewolf Hunters. There are all kinds of tales about that with things that scare humans. Look at Van Helsing and the vampire myth."

I smiled to myself. I loved when werewolves talked about other things like they might not exist. We were here. Maybe vampires were somewhere. Still, that was neither here nor there at this moment. The point was made. Humans made heroes of people who hunted monsters. We just happened to be one of those monsters.

"I don't know why they started doing this or what the point is. I'm afraid the good butchers in those labs didn't share the history of their organization with me. They did however have one thing they wanted very much."

Preston leaned forward. "What was that?"

"My sister. They want my sister. They want all the Omegas dead. They thought they had that. Now? They have to take out Kenzie. We have to keep her hidden."

Rainer's eyes turned wolf, and Kevin whistled. "I may never get used to seeing you guys do that. We never wolfed as easily as the five of you do."

My oldest mate ignored his father. "She's hidden. As hidden as I can make her with Loups showing up in the middle of the night and the Council getting involved in our lives."

The loudest noise I ever heard sounded through the room. It was mind shattering. Everyone at the table grabbed their ears, and before I could even think, I was on my knees next to the table, screaming. I couldn't hear myself yell, not even in my own head. What was happening?

I looked by the door. Standing there, wearing headphones, was Brennan. I growled, anger fueling me. What was he doing? Men rushed in next to him holding guns. They were humans. My ears were useless, but my nose was fine. Whatever this noise was they couldn't hear it. There was nothing stranger than not being able to hear what happened around me.

Someone grabbed me from behind. It was Rainer, and he dragged me backward. How was he doing this? I couldn't take my hands off my ears. His were totally uncovered. With a slight shove he passed me to Preston. Rainer hit the ground, but Pres was up. We were heading for the backdoor when the noise abruptly stopped.

That wasn't good news. The backdoor was blocked.

"Now everyone, calm down." Brennan took off his earphones. They had to be noise cancelling. What was that? Some kind of frequency only we could hear and not the humans? Like a fucking dog whistle? "Or we'll have to put it back on."

Kevin frothed at the mouth but wiped it away. He spit at the ground. "What the fuck are you doing, you piece of shit? I always knew I hated you. Running that Council like you were some kind of demigod of werewolves. What the fuck do you think..."

He never got to finish what he was going to say. Brennan nodded to the guy next to him and the man who was just another human scent in the room to me shot Kevin in the head. Rainer's biological father fell to the ground. Aurora started sobbing, and the overwhelming horror of what I'd just witnessed hit me like a sledgehammer in my gut. They'd shot him. They'd done that.

"Quiet," Brennan said again. Aurora dove for him, but Gus pulled her back, holding her so tightly I doubted she could breathe let alone get away. I reached for Rainer, but he wasn't close, and Preston pulled me back. Where were Anton and Jarret? By the table. I could see both of them. Okay. Okay. This was a nightmare, but they still breathed.

"Let's try this again." Brennan cracked his neck. "No

one else has to die, but I would like to point out that I have no problem killing everyone in this room except the Omega, and I am happy to make it so that every single one of you is dead except her. I don't think MacKenzie wants that. Do you, honey?"

I growled. "You would know, you piece of shit."

He sighed. "Everything I have done has been to keep us all alive. You think I like this?" He pounded on his chest. "You think this is fun for me? For decades, I have kept us alive by dealing with these people. Now, all they want to do is take the Omega. That's not a problem. They've taken every other Omega and managed to kill the others. Then the rest of us can get on with our lives. We give them a little. They leave the majority of us alone. We stay out of their way. We don't shift. I made this agreement with them, and they let us live. If we don't do what they want?" He pointed to Kevin. "That will be all of us. When we don't do what they say? They take our children. They kill us. One by one."

The man raved, and I wasn't sure he made any sense except that I was getting the gist of it. He'd made a deal. A lot of conditions. And somehow the fact that I existed meant that the deal had been broken.

I pointed at him. "What's the bottom line? They can kill and take the werewolves in Colorado and no one will care? Take them from... where else? Alaska? No one will notice. Just so long as your chosen few in New Orleans are left alone. How did you pick who got to live and who got to die?"

Tears rushed down my face. I didn't know when they'd started. I wasn't sad so much as angry and sometimes my tears didn't know the difference. I cried either way. Behind me, Preston's body vibrated. He held onto me like he'd never let me go, and I hoped he didn't.

"Whoever stayed with us got to live. Period. Your family left. They didn't like the swamp, didn't care for the way things were done. They thought they could make it better on their own. They left the pack. Don't you understand, MacKenzie? Pack is everything."

I wasn't going to dignify that with a response. This man was madness. I'd smelled it on him, I wasn't above believing he'd found a way to dissolve pack life just so no one would know how evil he had become. If I got through this, I was going to claw his eyes out. One at a time. While he stayed awake. My mouth watered. Then I might... eat his kidneys. While he stayed alive.

"They don't really want to kill us. Not all of us. They want to study us, to make us useful to society."

Jarret sucked in a large breath. "This is like a videogame. They want to make us what? Super soldiers for their wars?"

"Not the government." He kicked Jarret in the knee. "It's always corporations. There isn't a government in the world who can outdo the very rich. You know that, right? While we were living in this swamp, while we were shifting and killing those idiots with shotguns, some of their children grew up to be billionaires. Our fathers, our grandfathers, couldn't have imagined this. But it happened. They have money and they want us. To fight their wars. But not for the good of the country. It's always the almighty dollar. Or whatever currency they happen to prefer." He shrugged. "So now you're all going to go off quietly so that I don't have to kill anyone else. And do what they say. It hurts less. I am going to go back and reacquire the Council."

It was laughable except it wasn't. This had clearly been going on for a full generation now and there wasn't a thing I could do about it. Except die. Or not. They didn't want me dead? Why not? They wanted me alive?

"You'll never take her." It was Jarret who spoke. He didn't even smell scared. "Oh, you can shoot us. But not all of us. Not before some of us could take out some of you. Enough for Kenzie to get away. And you'll be dead. You and your plans. All the things you said you did for all of us. Keeping us weak so that we'd be easy to take. Whatever you're telling yourself. You sold us out. I don't know if it was fear. I don't know if it was greed, if you're getting something from this, but all I know is you just shot my father in the head, took my brother from his fucking crib and permanently changed him, and even if it wasn't you personally? You did it. And my love knew it the second she smelled you because she's just that good."

That was a lot for Jarret to have said. My heart swelled. He really wasn't scared. For all of his insecurity and worry, in this moment, he was as cool as I'd ever seen him.

"Oh, you can't get away. I'm sorry about that. But I don't even really need the guns. I don't even need the nifty little noisemaker. No, you see? The companies that have been taking us, working on us, using us? They've learned some things over the years."

Goosebumps broke out on my arms. I didn't like his tone or how profound his scent had suddenly become. This was an important moment for this little man, and one he'd been waiting to reveal for some time. He'd had this inside of him for too long, and he was finally going to get to say it aloud.

"One of the things they discovered about us didn't surprise me at all. They explained it, and I think they thought I'd be surprised. But I wasn't. It made such sense. In the end, it was all about the blood."

Well, I was glad that made sense to him because I was still clueless. It was Gus who finally spoke. "Blood? I think you might have us mixed up with a different monster myth. We don't have that much to do with blood. Not really."

"Blood. Like family. Like pack. And the ways we're all connected to each other. In the end, I won't have to do a thing because you will do it for me. And the few of you who won't? Well, there are guns."

He was delusional. There wasn't a wolf in this room who would hurt anyone but Brennan and his sick crew of humans.

"You see? We've always had an in to the powerful Lejeunes. Too important to take the Accords. Too proud to be members of the Council. The perfect, famous Lejeunes. Whatever name you take now, you're still them. And all those years ago, I waited. I watched. I called them and told them it was time to go. That Aurora Lejeune, so sure of her place in the world, had left her children home alone. All those years ago... they took Anton."

He reached for my love, and Anton swatted the man's hand away. "You may not know this? I mean, how could you, but all of these years? Silent. Hurting. Creative. Alone. Probably the smartest person in this room when it comes down to it. But unfortunately, all these years, you have ultimately belonged to us."

I could hardly breathe. I struggled in Preston's hold. "Don't touch him."

"All I have to do is turn him on. And then his blood will do the rest. All the people he shares blood with? All of them will do just as he does. We are pack after all. That's the issue with the Omegas. You just do nothing right. We can't have you here if you can't obey. Anton here. He is going to give you to me. He's going to turn you right on over."

CHAPTER 18

ANTON SHOT daggers with his eyes. If he could have burned Brennan to death from his glare alone, he would have done so. They stayed like that for a long second. Then Anton turned his head to look at me. I'd always been able to read him, to hear his thoughts, and now was no different. I didn't know if it was a mate thing or an Anton thing. They weren't wrong. He was exceptional.

But then so were Rainer. Jarret. And Preston. If they couldn't talk, I would be able to hear them, too. I could feel everything about them. There was something so fucking beautiful about that.

I love you. I could hear him as clearly as though he'd spoken that. The emotion filled me up before cold infected my soul. He wasn't saying that randomly. He was saying it because he thought he'd never get to say it again. Whatever nonsense Brennan spouted, Anton believed it. Which made it very likely not nonsense.

"Anton." I had to get to him. Preston held tight while I struggled in his grip. "Let me go. Let me..."

Brennan pushed a button on his remote. The loud noise

didn't come back. Instead, everything seemed to go quiet. I could hear Preston's breath in my ear. Rainer jumped to his feet. He rushed toward Anton. My youngest mate hardly seemed to notice. His gaze remained on Brennan. "When this is over, you will go back to them. To the men who made you like this. They've missed you all these years. You were so little. It only took them hours to do this."

My brother growled. "Leave him the fuck alone."

Brennan held up his hand. "You're next. It's convenient to have two of you in this room that belong to us.

"Anton, get me the Omega. I want her mine or I want her dead. Those are your two options." He looked over his shoulder. "I realize I'm going off book, but they're going to kill her anyway. Now watch this."

The man holding the gun didn't blink at Brennan. He kept his gun pointed at us.

"Brother." Rainer shook Anton's arm. "Whatever it is, it's nothing. Don't let him talk to you about nonsense."

But that button had been pushed, and as I watched, all the life seemed to drain from Anton's eyes. He stood there, but the bright, vibrant gaze, the one that let me hear his thoughts, was gone. Instead, he tilted his head, and his wolf appeared. But not the wolf I knew either.

"Fuck." My brother's remark seemed accurate. They'd done something to Anton. He wasn't here. Was that what my brother had meant about not being in control of his own thoughts?

"Hold on, Anton. I want the Omega to see. How blood always plays out."

Aurora gasped, loudly, grabbing her head. Her tears abruptly stopped and the same... nothingness... took over her gaze.

"His mother. No surprise. That'll go first." Brennan

sounded downright gleeful. I growled. If Preston hadn't been holding me, I'd have launched at him, consequences be damned. "And we've always suspected Gus was his father. Were we right?"

Gus groaned, and like Aurora, he was quickly on the ground. We were all frozen, watching. This was really happening. Some things seemed too surreal to actually be true and yet I viewed this with my own eyes.

Rainer grabbed his head. He doubled over, his gaze met mine and then over my head. "Preston, get away from her. I don't know what's about to happen. But if it's me... it's you, too."

"And there go the brothers."

Preston let go of me a second before he also writhed in pain. Jarret stumbled backward, hitting the couch and falling over the back of it. As Jarret went, a second later Brian hit the ground. It was moving, blood-to-blood. Son to mother to father to brothers to father. I broke out in a sweat. Oh fuck me, this couldn't be happening.

"Preston..." He was closest to me. "Don't do this. Whatever it is. They don't get to tell you what you're thinking... what you're doing."

My hands burned. In fact, my whole body did. I reached for Preston, but my brother yanked me back. Where had he come from?

Brennan's eyes widened. "You should be controlled, too. You're ours."

"Not anymore, motherfucker."

"That doesn't make sense," Brennan yelled as Cristian launched himself at him. He didn't have a blood son here. Rainer had been Kevin's son, who was dead. Preston had been Joe's, also gone, from the fight to recapture Anton. Jarret was Brian's. They were both taken. Anton had belonged to Gus. They were taken from me.

All of them were going and there was nothing to do but fight for our lives to get out of here. Those being controlled all turned to me.

Brennan got Cristian off of him for half a second. "Tranq the ones left and for god's sake all of you get the Omega or kill her."

My brother hit the floor as a tranquilizer whizzed past him, crashing into the fireplace. He darted to his feet, shifting as he did. Agustin charged the door. My heart was in my stomach as each of my guys and their parents shifted seemingly at the same time. They only had eyes for me, and it wasn't with their usual adoration.

Agustin leaped at the man blocking the door, tearing his throat out. I couldn't give this any more thought. If I stayed, they were taking me or killing me. I was certain of it, and I didn't think my begging or appealing to them to remember who they were or who I was would work right at that second. Agustin turned back, growling at me to follow him. I shifted into my wolf form, running after him as fast I could.

"Stop her."

I guessed my loves and their family were taking a little longer adjusting to their mind-controlled state than Brennan would have preferred. Guns were being fired. Tranqs for the other fathers. Noises sounded behind me as I ran with Agustin out into the woods, the same to our left.

I could smell him... it was Anton who had chased me outside. My love. But also somehow not. He didn't smell right, and I didn't have to turn to know what I'd find. Fuck me. He'd catch me no problem, and Agustin was still too new a wolf to count on in a fight. I didn't even know if

Agustin could beat Anton in a fight. This was all lunacy. I shifted back and jumped into Gus' car. It was such a shitty truck, half falling apart, but hell, it got him where he was going.

He never locked it and thankfully had done just what I remembered him doing the last time I was in it—he'd left the keys in the ignition. I guessed he didn't care if anyone stole it which was great since I was going to be doing just that. Agustin leaped in next to me, and I took off like I had some semblance of an idea of where I was going.

I didn't.

My brother shifted back, grabbing his head. "Fuck. The haze."

I grabbed a blanket from the backseat and threw it at him. "It's the new wolf problem. Close your eyes. Pass out if you need to." I couldn't make him feel better right now. I was too busy gunning it out of the area on roads I'd never personally driven on and checking my rearview mirror to see if anyone chased me. So far no one else was on the road. That didn't mean that they weren't in the woods. We were wolves. I'd not done so yet, but I imagined we could run a very long time chasing after cars. I took a deep breath. Truth was, I had no idea if Anton or any of them were there at all.

I'd just left them. Tears flooded my eyes and down my cheeks. My brother reached out and grabbed my arm. "I'm so sorry, Kenzie. I don't... I mean, I couldn't have imagined..."

I nodded. "Thanks for saving me."

"Stop. You're the one who saved me. I can't... They took your mates just from their hold on Anton."

I'd been there. I'd seen it. I didn't know what I would have said to Agustin because when I finally felt like I might be able to actually form words, he was out cold. I drove and drove and drove. Highways. I pointed Gus' car straight until there was no way any wolves could follow me in wolf form. There was nowhere they could have run to chase me. At some point I had my brother hold the wheel so I could put on some of the extra clothes Gus seemed to have in the car. They were too big on me, and I suspected they were meant to fit my brother since they did. He'd been prepared for shifting werewolves. Still, I was at least dressed.

I drove until we were almost out of gas and Agustin woke up, blurry but okay. How many hours? I didn't know. I just kept going because my entire world had shattered and what was a person supposed to do when everything they'd circled their life around was gone? I was an Omega, and my mates were gone. What was I supposed to do?

We stopped at a hotel. I didn't have cash, but once again, Gus came to my rescue. I owed that man. If I ever got out of this situation and somehow managed to save everyone, I would pay him back. I used the credit card and then chewed on my bottom lip as we walked quickly to the room we rented. This might not be safe. If Brennan was to be believed, and I did think he'd told me the truth, these were very rich men after us with a vendetta coupled with some kind of agenda I didn't yet grasp

They could probably trace Gus' credit card. Okay. I had to assume they weren't that organized yet. Maybe I was being too optimistic. But I was going to go with that for now. They knew I had Gus' truck. That Agustin was with me. I'd use the card tonight and maybe tomorrow before I never did again.

My brother rubbed his eyes. "Give it to me. That card we're using. I'll go get us food."

I nodded. "Okay. Then we have to talk. Be careful."

"I won't leave you, little sister. I promise. We're going to sort this out together."

I believed him. That didn't mean we didn't need to be careful. Once again, I found myself with no clothes or stuff. I took off the borrowed ones and walked into the bathroom. The motel was cheap, but it had hot water. I let that roll over me, washing away my terror, I hoped.

I had to think. I was bright enough. I could do this. Figure things out and save my loves, my family. I'd brought back Agustin. I could save the others. Not Kevin. I let out a sob. The guys, when they were back, when they were clear, they were going to be devastated. I hadn't known him, but I could smell their love for him. He'd been everyone's leader in that family.

Oh, poor Aurora. I gripped the side of the shower.

Okay. Okay. There were things to do. We needed to get rid of Gus' truck. They'd start looking for that, and I had to assume given the rich people after us that they'd have resources to check things like cameras and satellites. Maybe I was overthinking this but that was what I was going to do from this moment on—overthink everything.

I had to save my guys. That meant I needed somewhere to do that and also to keep moving so I couldn't be caught. How to do both of those things? I didn't have a clue. We needed help. Werewolves. Where were there werewolves? Where were the other places that we'd gone off to? I had to remember my history. I had to...

The pain hit me hard. My neck and chest burned. I cried out, falling out of the shower as I crawled along the floor to the sink with the mirror. What was happening? What was... I stared in horror after hoisting myself up to the mirror so I could see.

My marks. The bites my loves had given me were going

away, healing. They weren't supposed to do that. Permanent mate marks. Always with me. But no, they were... disappearing. What did that mean? I touched the mirror then my neck, my chest. Piece-by-piece they vanished. That had to mean the mating bond was gone, that somehow it had been broken. That my mates were gone.

Whatever I'd held onto that this could easily be fixed disappeared. I pressed my head against the cool porcelain of the sink.

That was when the emptiness hit. The last time I'd felt like this I'd begged Rainer to fill me, to make it better. He'd done just that. But that was gone now, like my marks, like my mates. My brother burst through the door

"Kenzie?" He knelt next to me, bringing a towel. "What is it?"

I was a mateless Omega. Alone. Empty. Hunted. And there wasn't anywhere I could go that I could stay hidden.

I stared up at my brother while he handed me the towel. "Agustin, things might get very bad for me for a while. Being an Omega... it hurts. I've been lucky thus far. When I come out the other end of what I think is going to happen, I'm going to be okay. Strong. But tonight? I'm not."

My brother nodded fast. "Okay. What do you need?"

I swallowed. "Revenge."

AFTERWORD

Dearest Reader,

Please don't fret. Pursued (The Swamp #2) is coming very fast. Please join my reader group on Facebook if you haven't already to get more news on this release (https://www.facebook.com/groups/rebeccasrandomness) or sign up for my newsletter at www.rebeccaroyce.com .

In the meantime while you wait how about checking out some of my other series?

I have over 80+ books released. Turn the page for more information about me and my books.

Hugs and Best Wishes, Rebecca.

UNTITLED

Please Turn the page for a complete list of my books

ABOUT THE AUTHOR

As a teenager, I would hide in my room to read my favorite romance novels when I was supposed to be doing my homework.

I am the mother of three adorable boys and I am fortunate to be married to my best friend. I live in Austin Texas where I am determined to eat all the barbecue in town.

I am in love with science fiction, fantasy, and the paranormal and try to use all of these elements in my writing. I've been told I'm a little bloodthirsty so I hope that when you read my work you'll enjoy the action packed ride that always ends in romance. I love to write series because I love to see characters develop over time and it always makes me happy to see my favorite characters make guest appearances in other books.

In my world anything is possible, anything can happen, and you should suspect that it will.

I'd love to hear from you! Please visit my website at www.rebeccaroyce.com to sign up for my newsletter and learn about my books!

Here's where you can find me online:

Rebecca's Randomness Reading Group https://www.facebook.com/groups/RebeccasRandomness/

https://www.rebeccaroyce.com

https://www.facebook.com/authorrebeccaroyce/

www.twitter.com/rebeccaroyce

Instagram: rebeccaroyce79
MeWe: RebeccaRoyce
Cheers!!
Rebecca

OTHER BOOKS BY REBECCA ROYCE...

Wings of Artemis

Kidnapped By Her Husbands https://amzn.to/2BQdUxy

Rescued by Their Wife https://amzn.to/2Rr9as4

Crashing Into Destiny https://amzn.to/2VkyXRL

Meeting Them https://amzn.to/2BLPaXm

Reclaiming Their Love https://amzn.to/2GKAw8E

Loving Them https://amzn.to/2BKDmEK

Ship Called Malice https://amzn.to/2BNputj

Saving Them https://amzn.to/2SsrBtH

Dark Demise https://amzn.to/2VidXv3

Light Unfolding https://amzn.to/2GO6Yqr

Still Waters https://amzn.to/2CFePT8

Rising Tides https://amzn.to/2MCdTlM

Lost Star (coming soon)

Pointed Arrow (coming soon)

Last Hope (completed series)

Tradition Be Damned

Past Be Damned

Destiny Be Damned

Compassion Be Damned

Future Be Damned

Dragon Wars (completed series)

Forever

Eternal

Always

Evermore

Endless

Wards and Wands (completed series)

Hexed and Vexed

Curse Reversed

Meow, Baby (novella, co-written with Ripley Proserpina)

Tragic Magic

Safe Haven

Everywhere and Nowhere

Dimension X (coming soon)

More coming soon....

Soul Bound

Prisoner of the Dragons

More coming soon....

Shadow Promised

Strange Days

Weird Nights

Bizarre Years

More coming soon...

The Warrior (completed series)

Initiation

Driven

Subversive

Redemption

Justice

Warrior World (spin off of The Warrior, completed series)

Deacon

Micah

Jason

The Westervelt Wolves (completed series)

Her Wolf

Summer's Wolf

Wolf Reborn

Wolf's Valentine

Wolf's Magic

Alpha Wolf

Angel's Wolf

Darkest Wolf

Lone Wolf

Fallen Alpha

Alpha Rising

Alpha's Strength

Alpha's Sacrifice

Alpha's Truth

Alpha Enticing

Hidden Alpha (coming soon)

The Capes (completed series)

Seductive Powers

Adrenaline Rush

Last Ascension

The Conditioned

Eye Contact

Embraced

Unlawful (coming soon...)

The Outsiders

Love Beyond Time

Love Beyond Sanity

Love Beyond Loyalty

Love Beyond Sight

Love Beyond Expectations

Love Beyond Oceans

Love Beyond Flames

Love Beyond Lies

Love Beyond Death (coming soon)

Cascade (completed series)

Haunted Redemption

Phoenix Everlasting

Fragility Unearthed

Persuasion Enraptured

Reverse Harem Story (completed series)

Unconventional

Unexpected

Undeniable

Kiss Her Goodbye (completed series)

Hard Truths

Dark Truths

Deadly Truths

Shifter World

Planet Bear

Planet Wolf (coming soon)

The Swamp

Hidden

Pursued (coming soon)

Stand Alone Titles

Under The Lights

No Quitting Allowed

Mr. Wrong

Bite Marks

Bitten Surrender

The Vampire and The Virgin

Demon Within

Crimson Lust

Call Me Crazy

The Storm (writing with Ripley Proserpina) **completed series.**

Lightning Strikes

Thunder Rolling

The Deluge